The Romance of TERESA HENNERT

The Romance of

TERESA HENNERT

Zofia Nałkowska

TRANSLATED BY
MEGAN THOMAS AND
EWA MAŁACHOWSKA-PASEK

FOREWORD BY
BENJAMIN PALOFF

NIU Press   DeKalb, IL

Published by the Northern Illinois University Press, DeKalb, Illinois   60115
Manufactured in the United States using acid-free paper.

All Rights Reserved
Design by Shaun Allshouse

Library of Congress Cataloging-in-Publication Data

Nalkowska, Zofia, 1884-1954.
[Romans Teresy Hennert. English]
The Romance of Teresa Hennert / Zofia Nalkowska ; translated by Megan
Thomas and Ewa Malachowska-Pasek ; foreword by Benjamin Paloff.
p. cm.
Megan Thomas–"a specialist in public education in underfunded schools, she
currently teaches English as a Second Language to recent immigrants in the
Detroit area ; is lecturer in Polish and Czech at the University of Michigan and
is a contributor to and co-editor of the first five fascicles of the Dictionary of
Polish in the Seventeenth and Eighteenth Centuries, a project of the Polish
Academy of Sciences.
Includes bibliographical references.
ISBN 978-0-87580-710-2 (pbk : alk. paper)—
ISBN 978-1-60909-168-2 (e-book)
I. Thomas, Megan, 1977- translator. II. Malachowska-Pasek, Ewa, translator. III.
Title.
PG7158.N34R6613 2014
891.8'537—dc23
2014025218

CONTENTS

FOREWORD

Benjamin Paloff

(RE-)INTRODUCING NAŁKOWSKA IN ENGLISH

Before Northern Illinois University Press committed to publishing new editions of the Polish novelist Zofia Nałkowska (1884–1954), beginning with Ursula Phillips' translation of *Choucas* (1927; 2014), the few readers in the English-speaking world familiar with her work were almost certain to have stumbled across it by one of two inauspicious routes. First, admirers of Bruno Schulz may recall that it was Nałkowska who arranged for the publication of his first book, the extraordinary collection of stories *Sklepy cynamonowe* (*Cinnamon Shops*, 1933).[1] Second, students of the Holocaust may be familiar with her slender book of reflections on Nazi atrocities, *Medaliony* (*Medallions*, 1946), misleadingly presented as journalism and, until recently, the only of her books in English translation still in print.[2]

These faint forays into the Anglophone consciousness—the professional (and, according to some sources, sexual) footnote to the life of a male author; the modest contribution to postwar reflections on the fate of Poland's Jews—provide a distorted, diminished portrait of one of the most surprising and influential voices in

Modernist literature in Central Europe. Nałkowska's intercession on Schulz's behalf, as well as her having been called upon to take part in the fact-finding mission fictionalized in *Medallions*, were hardly accidental. Nałkowska was unquestionably the *grande dame* of Polish literature in the interwar period—a prolific author whose diverse output has left a lasting impression on European letters and whose Warsaw salon was a meeting place for many of those who produced them. While her fiction, filled with incisive social observation and rare psychological insight, is an exceptional source of information about politics, manners, and artistic life in her time and place, it is more significantly a portrait of how that world looks from an intelligent, bold, feminine point of view.

Understanding the world by reflecting it back to herself was, in fact, a lifelong pursuit. Nałkowska started keeping a diary in 1899 and maintained it, with a few interruptions, until her death in 1954. The result is a document of rare value that traces the development of a girl in her early teens into an ambitious young author and eventually a major cultural force. In her *Dzienniki* (*Diaries*, 6 vols.), Nałkowska's life unfolds against the backdrop of politics, both personal and national, and events of global significance, including two Russian revolutions and two World Wars, yet these are all presented in their organic connection to the author's own consciousness. The text is as valuable a self-examination of feminine sexuality as it is a record of a woman's public life in the first half of a turbulent century. It is no wonder, then, that the strongest scholarly work on Nałkowska belongs predominantly to the subgenre of critical biography. For Nałkowska, the life and the literature truly go hand-in-hand.[3]

FROM LIFE TO LITERATURE

Zofia Nałkowska was born in 1884 in Warsaw, the second daughter of Wacław Nałkowski and Anna (née Šafránková). (Their first daughter, Celina, died in infancy.) Her father was a geographer renowned both for his scientific research and for his frequent contributions to the major periodicals of his day, in which he championed such progressive causes as gender equality and the abandonment of traditional aristocratic values. Her mother came from a Moravian family and instilled in Nałkowska a lifelong appreciation for Czech literature and culture.

The question of Polish nationhood, particularly of what constitutes Poland's national peculiarity, was never absent from the household. It was represented clearly in the ethnic and linguistic differences between Nałkowska's mother and father, certainly, but it was also the bridge linking her father's scientific and journalistic pursuits. More than a century after the Third Partition of Poland (1795) had wiped it from the political map of Europe, Wacław Nałkowski spent over a decade co-authoring the era's most detailed Polish atlas; it remained unfinished at his death in 1911. His treatise, *Terytorium Polski historycznej jako indywidualność gieograficzna* (*Poland as a Geographical Entity*), published posthumously in 1912 and quickly translated into French and English, makes the case for independence on the basis of Poland's geographic distinctiveness. The product of Positivist values, Nałkowski believed this to be a more scientific and objective basis for self-determination than the traditions and national myths glorified by writers such as Henryk Sienkiewicz, whose international reputation had been bolstered by the 1905 Nobel Prize in Literature. Nałkowski's popular work polemicized with this attitude generally and with Sienkiewicz specifically. Some of these conflicting notions of what Poland is or should be would resurface later in his daughter's fiction. As we shall see, they play an especially important role in *The Romance of Teresa Hennert.*

In 1895, Wacław Nałkowski moved his family to Wołomin, just northeast of Warsaw, where he had built a modest wooden house that would come to be known as the House on the Meadows. Zofia would compose several of her major works there and plan out *The Romance of Teresa Hennert,* as well as its follow-up, the autobiographical novel *Dom nad łąkami* (*The House on the Meadows,* 1925). As Nałkowski and his wife were constant hosts to artists, activists, and writers, the *House on the Meadows* was suffused with an intensely intellectual atmosphere. Zofia took an early interest in literature, while her younger sister Hanna (1888–1970) would become a famous sculptor.

The Warsaw of Nałkowska's youth and early adulthood was under Russian occupation. Instruction at the city's major universities and institutes was in the Russian language, unerringly czarist in its politics, and thus inimical to the leftist Polish intelligentsia to which Nałkowska's family belonged. She therefore received her higher education through the so-called Flying University, that is, from Polish specialists who, like her own father, taught illegally in private apartments and salons. This, coupled with her bohemian upbringing, fostered Nałkowska's independence of mind and a sharp eye for the gap between stated ideals and real-life practice. While some of Nałkowska's earlier biographers have extolled her home life as a natural incubator for a young woman liberated from traditional mores, more recent scholarship has suggested that it was the household's disjunction between ideal and praxis that had the most decisive influence on Nałkowska's personal development.[4] As Ewa Wiegandt demonstrates in her introduction to the definitive critical edition of *Romans Teresy Hennert,* which serves as the basis for the present translation, this is especially evident in Nałkowska's early rebellion against her parents' home, where her father's feverish activity in support of social progressivism came at the expense of her mother having to limit herself to tasks traditionally reserved for women, such as raising the children and maintaining the household.[5]

Eager to develop her own personal and professional life, in 1904 Nałkowska married Leon Rygier (1875–1948), a poet, and in the same year published short fiction that would form part of her first novel, *Kobiety* (*Women,* 1906). With a deeply independent disposition, Nałkowska anticipated the possibility that her marriage might not succeed—she and Rygier converted to Calvinism in order to facilitate a divorce, should the occasion arise—and took an active part in the burgeoning movement for women's rights. In addition to articles, short stories, and novellas, she produced new novels steadily: *Książę* (*The Prince,* 1907), *Rówieśnice* (*The Peers,* 1908), *Narcyza* (*Narcissa,* 1910), and *Węże i róże* (*Snakes and Roses,* 1913).

From the beginning, Nałkowska's work demonstrates its kinship with the late novel of manners, though with a distinctively Modernist twist that emphasizes the inner anguish of the struggle between personal desire and social convention. "In the consciousness of the era," Hanna Kirchner notes in regard to Nałkowska's intellectual pedigree, "this is a real dilemma:"

> accursed are the irrational, fatalistic, unfeeling powers of nature—and at the same time one struggles to return to it, for the freedom of instinct. One attacks culture as a source of lies, absurdities, the inner enslavement of man, but at the same time approves its artificiality, aestheticism, its dominance over nature's vulgarity. Nałkowska inherits from Modernism an ambivalent attitude toward both sides of this antinomy; her characters would be defined by the inner *impossibility* of following their instincts, by their consciousness of being bound by culture, or else by seeking within it an asylum from a "tough" life or love, that is, from suffering.[6]

At this early point in her career, still operating within the neo-Romantic aesthetic program of the Young Poland movement, which had dominated art and literature since the 1890s, Nałkowska was much less invested in presenting a total picture of a milieu than in probing individual responses to it, especially where the passage from innocence to experience leads to disappointment and inner turmoil. Her protagonists are typically young women who find that their ideals do not comport with the world around them. In this we can readily discern the early influence of Henrik Ibsen (1828–1906) and Stanisław Przybyszewski (1868–1927), as well as that of the outstanding novelist Stefan Żeromski (1864–1925), Nałkowska's older contemporary and friend. What makes Nałkowska's approach unusual is that her characters' problems often arise from the disjunction between a woman's intuitive sense of ownership over her own body—in as much an erotic sense as a political one—and her society's effort to wrest that control from her.

The war years saw aesthetic and personal changes that set the stage for Nałkowska's more sophisticated prose of the 1920s. Foremost among these was her concentration on the short story form, which allowed her to step back from her characters' sometimes tiresome philosophical ruminations and to imagine more fully the outward expression of individual personalities in gestures, utterances, and mannerisms. The apotheosis of this approach is Nałkowska's series of short stories collected under the title *Charaktery* (*Characters*), first published in book form in 1922 but expanded throughout her later career. In 1918, Nałkowska formalized her divorce from Leon Rygier—the couple had been separated since 1911—and shortly thereafter was hired to direct the literature section of the Office of Foreign Propaganda, a division of the Council of Ministers in the newly independent Poland.[7] Her office in the Palace of the Council of Ministers (formerly the Namiestnikowski Palace, today the Presidential Palace), in the heart of historic Warsaw, provided a perch from which the author could observe firsthand the pettiness, corruption, and confusion that plagued the reborn Republic: self-serving officials, befuddled bureaucrats, unscrupulous insiders, and those who jockeyed for access to them. This is precisely the scene that Nałkowska sketches in the fifth chapter of *The Romance of Teresa Hennert*, when a hapless, corruptible officer arrives at the Palace to do business with an already-corrupt official. But the author's vantage point was not merely professional. Having just remarried, in 1922, to one of Piłsudski's officers, Nałkowska was equally familiar with the rudderlessness and desperation of the very same men who had struggled so long for Polish independence.

These circumstances are easily legible to anyone wishing to give *The Romance of Teresa Hennert* a biographical reading. The text offers a biting (and rather fatalistic) satire of a claustrophobic community near the center of power, a milieu that bears more than a passing resemblance to Wołomin in the early years of Polish independence, which felt anything but secure. The Red Army's effort to retake Warsaw and its environs had only just been thwarted with the victory in August 1920 that has come to be known as the Miracle on the Vistula. Polish bureaucratic and military culture subsequently recalled the quip about the dog who, after chasing a fire engine down the street, finally catches it: now what does he do? The new state was rife with corruption and crisis, with unsettled borders, deep ethnic distrust, and a cartoonish rate of inflation. At its core, the officer class consisted of lifelong partisans for an independence that, once won, left them traumatized and without purpose.

Nałkowska was not alone in portraying this unease. In *General Barcz* (1922), Juliusz Kaden-Bandrowski's scathing assessment of what happens when military men assume the reins of state, the elation that accompanied the achievement of Polish independence is characterized as "delight in the trash heap regained." *Przedwiośnie* (*The Coming Spring*, 1924), Żeromski's last novel, portrays a young soldier's difficulty coming to grips with the economic ruin and social inequality he encounters when he returns to Poland from Russia. Nałkowska's novel differs from these, however, in both focus and technique. As Ewa Pieńkowska puts it, by the time she penned *The Romance of Teresa Hennert* Nałkowska had adopted "a more or less consistent restraint in judging reality and refrained from any kind of literary prognostication about the future."[8] Instead of placing Poland's political or socioeconomic trials at center stage, as Kaden-Bandrowski and Żeromski do, Nałkowska keeps them in the background. Her male characters talk politics in roughly equal measure, and with considerably less pleasure, to their talk of food and women. Backroom deals are kept to back rooms.

It then falls to the reader to interpolate from her characters' rich interactions what her early novels had imposed through first-person philosophizing. Bruno Schulz notes Nałkowska's stylistic change beginning with this novel. Even with the tortured psychology of her heroines, her earlier prose, most clearly influenced by the aesthetics of Young Poland, "pulses with the overwhelming aroma of the infatuation with life, rapture over multiplicity, an ardent affection for the world," whereas in her work from the 1920s on "this vernal enthusiasm is unbuttoned, no longer fitting within the frames of the narrative, the triumph of life all the more piercing because now it is endangered, delimited by the approaching night, marked for extinction."[9]

THE ROMANCE

From its opening passage, *The Romance of Teresa Hennert* suggests what H.G. Wells calls, in reference to Turgenev, "the novel of types." A distinctively Eastern European form—Wells laments its absence from English literature, though he would later withdraw this complaint—Wells uses the term to praise how Turgenev "can make his characters typical, while at the same time retaining their individuality":

They are living, breathing individuals, but individuals living under the full stress of this social force or that. The force is not the individual, any more than the voice of the preacher is the sounding board. But every note in the tumult of living opinion finds here and there through a country its own proper resonator, and Turgenev's seems to throw together in its own proper way a group of these resonators.[10]

Wells's characterization of Turgenev applies just as effectively to Nałkowska's method in *The Romance of Teresa Hennert*, in which "a group of these resonators" are cast together in various combinations, and their interactions prove comic and tragic by turns. (Without suggesting that Nałkowska was in any way imitating Turgenev, she had read his *Dvorianskoe gnezdo* [*Home of the Gentry*, 1859] and *Otsy i deti* [*Fathers and Sons*, 1862], Wells's holotype for the "novel of types," not long before she started work on *The Romance of Teresa Hennert*.)[11] These characters often appear together with or in close proximity to their foils, lending Nałkowska's tableaux their tension and spark and allowing her to explore what Bogdan Rogatko has termed "the *relativity of character,* or personality's dependence on external factors, above all on the nature of the community."[12]

Yet the author does not simply place incompatible personalities in conflict. Rather, Nałkowska allows her varied cast to accumulate gradually, introducing new characters one or two at a time.[13] By the end of the first chapter we are fully acquainted only with Julian Gondziłł, a disheveled lieutenant whose mediocrity extends from work to family life. Walking down the street, an alternative preferable to going home, he is thrilled to catch the eye, if fleetingly, of Józef Hennert—"Very nearly a vice minister! Who would have thought..."—a government insider roundly respected, just as his beautiful wife, Teresa, is roundly admired. In the second chapter, Nałkowska sits Gondziłł down to lunch with other types, each of whom might hold some advantage for him, if only he can figure out how to extract it: Professor Laterna, an older intellectual and idealistic patriot; Mr. Nutka, Teresa's father, and therefore a beneficiary of her husband's connections; and Colonel Omski, who, handsome and reserved, is everything that Gondziłł is not. Their initial scene of merriment calls to mind the format of the television sitcom: an otherwise unlikely gathering of personalities cram into a shared space, where they seem innocent of differences that are readily visible to the outside observer. As if to underscore the innocence of their camaraderie, the author calls the restaurant "Eden."

Nałkowska stages similar gatherings throughout the novel—a hoity-toity equestrian competition, an equally refined ball at the house of a general—at first to comic effect. Darker elements creep in as the cast grows. Their days of glory behind them, these men eat, drink, and sleep around, leaving the women—Omski's fiancée, Basia; Gondziłł's wife, Binia—to fend for themselves in a world where they have no real power of their own. Meanwhile, the younger men who have survived battles and revolutions to realize their fathers' patriotic ambitions—Laterna's son Andrzej strikes a terrifying profile of post-traumatic stress, long before such a term existed—are plagued by doubts about what it was all for. When Omski's affection for Teresa turns to obsession, the charade they have all been living begins to crumble. Such is the sense of the novel's ironic title, which refers both to Teresa's allure and to a knight's quest after an unattainable ideal. This is a chivalric romance gone horribly awry.

In orchestrating this drama, Nałkowska draws on her practice in sketching "types" in Characters and the work that followed. Instead of narrating the story from a fixed point of view, as we would find in a first-person novel or in a third-person narrative attached to a particular figure, the novel follows a different character in each chapter. In the study of narrative, this is usually called "focalization": the information delivered to the reader is projected from a particular point within the story world, which in a third-person narrative we might think of as having a camera propped over the shoulder of one principal character or another. By constantly changing the focalization, Nałkowska effectively allows us to peer over the shoulders and into the minds of multiple characters as the story unfolds. In fact, the only character who is not strongly focalized is Teresa herself. This is appropriate, since she serves as a screen onto which all the other characters project their own illusions. In full command of her body, which she does not hesitate to use for her own pleasure, she is robbed of a soul. This is not to say that she lacks an inner life. But

Nałkowska cleverly allows us to see Teresa as others see her, hinting at her interiority only through subtle gestures and details, most notably in the novel's climactic scene.

The novel appeared as a serial in the literary supplement to the Warsaw weekly *Świat* (*The World*), beginning in early 1923. It was reprinted as a serial once more the same year, in the Kraków-based periodical *Czas* (*Time*), before it came out as a book from the reputable publishing house Ignis. The history of its serialization is significant for two reasons.

First, the space allotted to novels serialized in these papers was so small, perhaps 600 words per installment, that an issue usually could not accommodate Nałkowska's already-brief chapters in their entirety. Although she was not unaccustomed to the restrictions and hard deadlines of serial publication—her preceding novel, *Hrabia Emil* (*Count Emile*), ran in *Świat* in 1917—*The Romance of Teresa Hennert* was at once a more ambitious work, both in its sprawling cast and narrative design, and a project into which Nałkowska initially struggled to find entry. On November 6, 1922, she noted in her diary that a letter from her editors "demanding the promised manuscript found me with the first, unfinished chapter."[14] The pressure she felt in producing the text helps account for its highly condensed, urgent, and at times frenetic prose, something today's reader will appreciate: eighty years on, Nałkowska's novel remains a page-turner.

The second, more consequential implication of the novel's serialization is much more difficult to replicate: in its original setting, the text is accompanied by the very same socio-political debates with which it engages directly. Even as it depicts the social dysfunction of the military classes in the early years of the Second Republic, each installment could be read as a fictional portrait, often satirical, of the kinds of figures one might encounter in everyday life, and who were otherwise discussed elsewhere in the same publication in which the text was serialized. Set in the same milieu as that of its real-life readers—that is, in an urban society on the periphery of political or cultural power, where the number of those who were benefitting from pervasive corruption was dwarfed by those who watched it happening and perhaps jockeyed for access of their own—*The Romance of Teresa Hennert* was an unflattering mirror in which many of its readers might have seen themselves. In its original printing, it carried the subtitle *Powieść dzisiejsza*—"A Novel of Today."

AFTERLIFE

The Romance of Teresa Hennert received considerable critical attention upon its publication in book form, some of it negative. Nałkowska had, of course, violated the patriotic imperative that still plays a significant part in Polish culture, and some readers simply objected to her unrelentingly dark treatment of the newly independent state. Others objected to the novel's departure from the convention of narrating from a single perspective. As was often the case with reviews in the interwar period, however—Witold Gombrowicz's work from the 1930s has come down to us as the glaring example—conservative critiques had a funny way of justifying the work's lasting value. Nałkowska would continue to address such sensitive topics as economic inequality and the disconnect between national values and private practices, especially as regards the treatment of women, so that the abundant public discussion of her work over the following thirty years concerned its social critiques as much as its aesthetic achievements. And she would still allow her readers to infer those critiques as they unfolded in engaging interpersonal dramas. Nałkowska would frequently revisit the method of *The Romance of Teresa Hennert* that had initially caused consternation among partisans of a more orthodox literary realism. Her brief chapters, spare prose, and refocalization of the narrative among several characters draw readers into the text. At the same time, the approach to the psychological novel that Nałkowska develops in *The Romance of Teresa Hennert* maintains its resonance. We see enough of the inner lives of her characters to understand them as individual, idiosyncratic personalities, but ultimately we can know them only so well—just as it is in our actual lives. Schulz's formulation of Nałkowska's approach is especially apt:

> At the center of her concept is the human drama, in which roles are
> not clearly delineated in advance, but are to a certain degree prone

to shift and blur into each other, and whose instrumentation allows for a range of variation. In Nałkowska, characters serve only to orchestrate an impersonal drama, they are the polyphonic unfolding, to put it in musical terms, of its content.[15]

The Romance of Teresa Hennert was made into an unremarkable film in 1978, directed by Ignacy Gogolewski and starring Barbara Brylska. This was during a brief spate of interest in adapting Nałkowska's work for the screen that also saw productions of *Dom kobiet* (*House of Women*, as *Haus der Frauen*, dir. Krzysztof Zanussi, 1978), based on her play, and of *Granica* (*Boundaries*, dir. Jan Rybkowski, 1978), that novel's second adaptation after Joseph Lejtes's 1938 film. There have been numerous other productions of Nałkowska's fiction both for the stage and as teleplays, a performance genre that has enjoyed far greater longevity in Poland than in the United States. But none of these can really approach the power of Nalkowksa's prose, and not only because she is a witty and engaging writer. Oddly enough, despite the critical tendency to speak of Nałkowska's fiction in terms of "drama" and "staging," and despite my own emphasis on "focalization" and the "camera over the shoulder" of Nałkowska's characters, her fiction does not film well. This is perhaps because it cannot be reduced to its externally dramatic elements. Indeed, such a reduction inevitably transforms it into a domestic melodrama, a parody of itself. Only Nałkowska's particular style of storytelling can make us feel that we are in the middle of the action—on stage, as it were, with people who are in many ways just like us.

With this new, vibrant rendering of one of Nałkowska's most enduring works, we are finally allowed entry into her world of wonderful characters and conflicts, a world we may find to be delightfully, frighteningly similar to our own.

NOTES

1. For a detailed reconstruction of Nałkowska's patronage, see Jerzy Ficowski, *Regiony wielkiej herezji i okolice: Bruno Schulz i jego mitologia* (Sejny: Pogranicze, 2002), 59–60. Ficowski reports that Schulz later presented to Nałkowska a

unique edition of the book with original illustrations pasted into the text, but this copy was later lost. Ibid., 463.

2. Diana Kuprel's introduction to *Medallions* describes the book's brief narratives variously as "witness reports," "more than a mere historical record," and "reportages"—a word whose meaning is somewhat different in Polish than it is in English. But the text is a fictionalized representation of testimonials the author heard while serving on the Main Commission for the Investigation of German War Crimes in Poland, not a direct record of wartime atrocities. See Diana Kuprel, "Introduction," in Zofia Nałkowska, *Medallions*, trans. Diana Kuprel (Evanston: Northwestern University Press, 2000), xi–xxi. Besides *Medallions* and, quite recently, *Choucas*, the only of Nałkowska's book-length works to appear in English is her early text *Women*, translated by Michael Henry Dziewicki and published in 1920 under the title *Kobiety (Women): A Novel of Polish Life*. It is long and mercifully out-of-print.

3. For the most perceptive recent studies in this vein, see Hanna Kirchner, *Nałkowska, albo, Życie pisane* (Warsaw: W.A.B., 2011); and Paweł Rodak, *Między zapisem a literaturą: dziennik polskiego pisarza w XX wieku (Żeromski, Nałkowska, Dąbrowska, Gombrowicz, Herling-Grudziński)* (Warsaw: Wydawnictwo Uniwersytetu Warszawskiego, 2011).

4. For the rosier vision of Wacław Nałkowski's house as "famous for its atmosphere of trust, good cheer, and tolerance," see, for example, Jan Z. Brudnicki, *Zofia Nałkowska 1884–1954: Poradnik bibliograficzny*, 2nd ed. (Warsaw: Biblioteka Narodowa, 1969), 11.

5. Ewa Wiegandt, "Wstęp," in Zofia Nałkowska, *Romans Teresy Hennert*, ed. Ewa Wiegandt (Wrocław: Ossolineum, 2001), vii–ix.

6. Hanna Kirchner, "Modernistyczna młodość Zofii Nałkowskiej," *Pamiętnik Literacki* 59:1 (1968): 77.

7. Sources provide conflicting start dates for Nałkowska's work at the Office of Foreign Propaganda. Bogdan Rogatko suggests that she started as early as 1918, whereas Hanna Kirchner puts it as late as autumn 1920. See Bogdan Rogatko, *Zofia Nałkowska* (Warsaw: Państwowy Instytut Wydawniczy, 1980); Zofia Nałkowska, *Dzienniki*, vol. 3: 1918–1929, ed. Hanna Kirchner (Warsaw: Czytelnik, 1980), 75.

8. Ewa Pieńkowska, *Zofia Nałkowska* (Warsaw: Wydawnictwo Szkolne i Pedagogiczne, 1975), 53.

9. Bruno Schulz, "Zofia Nałkowska na tle swej nowej powieści," in his *Opowiadanie, wybór esejów i listów*, ed. Jerzy Jarzębski (Wrocław: Ossolineum, 1989), 392.

10. H.G. Wells, *H.G. Wells's Literary Criticism*, eds. Patrick Parrinder and Robert M. Philmus (Brighton: The Harvester Press, 1980), 68.

11. Nałkowska, *Dzienniki*, 3: 67.

12. Rogatko, 123. Author's emphasis.

13. The novelist and critic Karol Irzykowski notes this approvingly in his

review of *The Romance of Teresa Hennert,* in which he also refers to "characters" in much the same way as Wells refers to "types": "In *The Romance of Teresa Hennert* we ostensibly get a slice of contemporary, postwar life in Poland.
It's a fine task, but Nałkowska's power does not rest in painting the so-called
background. Perhaps others do this in a fuller and more popular way, since they
gather types where Nałkowska gathers characters. I say that she 'gathers' them,
because she doesn't think them up herself but 'sets them up' clearly according to
certain actual models. Is this invention? For doesn't it echo life?" Karol Irzykowski,
Wiadomości Literackie 1:3 (1923): 3.

   14. Nałkowska, *Dzienniki,* 3: 96.

   15. Schulz, 396–97.

The Romance of TERESA HENNERT

1.

Julian Gondziłł, already-graying infantry lieutenant, was not happy in his family life. Perhaps the state of matrimony simply did not agree with him. The mere act of crossing the threshold of his house was enough to make his good humor melt into air. He was a fair man, however, and admitted that some of the blame lay with him.

But the woman who greeted him there—my God, how could this possibly be his wife?

She was a maid, a cook, a laundress—every bit the slave, concerned only that dinner might be left standing too long.

As a matter of fact, dinner was always left standing too long.

Indeed, it was literally through the kitchen—where the smell of food thrust itself upon you from the moment you entered—that one accessed the apartment.

What's more, there were two lines stretched across the kitchen on which linens were hung to dry at all hours of the day and night. Damp sheets, various dangling sleeves, trouser legs, and drawstrings caressed the lieutenant's face, though he ducked his head in an effort to avoid them.

He had two small boys. If Konrad, the older child, was healthy, the younger one, Wituś, was sure to be sick. At least that's how it seemed to the lieutenant's wife, who immediately put the child to bed. It was often the case that both boys were in bed. Such were the joys of fatherhood.

His wife, unfortunately, was never idle. When all her work was finally done, she always somehow found still more to do. Usually, that meant embroidering *filet* or, even worse, weaving intricate Spanish lace.[1]

Sometimes the lieutenant said of her, "Her little horizon—it's like this!" And he traced a circle on his palm with his finger, indicating that the scope of his wife's interests was precisely that small. Sure enough, airing the rooms and the linens, beating the carpets, mending and patching, scrubbing everything in sight—these were her life's objectives; her entire world boiled down to this.

Lieutenant Gondziłł had once harbored grave delusions about his wife, since he'd married her out of passionate love. A few years were all it took for his passion to disappear without a trace. The wings of his wife's soul, like a hen's, were used not for flying but for wrapping around her little chicks.

These days the lieutenant believed only in friendship, valued only the society of his close comrades, and was fond only of good company.

He maintained that his fate had gone off the rails. He had a hereditary proclivity for working the land, but the war had torn him away from the agricultural studies to which he'd finally devoted himself after several unsuccessful attempts. The swiftly passing years, along with his marriage and all it entailed, thwarted any resumption of his previously chosen path.

The lieutenant was a tall man, and he was already putting on weight. His face—full, flat, and, despite life's adversities, cheerful—was carelessly shaved, and he wore his thin mustache just a little bit longer than fashion dictated. His uniform—too short and too tight—was completely filled out by his doughy body. When he sat, the second-rate cloth managed both to stretch and to wrinkle. When he stood, the creases refused to go away. Even his thick winter coat could not hold out against these transformations. His army cap had also lost its basic shape and drooped in soft folds toward his neck.

So attired, Lieutenant Gondziłł was coming from work along a wide city street flooded with sunlight. The black hands of the clock suspended above the sidewalk clearly indicated that dinner had once again been left standing for too long. His pace didn't quicken.

Crowds of people swept past him almost capriciously. The strong, ardent wind of the unseasonably warm spring day lifted hats off heads and tousled the coattails of those still dressed for winter. The sun blazed in the sky, the smell of dust was everywhere, and the black trees' short, naked branches tossed and swayed. Spring had taken the world completely by surprise. As always, only the vibrant blue sky and the fresh, joyful air had been ready.

Proceeding through the crowd, the lieutenant offered military salutations carefully calibrated to various ranks.

He valued the structure of military hierarchy, its wise and implacable architecture. When he considered his own rank, low for someone his age, a secret bitterness welled up within him, as if from a poisoned spring. At the same time, though, it allowed him to experience an exquisitely complicated delight, the delicious merging and intertwining of superiority and subordination, submission and dominance, raw generosity and the veneration of absolute obedience.

The rank of lieutenant was for him a geometrical space that occupied a position between life's upper and lower levels, a sort of zero on fate's thermometer. It was an inalterable point amidst the constant flow of existence, the fundamental base from which to orient himself.

Gondziłł, raising two fingers to his cap again and again, was particularly attuned to the warm, panting thud of automobiles, in which the highest-ranking military personages sat dull and motionless as they were carried past.

He was disappointed when it was only a state dignitary or some unfamiliar, unimportant civilian type.

In one of the cars, he saw a familiar figure. It was Mr. Józef Hennert, who was returning from the ministry. Gondziłł managed to offer a bow of greeting, which Hennert returned, fleetingly lifting his matte bowler with a touch of his dark, impeccable glove.

"My God," Gondziłł murmured to himself. "Very nearly a vice minister! Who would have thought..."

Their encounter reminded the lieutenant that Hennert's father-in-law, Mr. Nutka, an old *bon vivant* and a splendid companion, would most certainly be dining at Eden at that very moment. Yes, Mr. Nutka, and perhaps with him, Laterna: philosopher, globetrotter, all-around eccentric, whose appreciation of a good drink was second to none. Even General Chwościk had recently begun to frequent the restaurant.

Gondziłł sighed as he thought of a certain beloved dish, salted mushrooms with meaty pasties. If that weren't reason enough, today Eden was sure to have Lithuanian dumplings. No. He sighed again and began heading in the opposite direction. He walked faster now. Having made his decision, joy coursed through his entire body.

Though fate, to some extent, had done him wrong, Gondziłł had an utterly underdeveloped sense of envy. Coming into contact with other people's happiness and success, even from a distance, heartened him. It fueled his admiration for the extraordinary ways of the world. Basking in the fantasy-filled air of these good fortunes, the lieutenant could justify any recklessness or irresponsibility. For a moment, he could breathe deep an atmosphere in which anything was possible and nothing was really necessary, an atmosphere that was most agreeable indeed.

And now, thanks to his encounter with Hennert, here he was—headed for dinner at Eden in the highest of spirits.

If he'd wanted to, Gondziłł could tell some stories about that Hennert and his marriage. He had known Teresa since she was a schoolgirl, when her mother often sent her to the Laternas' house to borrow a few pennies for dinner. And now—a grand couple, an elite position… Gondziłł mused about it good-naturedly, without a hint of jealousy. He didn't impose his acquaintance on them. He was close only to old Mr. Nutka, who, despite his change of fortune, had not become proud or aloof.

Hennert himself wouldn't have believed that he could have attained such heights, Gondziłł thought. He was basically a nobody when he'd married little Teresa—and the role he'd agreed to in becoming her husband… The actual vice minister—well, it didn't mean anything, he was merely playing politics. Everybody knew it was Hennert who made all the decisions. Everything depended on him…

The lieutenant suddenly stopped and stiffened to attention, preparing to salute again. But it wasn't a typical salutation. One moment the picture of military rigidity, the next moment he was transformed: having fulfilled the ritual's requirements, a hearty exclamation burst from his thick lips, and he spread his bearish arms for an embrace.

"Well, look who it is! At your service, colonel!" He greeted the elegant young officer with the exuberance of an exile meeting a fellow countryman. His entire soul rejoiced, and he simply glowed with the guileless delight of the quintessential "nice guy." It was enough to disarm anyone.

The colonel, who—unlike Gondziłł—was slim and starched, an immaculate leather holster fitted tightly around his waist and across his shoulder, brightened noticeably. He flashed his teeth, beautiful but a little too long, in a smile. His smile was almost charming, although a shadow of indulgent superiority played on his face.

Embracing one another, they stepped to the edge of the sidewalk, where Gondziłł issued a categorical declaration: the colonel would not be allowed to slip away, and together they were to head to Eden for Lithuanian dumplings.

Gondziłł's relationship to Omski was rather peculiar. Gondziłł sought out his company and missed him when he was gone. To a certain extent, he even worshiped him. The colonel's outstanding military service, his distinguished decorations, and his excellent social connections, all remarkable for a man at such an early stage in his career, obviously played a role in the lieutenant's adoration of him.

But it was actually something else that impressed Gondziłł. Like other officers, the colonel was able to drink a great deal. However, there was always a point when he finished that one last glass, after which—regardless of circumstance or situation, impervious to persuasion—he would drink no more.

Gondziłł knew people with stronger heads and could drink even the most dauntless companions under the table, but he was never able to conquer the colonel. More than once it seemed to him that he had done it, that he finally had the colonel firmly in hand—but at any given moment the colonel again became enigmatic, unattainable, indomitable—while all around him the others plunged headlong into the abyss of a drunken spree. Gondziłł spent a lot of time pondering this strange case. He dreamed about the colonel as if he were a woman he could not win.

Fortunately, Colonel Omski happened to have no other dinner engagements that day. So, remembering that he had refused the last several times, he consented to Gondziłł's invitation.

They didn't have far to walk. Soon they turned onto a less crowded street.

"Everything would be fine, if it weren't for the money issue," Gondziłł was saying. "While we were needed—'Oh, please, by all means!' Empty promises, fine words, flowers—heroism, et cetera… the thanks of a grateful nation, new settlements for soldiers, God knows what else![2] But nowadays, when the situation no longer makes our countrymen's skin crawl—you're on your own, my fine feathered friend! Poverty, plain and simple—searing poverty."

Gondziłł's monologue did not resonate with his listener. The colonel's long, narrow face, with its vulturine profile, slightly protruding lower jaw, and gloomily knit eyebrows, showed no trace of its previous smile.

"Surely the bonuses were paid," he said in a studiously unconcerned tone, as if he himself could only vaguely remember it.

The poverty of military life was widely known, and to the colonel, it was a matter both embarrassing and indecent. He was clearly uncomfortable when the subject was raised.

Gondziłł, with his benign "jolly old fellow" appearance, loved to complain, criticize, and generally bemoan. The somber colonel, meanwhile, held the loyal opinion that everything was for the best, and besides, such deliberations were somebody else's job.

"Bonuses?" Gondziłł was instantly appalled. "Bonuses!"

They'd been small, late, and had a number of other deficiencies.

Gondziłł, for his part, clearly relished this topic. He was no worse off than others. The humiliations and woes were not his to suffer alone. In his affliction, he felt a reassuring kinship with both the highest and the lowest ranks. He was elevated by this brotherhood of fate, which he shared with dignitaries.

Omski bowed to a beautiful young woman. The street was empty, and it was taking some time for her to pass. Feasting his eyes on this vision, Gondziłł fell silent. Blushing cheeks, enormous black eyes. Ash-gray suit of English corduroy, small red hat.

"Colonel, sir! What a choice woman!" Gondziłł exclaimed with enthusiasm, not caring that he could be heard.

The colonel's face was like stone.

"What luck!" The lieutenant was relentless. "Such eyes! Such a figure! The way she moves, her legs, her style—Holy Mother of God!" He looked back again, nearly stopping.

"Who the hell is she?"

"I don't remember her name."

"My God." Gondziłł shook his head in reverential delight. "An actress maybe, or something of that sort."

"No, what are you talking about? She's not an actress. She's only a clerk. All the girls work at the ministry now...It's just come back to me, her name is Sasin. Elżbieta Sasin."

Gondziłł was still looking back—whether more in admiration or curiosity, it wasn't quite clear.

She was already some distance away, although perfectly visible against the bright, empty street. The ardent wind roused the folds of her dress. Above her matte, ash-gray kidskin pumps you could see her slender ankles, sheathed in shimmering ash-gray stockings. She had a nimbly swaying gait, the back and forth of her hips almost dancelike. She moved as though consenting to have the wind carry her.

Like the sky and the air, she was in perfect accord with this spring day.

"A clerk." Gondziłł was impressed. "She doesn't look like one! Oh, my dear colonel, if only I could meet her somewhere!"

The colonel was slightly astonished, but he didn't seem to be offended.

"What are you saying? She's not so—you can't just—she's not without a sense of decorum. She's from the Borderlands.[3] Her family is respectable, all things considered, though they're impoverished. Besides, I hardly know her."

Omski fell silent. He really was being too persistent. But he couldn't figure out what the hell sort of relationship linked the colonel to this person.

Then he looked at Omski's dry profile as if with opened eyes, with a new shade of respect. Indeed, who could deny that a man like him was worthy of such a woman?

"Perhaps that's just it," he thought, and was very nearly pleased.

Yes, Gondziłł's soul was devoid of envy. Proximity alone, just the possibility of someone else's triumph and good fortune, filled him with joy.

2.

They descended a few wooden stairs covered in threadbare carpet and entered the establishment, removing their coats and entrusting them to the glum, gray-haired, dirty-looking servants. The colonel paused for a moment before a cloudy mirror and smoothed his hair.

They had scarcely crossed the threshold when, rising up from a table deep within, there emerged the great bulk of Laterna. Gondziłł saw him at once. They quickly passed the reveler-filled tables, and the lieutenant introduced the strangers as though performing some triumphal rite.

"Why, professor, sir," the colonel said to Laterna with polite ease. "We are neighbors, I think. I'm so pleased."

"Who would know better than I?" laughed Gondziłł, glowing with happiness. Matching up friends, assembling good, cheerful company—this constituted his life's passion.

Professor Laterna declared that he was also very pleased and vigorously shook the colonel's hand with his great right paw.

The dimensions of his body dwarfed the others. Fat and soft, quick to laugh, he had a huge face, eyes full of youthful liveliness, and a head sprouting short, gray fluff. Despite his age, he was curious about the business of humanity and seemed to take an interest in everything.

Indeed, Colonel Omski had only very recently taken a room that was adjacent to Laterna's small apartment, but he had already managed to attract the professor's attention.

The fourth member of their circle was a slight, wizened old man, Mr. Seweryn Tarnawa Nutka, "Hennert's father-in-law," as the beaming Gondziłł discreetly informed the colonel.

It turned out that their arrival was not disruptive in the slightest. Quite the contrary: "We were just about to start," Mr. Nutka said benevolently, inviting them to the table where—Gondziłł had just noticed—there rested a plate of his favorite mushrooms.

The men often met here for breakfast. It was an old place, dark and less than perfectly clean, but full of tradition, enticing patrons with quality house specialties that had weathered the test of time, renowned for its strong vodka and, in general, a solid fraternal atmosphere.

The distant midday sun filtered in as if into a cellar. The air was heavy with the smell of food and the stale tobacco smoke that clung to the thick walls.

Everyone who sat at the tables that filled the few small rooms was male, old men mostly, connoisseurs and gourmands who didn't trust the cheap showiness of the huge newfangled restaurants.

When both officers had settled into their chairs and expressed their wishes to the exceedingly obliging servants, Mr. Nutka turned to Gondziłł.

"My son-in-law asked about you yesterday," he said confidentially, leaning closer. "I don't meddle in his affairs—God forbid—but I think he must have something for you."

For Gondziłł, this news was downright sensational. And here it was, completely unexpected!

"I saw the director just a moment ago!" he said. "Well, in his automobile, at least."

Mr. Nutka continued. "Hennert—" as he called his son-in-law "—doesn't know you very well, but he's got a nose for people. I don't want to give him too much credit, but he's actually quite a good fellow, very helpful. And if he wants to do you a favor…he has the means."

Gondziłł didn't doubt that. He was truly happy and made no attempt to conceal his interest.

"Hennert wants to meet with you one of these days." Nutka suddenly shifted from the general to the concrete. "What is the number to your office?"

"I am always at his disposal, the pleasure is all mine!" Gondziłł assured him fervently.

Just then, a waiter they'd summoned bent toward Nutka, and with eyes partially closed in concentration, hung on the old man's every word as he ordered. The captivated servant's entire bearing radiated only one concern: to understand precisely, to penetrate the very depths of his guests' whims and indulge them in every way.

Meanwhile, Gondziłł was collecting his thoughts. He was recalling that today's encounter with Hennert made an especially pleasing impression on him, that his fleeting gesture revealed something enthusiastic, eager, very affable indeed. Something that even seemed to suggest his desire to stop the chauffeur—didn't it? At the time, he thought it was all in his head. But now everything had become clear. Clear? But no, he understood nothing. What could Hennert possibly "have for him"? How could he—someone of so little significance—be of any use to Hennert?

Well, it just goes to show you: insignificant today, significant tomorrow. You never know, anything is possible.

He wrote his telephone number on a sheet from a notepad and outlined, in detail, his working hours. He awaited further explanations and instructions—in vain. Mr. Nutka didn't know anything and didn't *want* to know anything. He never meddled in his son-in-law's affairs and generally washed his hands of it. So Gondziłł resisted the urge to ask questions. He was patient and cheerful.

Upon the tablecloth there now bloomed colors of every type: salad, chilled meat and fish, cold cuts, pickles, and other appetizers. The men's eyes shone with delight at both the simplest and the most refined dishes.

Gondziłł filled their glasses. As one, they drank—and looked at one another with sudden smiles of disbelief. Could it be? After all, they had been expecting to drink something completely different. Gondziłł took the bottle and, noting the label, wanted to show it to the others. But Laterna, with his great meaty hand, motioned for him to be quiet.

"There's no need, Julian. Without a doubt: it's authentic aged Marcelain."[4]

It was as he said. Professor Laterna was never mistaken about such things.

Once again they all looked around at one another, this time in search of the culprit.

It was Mr. Nutka, who smiled modestly and, giving his companions a disarming look, begged their pardon. "Gentlemen, you won't hold it against me that I took the liberty of celebrating a little…"

No, they did not hold it against him. Quite the contrary.

But their attention had already turned to a matter of utmost urgency: the hurried selection of their first appetizers. Like the beaks of birds, their small forks descended on the pink meat of salmon and the pale violet slabs, thick as rolling pins, of herring. A moment later, elaborate decorative pyramids of cubed vegetables collapsed and the mayonnaise glaze covering cold sturgeon and lobster was broken and ruined. This will certainly end merrily, Gondziłł thought.

All around them, servants—solicitous, intent, celebratory—were on the alert. No one had a chance to experience any inconvenience; they wanted for nothing. Plates were changed unseen and unheard. Off to the side, two bottles of Chambertin had already been immersed in lukewarm water.[5]

Meanwhile, Laterna and the colonel continued the conversation they'd started earlier.

For it happened that today, in the office, the colonel had received as-yet unpublished details of the most recent enemy attack on the northern Borderlands.[6] The professor's interest was on full display. Yes—it was no longer a handful of armed bandits, sowing fear and eluding pursuit. It was a regular army, troops numbering several hundred men, looting, murdering, torching everything in their path. The exchange of fire had lasted several hours; there were casualties.

The impunity of these crimes, the particular passivity with which they were treated, was simply incomprehensible to the colonel.

He said nothing more. His officer's loyalty did not permit him to reveal everything he felt.

Having overheard what was going on, Gondziłł eagerly seconded him.

"Exactly! They'll issue yet another diplomatic note and it will all be over and done with."

Laterna spoke with deliberation. "It's difficult—we can't always be at war."

The colonel suppressed his internal agitation. Sullen and mistrustful, he remained silent, occupying himself solely with the Lithuanian dumplings, a tureen of which had just been set upon the table.

"Unfortunately, the army means nothing anymore," said Gondziłł. "The diplomats are in charge now."

Gondziłł didn't wear cuffs, so when he reached for a dish or picked up his glass, his forearms extended well beyond the sleeves of his uniform, revealing a lush growth of golden hair.

The professor was just finishing the fresh, fragrant mushrooms stewed in butter. Eating with gusto, he spoke mildly—as though trying to strike a persuasive tone:

"It figures, because we're now at peace. There's disappointment and tedium, it's true—but, after all, the war is over. You've experienced everything already, gentlemen. Your years of heroism and service are past, your honorable wounds have healed—and now there are decorations on your chests and safe work in offices. So much was expected…and now? Contracts were drawn, treaties were signed—and the great waves came back to a dirty river bed. The whole world has become 'the rearguard.'"

An untouched glass stood before the colonel. Mr. Nutka—who set an example for the younger men and in fact put them to shame—gave him no peace about it.

The way Mr. Nutka drank did inspire awe: with every glass, his good humor and self-satisfaction only increased.

The colonel yielded to the old man's exhortations and belatedly knocked back his drink. A blush darkened his thin, swarthy cheeks.

Yes—he felt with renewed intensity what he'd felt since morning, on this day that heralded the return of spring. His life was agony. He was just standing still, holding his breath, nostrils quivering—chained, by others' blunt will, to a great prison filled with military paperwork.

He thought he knew exactly how a setter must feel when it has caught the scent of a covey of partridges, has crept closer, has raised its paw, and is petrified with apprehension, subordination, and anguish. Not permitted to budge, not permitted the slightest movement from that particular spot. And the hunter never comes, and the awaited shot is never fired. And the moments pass, they pass…

From time to time, one heard the distant rattling of weapons—now from the east, now from the west. Ah, there was no shortage of pretexts! An insulting note, an unfulfilled contract, political assassination, armed gangs. Each case in its own right would be sufficient as *casus belli.*[7]

And nothing! Nothing! He was slowly dying from comfort, from safety, from—peace.

There, back then: the momentum of his self-confidence, the certainty of his decisions, his unshakable will. He had been swept forward toward ecstasy and victory. One, two more years of war—and his ambitions would brook no limits. He had the most exalted reputation among his entire circle, of the entire military coterie. On the fine worsted wool of his uniform, hanging from a metal bar that ran underneath the length his collarbone, was a series of colorfully beribboned military decorations, several of which denoted foreign orders of the first class.

There, back then: amidst hardship and the grim travails of war, he had been young, cheerful, and full of pluck. Grueling marches through rainy fall nights, his heart—replete with duty and responsibility—pounding with grave emotion, spring gales teeming with lead bullets, the smoke blackening the sun—*that* was happiness.

These days, he was suffocated by torturous boredom. It gnawed at him. He lost weight, his brow darkened. He smelled gunpowder and—he shut his eyes.

"Well said, my dear professor!" enthused Gondziłł. "The whole world has become 'the rearguard.'"

And he burst out laughing, like a big child.

3.

"The thanks of our countrymen!" Gondziłł was bellowing in indignation. "I'm sorry, gentlemen, but these things are unheard of! All winter long, General Chwościk's wife doesn't once appear with him. Why? He simply doesn't have enough to buy her a fur. Major Bielski sells off his furniture piece by piece so he can send his son to school. And poor General Uniski's wife!" Gondziłł moved in only the highest military circles. "The general dies and leaves her nothing but their fine furnishings—you know, silver, crystal, paintings… really, everything her dowry brought along, being as she was from a noble family. They're ruined now, of course. And so what happens? There had been no prenuptial agreement, so the furniture is considered her husband's property—and treated like some fabulous inheritance. This poor woman, still young, is left to raise two little children all on her own—and on top of that she has to pay an enormous inheritance tax."

"This is a good temperature." Laterna's words had the weight of authority. He'd taken his first sip from the glass of burgundy and expressed his approval.

Gondziłł was still telling a story—merely a captain's wife this time, a Mrs. Wygienacka, who, a full year after her husband was killed on the battlefield, had not received a penny of his pension. Luckily, she was from a well-to-do family—this one wasn't ruined—and found refuge from poverty under the roof of her ancestral home.

The storyteller's voice quavered with the warmth of genuine emotion. It was solidarity, so to speak, although it steered clear of over-familiarity, mitigated as it was by the deepest respect.

Mr. Nutka arranged his withered face, furrowed with wrinkles, into an expression of interest and concern. He personally knew and liked some of the people Gondziłł was talking about. He was not indifferent to their fate.

Besides, because of his own experience, Gondziłł's tale had struck a chord. Despite being "Hennert's father-in-law," Mr. Nutka was constantly having minor financial troubles of some kind or another, and was not in the habit of hiding it. He was always worrying himself about something, always looking for something; he was never at rest. Gondziłł, with no small measure of surprise, had heard that Mr. Nutka was simply "writhing" over some silly amount, and—here was the peculiar thing—it wasn't even for himself. Mr. Nutka freely admitted that, in all honesty, he had nothing—but he also didn't owe anybody anything.

Self-satisfaction, growing in direct proportion to the number of glasses he drained, appeared to be the old man's dominant feature.

In answer to a question, Gondziłł enumerated without hesitation the amount paid to officers of various ranks. "That can't be—it's unbelievable!" Mr. Nutka wrung his hands conspicuously. But Laterna topped them all when he revealed the monthly salary he received in his capacity as a university professor.

"It's the times we live in, the times…" And everyone agreed that nowadays it was better to be a street sweeper than a government minister.

Clearly, only the most down-and-out paupers were seated around this sumptuously laden table.

As for the colonel, refusing to take part in this rivalry, unwilling to join the gentlemen's boasts—or rather, embarrassed by them—if that fine, fresh, dazzling officer uttered not a single word that betrayed his woes, he was by no means free of them.

Laterna observed the younger man, proud and self-contained, with approval.

He knew that despite the colonel's refined manner and lordly habits, he came from a kind of minimally educated sphere, from a shabby family that accorded him no honor. His father, who fortunately lived far away in a remote provincial town, had lost his position after his abuse of it had been exposed, and now he was doing some business on his own. He inspired neither confidence nor trust. With this dubious source of income he supported a sick wife and the younger children, although at critical moments the colonel was obliged to send help to his family.

Laterna, as his close neighbor, was aware that his room was small, dark, and sparsely furnished, its window facing the interior courtyard.

Furthermore, the colonel did not smoke, did not drink with abandon, did not play cards, and was not fond of loose women. With regard to the matter of finances, he was generally quite scrupulous; he did not have debts and was reluctant to lend money.

Immaculate cleanliness was the only luxury he didn't deny himself. Half his salary was spent on linens, gloves, and items for his toilette. He was also in the habit of sending large baskets of flowers to his female acquaintances on their name day.

The professor knew all this from his brother-in-law, one Julian Gondziłł.

Colonel Omski had fascinated the professor for some time. Laterna described himself as "an aficionado of humanity" and, in his eternal desire to know more about other people, was by no means dismissive of gossip. What on earth could interest a man more than the soul and fate of another man? What on earth could be more instructive?

He listened with pleasure to indiscreet snippets of news about others' lives. He prized the documentary value of gossip. He was intrigued by the furtiveness with which cultivated people spoke about one another.

The gospel of personal privacy did not find a believer in Laterna: secrets were made to be unearthed, not to be respected. The only private life that might have a right to inviolability was one that exerted no influence on anyone else's. For Laterna, the web of gossip woven between people simply regulated this influence. He considered it a manifestation of the collective's organization, a crucial element of society.

Going further, Laterna maintained that listening to gossip arose from the same need as the reading of novels, likewise the writing of them, which was merely a more sophisticated desire for revelation. Theater similarly fulfilled this innate humanity; it was by no means an affront to it, this penchant for eavesdropping and sneaking little peeks. Indiscretion with regard to neighbors—well, the instinct for self-preservation prescribed the need to be cognizant of the environment in which we live and operate, the need to illuminate the darkness that surrounds us. Gossip that reflected the actual state of things—"a record of humanity"—was a rudimentary part of social affairs. And from untrue gossip, well, there you had the genesis of fiction, of all myth and legend.

Laterna considered himself a moralist, but hardly in the traditional sense: loving mankind, he attempted not to elevate or ennoble it, but only to rehabilitate its weaknesses.

Armed with such notions, as well as with the information he'd obtained from Gondziłł, the professor endeavored to learn about the colonel's personal life. For one thing, his relationship to women merited attention.

Not given to partake in the decadence of the big city, Omski also avoided young society ladies—fearing, perhaps, that his attention might be misinterpreted. As a guest in the family home, however, he basked in the warmth of assorted opulent interiors, spoiled the children and petted the dogs, and strove to befriend the lady of the house, becoming her trusted advisor, a fine ornament for parties and gatherings…and never anything more.

He was immune to temptation—but he danced passionately. He spent every night sweeping the pliant, satiated bodies of women across the ballroom floor. Between dances, when the other officers headed together to the buffet, the colonel would stay put. Gondziłł supposed he was simply saving his money. Because, despite his appearance of extravagance, he was quite economical and always managed to stretch the last few pennies of his latest pay all the way to the first of the month. Brooding and hungry, he danced until morning, the grace of his movements and form arousing aesthetic delight in all who saw him. Charming, well-mannered, bitingly ironic, with a cool temperament and fire in his eyes, there seemed to be something hidden and unsaid within him, something steeped in torment and bridled rage.

Women were very fond of his company, but they didn't fall in love with him. His erotic chill puzzled and discouraged them.

Despite his curiosity, perspicacity, and vigorous efforts, Gondziłł couldn't unearth any women in Colonel Omski's life. Every suspicion turned out to be baseless, no one turned out to be *the one*.

Laterna considered it most satisfying to drink good wine and watch this beautiful man. To him, there was no such thing as a trivial matter or an uninteresting person. He loved life and enjoyed it to the fullest.

Time passed. Minutes turned into hours. The drinking continued. Nutka's creased yellow face was now flushed blood-red, but he refused to call it a day.

"To the professor's health!"

"To the colonel's health!"

"To the lieutenant's health!"

Proposing toasts again and again, he spurred them to drink still more. When he succeeded, he was quiet for a moment and, slipping into a reverie, crooned in a soft, senile voice:

She danced lightly and such singing…

Just then Gondziłł spoke. "To our beloved Nutka's health!" He raised his glass gleefully. And that magical incantation was enough to rekindle any waning desire.

Again they raised their glasses to their lips. Mr. Nutka, deeply moved, immediately rose from his space and, glass in hand, made the rounds of the small circle. One by one, he kissed each of them, thanking them from the bottom of his heart like someone who has received far more than he expected or deserved.

It was at this moment that the colonel reached that critical point—his last glass of the evening—and indicated that he would drink no more.

"Oh, you see!" Gondziłł crowed triumphantly, for God only knows what reason. "Didn't I tell you?"

But Mr. Nutka could not accept it. He felt personally wounded by the colonel's obstinacy, and he was deeply saddened. What did he do to deserve this? Surely no one could accuse him of being offensive in any way...

But the colonel was unmoved. He was already listening only to Laterna, with whom he discussed, in a quiet voice, his long-standing dream of hunting tigers in the jungle or taking a trip to deepest Africa. He admitted his fierce desire to participate—somewhere, in some colony—in quashing some savage natives' rebellion...but it was all beyond his grasp, everything was impossible. Everything was impossible!

The professor listened to this confession with pleasure, only occasionally uttering, in a soothing and almost tender tone, some innocuous little pacifist truism. This mortal fever of youth was far too appealing for him to seriously want to quell it.

But the moment arrived when it seemed they should rise and take their respective leaves. Dusk fell, and the electric lamps flickered on.

The gentlemen demanded the bill—and a certain chill descended over the table. But here it came to light that everything had already been quietly taken care of by Mr. Nutka.

"Nutka? What a devious trick!" The indignation was universal. Laterna protested. Gondziłł could not be pacified. Not until the last minute did the colonel consent, coldly thanking him with a mute nod. Gondziłł finally agreed, but only on the condition that they would all adjourn to Lamus, where it would be his treat. "'Just for black coffee,'" he beseeched.

Hesitation briefly set in. But they were able to shake off their doubts quickly, leaving behind no trace of reluctance.

As they were making their exit, there appeared in the doorway of the neighboring room, in the full splendor of his epaulettes and medals, a short, stout general with an extremely red face and, behind his *pince-nez*, small, drowsy eyes. At the sight of him, both officers simultaneously froze in their tracks, as if dazzled by a sudden illumination. It was General Chwościk—the very man who, since he didn't have enough to buy her a fur, had not appeared with his wife all winter. Sure enough, he was completely alone this time, too.

Greetings and salutations went around. Gondziłł offered an irreproachable salute and immediately entered a state of peak enthusiasm. It was already truly providential that everything should fall into place so perfectly: meeting the general while he was here with everyone, right as they were heading to Lamus "for black coffee, for simple black coffee, nothing more." He dared to believe that the general would not refuse all of them at once, and he begged the general to do them the honor as if he were begging him to spare his life.

Not so, Omski. The sense of distance and subordination that manifested itself in Gondziłł as ecstasy, in the colonel took the form of a kind of stony determination. In the presence of authority's warm glow, so simply incarnate in a living person, Gondziłł completely melted. But the colonel stood like a devotee in the presence of the Holy Gospel—spellbound by terrible awe, steadfast in his reverence for this symbol.

The general did not refuse and, indeed, joined their company. He was enveloped in the warm, heartfelt words of the professor and Mr. Nutka, who followed Gondziłł's lead. He wore his familiar, well-established popularity with comfort and ease, which—judging from the expression on Omski's face—the young colonel was completely incapable of doing.

They left in the highest of spirits, Gondziłł distributing coins to the servants in the hallway to retrieve their coats and holsters and locate their hats.

Their little band drank black coffee all night long. And when the check arrived at dawn, it was revealed that, once again, Mr. Nutka had already taken care of everything.

4.

The state of Mr. Nutka's affairs had not always been so rosy. Years ago he had been a miserable railway clerk, and together with his wife and little daughter Teresa he truly had endured poverty. Yet he'd always been marked by a heightened sense of personal dignity and intensely expansive ambition.

It wasn't just hopes and dreams about the distant future that fed his imagination. In every detail of his pitiful life, he found some dazzling, unexpected pretext for intoxicating self-regard. He prided himself that he'd never go to anyone for anything or ask anything of anyone. From time to time he went even further, asserting that no one could say of him that he needed something from someone or that he asked somebody for something.

He dealt in vague, inept boasts about unspecified circumstances beyond his control. What's more, they were insufficiently grounded in reality. Because it turned out that Mr. Nutka had debts that he had not paid back in a timely manner—or at all, actually—and was suffering the subsequent distress. And then, of course, he maintained that no one could say of him that he had debts that he didn't intend to pay back soon, or that he wouldn't, generally speaking, pay back eventually, or finally, that he would not pay back if only he had a suitable sum at his disposal.

He had a whole collection of such expressions, full of dignity and pride, at the ready for any life situation.

In the face of incontrovertible failures and undeniable humiliations, Seweryn had found refuge in the conviction that the noble jewel of the Nutka family name was certainly no worse than anyone else's. It was the ultimate argument, the highest moral authority, with which it was possible to triumph over all of life's painful adversity.

Laterna, then a young idealist working as a high school teacher, remembered the Nutka of this era very well.

It was just unbelievable, the pride and ambition that burst forth from the miserable, shambling, tormented life of that man.

If someone came to visit, he bowed and scraped and fairly

squirmed before them with the desire to please, but at the same time—and there was no telling how or with what—somehow to impress. The grim, dirty hovel on the lowest floor, set way back in the depths of the courtyard, aroused visitors' pity and disgust. And Nutka, with secret vainglory that assumed the form of spiteful humility, would say that here he lived with his wife, poor thing, and they didn't grumble about their fate, in fact they thanked God because they did not deserve anything better. He begged guests to not spurn him, and to pardon the mess, and to please sit down and share a meager supper (for which they had been preparing since morning, and, at the time, seemed to Nutka quite a feast), and that what's ours is yours. "We're humble people, we don't aspire to much..." And everything positively seethed with unwholesome pride, with the willingness to ridicule, humiliate, and demean.

Among his colleagues at the office he occupied the lowest rung, disdained for his lack of education and his drinking, his slovenly attire and his obsequious manners, for bowing too eagerly, even for the way he shook hands, which seemed a definitive statement of poverty and anxiety.

Nutka had found an ideal wife in Teresa's mother. She took everything seriously, and everything impressed her. She was perfectly suited to her situation. Without a murmur of protest, she lived in squalor—dirty, ragged, and inadequate, unaware that scrubbing the floors might help to keep them clean, unclear about how to get the stove to stop smoking, how to rid the house of vermin, how to prevent her dress from becoming threadbare. In fact, she did do the laundry, and cooked and cleaned as well, but all this she performed as if at the last minute, as if it were all in vain, as if nothing she did could possibly be of any use.

The money went to vodka, which the Nutka of that time already drank immoderately, and to the types of spicy snacks that only men ate, an assortment of mysterious tidbits that he kept sealed up in tin cans.

In this dismal life of theirs, in this hopeless decay, there was still a sort of tragic cheerfulness, a keen and chronic optimism oblivious to everything, that Nutka imposed on his family and which seemed to rule out any change for the better. Mrs. Nutka could lament the smoking stove, the inexplicable speed with which everything in their house got so dirty, the perpetually scalded milk. But she never said that such a life was terrible.

Thanks to her father's ambition, Teresa attended a first-rate boarding school, where she did very well. But after talking with her classmates she began to look with horror upon the poverty of her home, which she hadn't really noticed until then. It shamed her, and she lived in constant fear that someone would visit her house. She was afraid that people would see her parents; she was mortified when her father personally met with the principal to pay her tuition and to exult in hearing praise for his daughter. At school, she never let on that all three of them lived together in one room. She felt marked by the bitter brand of poverty, and this set her apart from her young friends. When she complained about it at home, nobody understood, and her mother was incapable of mending a torn stocking.

Teresa was alone among her household in her commitment to cleanliness. She bathed thoroughly every day, hiding herself behind an old screen draped with tattered clothes, which required cunning and no small amount of time to set up so it didn't topple over. She taught herself to sew. Late into the night, lying behind that same screen, she deliberated over how to alter a dress, how to improve a cheap and ugly hat. She would have given her soul for a fashionable spring hat, for leather gloves instead of cotton ones. Even as a child, she'd had an acute sensitivity to luxury. It gave her joy just to look at high-quality fabric with its matte sheen, at stylish little yellow shoes. She had an innate sense of the aesthetics of everyday life. She couldn't stand it when, at home, the ham was eaten directly from the paper unfolded upon the oilcloth, when the sugar cubes were picked up by fingers greasy with food. She understood that this was not simply for lack of money, but something much worse, much more degrading.

Nutka was unwavering in his cheerfulness, even in the face of the teary little arguments that Teresa tried to start with her parents. "If you were dressed entirely in gold, it would make me no happier than one of your excellent grades," he used to say. Teresa would smile bitterly and make no further attempts to explain herself. She knew how moral value measured up against the material kind. She understood that life offered a particular kind of marvelous beauty accessible only to those with money.

Teresa often came to the Laternas' house in those days, dispatched by her mother on her pitiful mission. Laterna enjoyed talking with this slight, well-mannered, private young girl. He saw in her the excessive ambition she'd inherited from her father; but while Nutka's ambition was satisfied by delusion, his little daughter craved the real thing.

At any rate, Laterna didn't have the opportunity to indulge his interest in the plight of the Nutka family for very long. Shortly thereafter he was imprisoned for illegal educational activities and then sent into exile.[8] Laterna's young wife (née Gondziłł), enthusiastic and cheerful companion in his work, went with him to endure her share of this unfortunate fate.

Teresa Nutka was in the eighth grade when she suddenly started to become pretty. Her thin, swarthy face grew fuller and brighter, and her delicate nose and the subtle lines of her lips gained considerable charm. Though she wasn't tall, she was quite shapely. Her influence on the household was already fairly established by this time, and her parents were willing to do without so that she could wear good-looking clothes in the latest style.

She was proud and standoffish in the presence of other young people whom she happened to meet at her classmates' houses. She avoided making close friends out of fear that they would then want to visit her. After all, she couldn't invite anyone to such a home. On the street, she greeted male students with a cold nod so they wouldn't dare to approach her and start a conversation.

But one of them—bold, rich, spoiled by popularity and success, beautifully attired, daubed with cologne—dared to do just that. When he asked if he could accompany her on her way home, Teresa couldn't refuse. She was uncompromising, though, in the face of his attempts to pay her a visit. She insisted that she had very strict parents who would disapprove. It's anyone's guess if he believed her. After a while, though, she consented to go with him to the café, to the theater. Finally, he accompanied her home so late at night it was no longer possible to believe in the strictness of her parents.

When she finished school, there were decisions to be made. He could not marry (yet). His wealthy family was making plans for him, plans that were being thwarted by his love for Teresa. In the meantime, they secretly got engaged, and she—still fearing her parents' strictness—began visiting him at his apartment. At the same time, she took private language classes with the thought that she might become a teacher. Her clothes were beautiful and expensive now. She'd become a kept woman. Dazed by luxury and flattery, lulled by the hope of marriage (someday), she agreed to everything.

When the secret was revealed, Nutka accepted the excuses easily enough. Her mother was more alarmed. Their daughter's fall from grace was not cause for despair; that particular point didn't register. Rather, the issue here was that a well-to-do young man, endowed with certain merits, had gotten engaged to little Teresa—but "obstacles" could always come up.

At first, Teresa's parents awaited the removal of these obstacles, but they soon became accustomed to the state of things. Teresa moved in with her lover. Nutka kept saying the era of superstition and prejudice had passed, thanks be to God, and that it wasn't convention that mattered so much as the actual essence of it all. He ruminated on how this young man loved little Teresa, how he had completely lost his head, how he'd ruined himself for her, acted the fool, fallen out of favor with his family. More than once, Nutka maliciously rejoiced in the thought of those moneybags' impotent anger as they attempted in vain to separate their son from Teresa. And, once again, he'd found a reason to wallow in unwholesome pride.

This idyll lasted two years before it went bad. At home, Teresa— with reddened eyes—claimed she was tired of the constant parties and wild revelry; she'd had enough of that life, and all she wanted now was some peace and quiet.

She moved back in with her parents, whose house had expanded to two rooms and a kitchen. She deposited the money she had received during the separation in a bank. She became sensible and industrious. Now the house was always neat, pleasant, and clean. There were flowers everywhere. Her parents' admiration was stoked by the beauty of her dresses, her nightgowns, her jewelry, her habits and mannerisms. They were proud of her. As the head of the household, she reigned over them—but she was by no means spoiled or temperamental. She required only order, beauty, and comfort; her feverish love of luxury had died down.

It turned out that Teresa, quiet and reliable by nature, was born for the job of orchestrating domestic life, for legitimate love. It turned out that she was virtuous.

Was it easy for her to bear her life's crushing disappointment? She wept, but in secret. She had been deceived, but she was not fully aware of the extent. She didn't see her lover's conduct as a premeditated act, a plan hatched in advance. Instead, she wanted to excuse him. The only grudge she bore was against his family, about which she actually knew nothing at all. But they had made so many efforts to sever them, to induce him to leave for further studies or a career. She remembered how much distress he had suffered. In the end, he was too weak not to surrender.

Despite her worldly experiences and innate sensibility, she retained a certain naiveté and good faith, which allowed her life to be bright and hopeful.

She was young, she was beautiful, and she was no longer poor. She shared her parents' optimism. She knew that marriage was still a possibility for her.

In the face of reckless advances from various men, whom she met very rarely these days, she was unswerving and invulnerable. She didn't believe that any exceptional fate awaited her. She didn't lose her head.

Her marriage to Hennert was a result of matchmaking. An acquaintance of her mother's arrived with the news that a merchant who lived in her building employed a senior clerk who was interested in "going into business himself," that he was sober, hard-working, clever, that he had managed to put himself through school. Teresa knew him by sight. She'd realized, doing the shopping there, that she'd been noticed and singled out for favor. Arrangements were quickly made. Teresa gladly entered into marriage. She didn't mind the difference in "spheres" (she had in mind the noble jewel of the Nutka name), just as Hennert didn't mind her past, which was no secret to him.

They went abroad right after the wedding. Hennert completed commercial trade school, and Teresa gave birth to a daughter. Upon their return, they opened a store. Prosperity was not immediately forthcoming. But Teresa wasn't afraid of work. All day long she sat at the cash desk—always pleasant, polite, and full of placid cheerfulness.

The social sphere in which she now lived, and to which she belonged through her marriage, was one which she hadn't much appreciated before. There were burghers who had become wealthy; impoverished gentry making their way back up; merchants, traders, even craftsmen who were transforming themselves, thanks to their growing fortunes, into manufacturers and industrialists. Among the names announced broadly by the signboards along the street, some were better and some were worse. Those in established old firms, with substantial fortunes—they were regarded as aristocratic and affected a particular social flair that inspired thrilling shivers of respect, curiosity and, masquerading as ambition, envy; they were the source of a distinctive class culture, a particular etiquette, a specific lifestyle.

This insular world was completely self-sufficient and had its own set of traditions, ideals, and prejudices. There was no jockeying for higher status. Marriages, the aligning of fortunes and affections, were conducted only between members of the sphere. Fur manufacturing formed an association with a knife company, silver- and gold-plated goods with a jewelry store. Within these boundaries, both great matches and misalliances were made. The fundamental need for vanity was satisfied by vying for the highest standard of living: elegant parties, fashionable furniture, expensive clothing, sometimes even a library or a painting collection.

Etiquette decreed that one shouldn't wear jewelry if one was married to a jeweler, and exceedingly nondescript clothing was in order if one was a tailor or a proprietor of a clothing shop. Giving people gifts from one's own store also simply wasn't done.

Here was exactly the same social hierarchy, with the same ever-present emulations, rivalries, and grudges, with the same exclusivity and clannish pride, as was found among the landed gentry and aristocracy.

They engaged in philanthropy, read each other's names in the newspapers, filled the theaters, concert halls, and cinemas; they gave the capital's face its character. They were the highest adjudicating body when it came to the success of a new play or opera, the popularity of a new book. The social elite, meanwhile, the world of old families and big names, the world of scholars and connoisseurs, was floating like a little drop of grease on this ocean, not even remotely aware of its own insignificance.

The solid reputation of Teresa's husband, her innate modesty and tact, and especially her personal charm, allowed her to slowly carve out a position for herself in this world.

The outbreak of war brought unexpected change to their quiet, predictable, industrious life. Hennert handed the shop over to his younger brother. He joined, as a shareholder, the boards of various industrial and financial institutions. He had no official title, no office of his own, and did nothing in particular. He made money. He bought an apartment with eight rooms, which he furnished lavishly, and gave Teresa expensive furs and new, far more beautiful diamonds. This time she was neither surprised nor stupefied by fortune—she was simply satisfied. She bought silver and crystal, she had beautiful china and exquisite table linen; she was particularly enamored with the refined aesthetics of everyday life, the quiet, intimate personal luxuries: the way her bedroom and bathroom were appointed, with embroidery and the finest linen covering the eiderdown bedding. Art objects were less impressive to her—in the Hennerts' apartment, paintings and sculptures were just another part of the furniture.

Old Mrs. Nutka did not live to see this splendor. Having contentedly laid her eyes upon her daughter's tranquil happiness and her thriving granddaughter, she fell victim to the first wartime epidemic.[9]

Mr. Nutka, on the other hand, found that as his daughter's prosperity increased, so too did the quality of his drinks, and that was just fine with him. He served as a relic of nobility's faded glory at all the Hennerts' parties, and, moreover, in his role as the exalted father he was treated with particular ceremoniousness. Despite his distinct claims to the contrary, his son-in-law's dealings were not so foreign to him. Quite the contrary: he involved himself to a certain degree, and sometimes even played an active—albeit minor—role.

5.

Gondziłł waited for Hennert's telephone call in vain. But the hopes roused by his conversation with Mr. Nutka hadn't faded. "Clearly he didn't have time today, he'll surely call me tomorrow," he told himself.

After a week, however, he lost his patience and decided simply to go to Hennert's office. His receiving hours were well-known. Gondziłł excused himself from his own work and, filled with joy by this act of vitality, set off to a certain old palace, in whose large, beautiful rooms Hennert's office was located.[10]

He entered an immense, high-ceilinged vestibule, recently renovated, that was covered in white stucco. The bright air smelled of linseed oil. A large balustraded staircase, splitting off in two directions, led to the rooms on the second floor. The lieutenant was familiar with this place, since this was where his young niece—Laterna's daughter, recently arrived from Russia—worked.

He found himself in a broad, light-filled hallway. Vases of flowers stood on the windows, and the walls above were embellished with colorful modern frescoes. A row of double doors with frosted glass panes led to the individual offices.

The opposite wall was lined with mahogany Biedermeier chairs.[11] A crowd of elegant people was sitting there or milling around nearby—dejected, ill-treated, rendered equals by their shared lot of interminable and fruitless waiting. Over and over again, someone stepped to the side for a furtive word with the steward. Now and then somebody importunely poked his head through a door slightly ajar. Everyone had some urgent matter to settle, everyone was fretful and on edge, everyone cursed the waste of time, and—despite their identical experiences—everyone felt individually afflicted and personally demeaned.

Gondziłł approached the steward and quietly, confidentially asked if he might be received by the director.

"He's not receiving anyone else today," answered the unpleasant old man, without even bothering to look at the petitioner. Gondziłł was angered. What did he mean? Why not? He wouldn't receive him? But he didn't come here on his *own* business. As a matter of fact, he was summoned, commissioned. Mr. Hennert was surely expecting him.

He attempted to press his calling card into the steward's hand. If only he would pass it to the director—he'd certainly be received then. But the old man was uncompromising. He was expressly forbidden to let anyone in and was not willing to make an exception.

"Look how many people are waiting." He motioned to the masses assembled in the hallway and refused to reply to any further appeal. Gondziłł, like the others, felt personally insulted. He hated this lout, who had become, in this situation, someone who could pass judgment from on high, enjoying his dominance over the crowd of people—all more educated than he—who, with resignation, had surrendered themselves to his supremacy.

There was nothing to be done. Like anyone in his situation, his thoughts turned to "connections" he might have in the office. He went to look for little Zofia Laterna. Maybe she could be of help.

At the far end of the hall, a door opened onto a large room, from which could be heard the raucous clatter of typewriters. It occupied the corner of the building and had two walls full of windows. Running through the center of the space was a row of white pillars. The sun, from which the blinds provided scant protection, streamed through the windows.

This room was both the nicest and the noisiest, home to the youngest and prettiest office girls. The heads bent over the little tables had hair set in permanent waves, the fingers tapping on the keyboards had lacquered fingernails and were decorated with rings. The young women wore crisp English-cut blouses, pleated skirts, tunics and dresses made of bright silk. Their elegantly shod feet gleamed with freshly polished leather or softly glowed with suede. The silk stockings on their exposed legs shimmered from underneath the tables. One could feel an acute sense of spring in these rosy young women, in their restless laughter, in their playful and impatient movements.

Their attire had no correlation to their salaries. Some were married women, supported by their husbands but working, during these lean times, for extra money to pay for new clothes. Here at the office they had their own world full of lively interests and little matters to attend to, a world that gave them a sense of independence and interfered with the harmony of their families. There were also several divorcées, as well as a host of girls who had taken a lover or two. No one was offended by mascaraed eyes and rouged lips here. The girls had mutual male acquaintances, arranged double dinner dates and trips to the cinema, showed each other the jewelry they'd been given, facilitated each other's purchases of second-hand boots, coats, and suits. The young married women and the girls who couldn't be bothered to hide their lifestyle were on a first name basis, casually kissing each other hello. Here—in the realm of independent employment—there was a blurring of their different worlds, a falling away of prejudices.

This room was home to the least efficient work in the entire office. From time to time there would be a great storm of exasperation. The office manager would burst in unexpectedly and, his voice raised, express his displeasure in the harshest of terms. The women's faces would flush, and they would fall silent, sulking. The very laziest among them would receive dismissals. For a few days, they would be more productive. But the general atmosphere of the room remained unchanged.

Male clerks from various departments, bearing documents that required copying, entered the room with curiosity and excitement. They bent low over the fragrant heads of the typists as they dictated, bantering and cracking jokes between lines. The girls flirted languidly, without conviction: the clerks were not rich; they had families and other responsibilities; they didn't move in the right circles. They weren't worth the trouble.

Exceptions were made, however—when it was one of the bosses, someone who was particularly distinguished or influential, or one of the several young noblemen who were preparing themselves for diplomatic careers or high-level civil service. In this last category was a young baron—beautiful, spoiled, and lazy—who was deigning to toil at translating telegrams, as well as a small, stern, meticulous pedant of a count. When any of these men came through the door, the room became brighter and more boisterous, with little bursts of teasing laughter. A whole world of possibilities arose from this room of typing machines; everything was easy and available. Gondziłł, not without a pleasant thrill, entered this atmosphere. He paused meekly at the threshold and looked for his niece, but he didn't see her at her usual spot. A young woman who was idly standing nearby asked if she could do something for him.

"Miss Laterna?"

No, this was already her second day of missing work. She was sick, supposedly.

Gondziłł was out of luck. He turned and went back into the hall, still filled with the waiting masses. But he suddenly came to a standstill, more shocked and amazed than delighted: the door of Hennert's office had opened and emerging from inside—*her!*

There was no doubt that it was her—the woman whom Omski had identified as Elżbieta Sasin. Now she was walking in his direction, tall and slender, with her hair swept back and those black eyes—what a stunner! Proceeding through the hall with a thin sheaf of papers in her hand, she made an impression even among this malcontented crowd. Her lively gait caused the papers, which she held by one corner, to rustle and flutter. Glancing around as she passed, she noticed Gondziłł, and, perhaps remembering his admiration in the street, she smiled slightly.

Lashed by the whip of sudden decision, he turned to her and bowed.

"I beg your pardon for daring to interrupt you. My name is Gondziłł. You've just come from the director's office, and I've been wasting my time trying to get in there. Could I possibly ask for your help, your patronage? It's an urgent matter!"

At that moment, Gondziłł really did seem to think that this matter was of the utmost urgency.

"You want to see the director? Ho ho—you'll have to wait a week, a few days at the very least. Perhaps some clerk...In this office, you have to apply in writing to the minister himself!"

She laughed. He looked at her lovely mouth and white teeth. Her diamond earrings sparkled, setting off her olive complexion and her rosy cheeks.

He stood and gazed at her helplessly. With an acute sense of poignancy, he noticed that the fingers with which she held the fluttering sheaf were stained violet from carbon paper.

"Let's write down your name—that will be a good start," she said, still smiling.

She was either in an excellent mood or, as he supposed, she was simply making fun of him. He was emboldened.

"I have a niece here, Zosia Laterna, she's a typist." He attempted to embark on a new conversational thread.

"Oh, I know. That feeble little blonde girl..."

"I was told that she's sick. Is she really sick? Do you know?"

The pretty young woman laughed unabashedly. "No, that I don't know, Lieutenant."

He thanked her and begged her pardon again. He bowed and she extended her hand. So now they were acquainted! He was most pleased.

"Do you see Colonel Omski often?" she suddenly asked. She looked into his face, her enormous eyes flashing mischievously.

Gondziłł immediately turned red, which was particularly endearing given his graying hair.

"Me?" he mumbled, caught off guard by the allusion to their first encounter.

"Ah, he's a very dangerous man," she added.

She walked away briskly, papers rustling, nodding her head a few times like they were good friends. Gondziłł left the building without writing down his name. He'd forgotten the purpose of his visit. Their exchange had left him strangely dazed, and his mind raced with thoughts that chased each other away, one trailing after the other.

He knew—he could feel it—that this was not the end. Such a powerful impression was never wrong. Something must surely happen between the two of them! At the same time, he didn't get his hopes up. He wasn't that deluded about who he was.

He recalled Omski's words: "She's not without a sense of decorum." All evidence suggested, however, that great decorum was not entirely necessary. Or, rather, what was necessary was something other than decorum.

Gondziłł didn't have much respect for the women to whom he was attracted. It would be rather funny if he did, considering his age and appearance. Respect was reserved for his wife alone, despite her limited range of interests. "Why did she ask about Omski," he thought suddenly. "So perhaps she *is* interested in him?"

He remembered that, in the moment before she asked this question, she'd been gazing down at him, her head slightly tilted. Ah, how pretty and charming she was.

He resolved to go to Zosia Laterna's home and inquire about her health. But he didn't even know where, strictly speaking, she lived. He wracked his brain for a way to get closer to Elżbieta, something that could facilitate the first steps.

Meanwhile, he found himself on the street at a much earlier hour than usual, on a beautiful day that was undeniably springlike. It was still too early to head home. Besides, he had no desire to go there. All week long he'd been a stern and exemplary family man: he'd eaten dinner at home, he'd been quick-tempered with his wife and children, he'd been overworked, he'd had a head full of problems and didn't want to be pestered by anybody or anything. But the sensations he'd experienced this afternoon and the fantasies that were now pleasantly hovering around him in no way disposed him to the tenor of family life.

As was usually the case in such circumstances, he suddenly felt the need go somewhere and drink something.

He was confident that, wherever he went, he would meet friends and be warmly welcomed as a fine fellow and excellent companion. It was widely known, after all, that he never refused anything, that he was always ready and reliable. Gondziłł liked this particular brand of popularity, the kind which grew from the brotherhood of the glass. He savored these sudden friendships, grounded in very little, based on a kind of limitless trust, but free of any binding obligations during the following month, or even the very next day. When such friends met once again in the vicinity of an opportunity to drink—and, strictly speaking, this opportunity could occur anywhere—their friendship instantly came back to life, picked up exactly where it had left off when it was cut short by sobriety. And so there was a distinct alternate reality of intermittent continuity which, though often interrupted by his other, primary reality, was capable of full and joyful resurrection at any moment. Gondziłł's heart, soul, and imagination belonged to this special world that was born of alcoholic haze, that world where everyone was friendly and even the most difficult plans were realized, where life's unfair distinctions, its disparities and antagonisms, faded away.

It was different in the real world, which seemed to have formed from some resistant and hostile element. There, certain acts resulted in predictable consequences: the children got sick, the wife wanted money, debts rained down upon his head, promotions and medals were distributed unjustly, things were always going from bad to worse...

It was too hard to fix this life completely, to render it joyful and carefree. But that other life that was waiting for him—good-natured, friendly, wholeheartedly happy. All you had to do was stand around the bar with good company.

And, after meeting Major Bielski along the way, Gondziłł did just that. The two men instantly understood one another in their resolve, recognized each other as devotees of the same cult, united by a common credo. It wasn't even clear who had proposed what, who had invited whom; they bought each other round after round, overflowing with mutual devotion. Their altruism, their desire to give their friend the shirt off their own back, knew no limits. When Gondziłł protested, the major mollified him:

"I sold the grand piano yesterday."

For he was the very same major who'd had to sell his furniture in order to send his sons to school.

So Gondziłł gave in and accepted another round.

When they left this bar, they headed off to another for dinner. There they found a large group of friends gathered at adjoining tables and were admitted into their company with open arms. For supper, they moved to yet another room. Finally, they were invited most heartily to black coffee and cards at the home of a friend whose wife had just left town that day. They spent the rest of the night there in splendid humor, and the major gambled away two thirds of his piano.

Gondziłł, however, was on a roll. All in all, it was a thrilling night. There was a moment when he held in his arms a general, drunk as a lord, whose last name he didn't even know; the dignitary, as was typical, had a weak head and was about to lose consciousness, whereas Gondziłł still felt strong as a lion. It was a marvelous moment. Gondziłł felt affection toward this drunken old man, an almost filial tenderness—but at the same time he was blissfully aware of his own superiority, of how kindly he cared for and protected this potentate. Now he was shielding him from the evils of the world, from the table leg, against which he nearly hit his temple, from the floor, upon which he seemed to want to collapse at any cost. Now he was gently leading the general to a sofa and laid him down as carefully and lovingly as a jewel.

Gondziłł achieved a particular spiritual elevation at these moments; he had the sensation of being at some dizzying height. Something important was happening, something crucial that indicated how, from now on, everything would change, that henceforth a new life would begin.

At dawn, he took the general home himself. He discreetly led him up the kitchen stairs and, in the semidarkness, issued instructions to the unfamiliar servants. He saw to it that the general was undressed, put to bed, given black coffee.

It was already light when he set off for home. He rode along the sleepy city streets in the general's weathered carriage, pulled by skinny horses—still drunk on good wine, cooled by the spring breeze, everything cheery and kind.

With regard to these endeavors and elations of Gondziłł's, it is worth noting their total selflessness and noble perseverance. Because in this case and in other, similar moments of fraternity and mutual understanding with high-ranking acquaintances and friends, there was no benefit, in the grim world of reality, to his personal or professional life. Quite the opposite: when the moment of sobriety arrived, there was no sense of obligation. Disparities became larger and distances more strictly observed, and promotions and medals were still distributed unfairly.

Shortly after this pleasant ride home, when a tired and sour Gondziłł, his head full of problems, was "slaving for everyone" in a gloomy office, he was suddenly summoned to the telephone. He rose heavily, without faith that it could be anything good.

Contrary to expectations, this time it was the call he had long awaited. It wasn't Hennert, though, but rather someone speaking on his behalf: Mr. Nutka.

Spilling over with expressions of gentility, Nutka explained that Hennert didn't want to put Gondziłł through the trouble of visiting him at the ministry, since there he was besieged by applicants waiting their turn for an audience. And he didn't want to waste Gondziłł's valuable time.

"You can simply stop by the apartment sometime for a little chat. He can always be found there at six."

Gondziłł thanked him and promised to do so. But he was a little surprised. So many declarations and pleasantries, so much verbiage— but so far nothing specific. Mr. Nutka hadn't even set a day. Gondziłł wasn't sure how to proceed.

But the very next morning Hennert himself called. It may have just seemed that way over the telephone, but Hennert's invitation was neither pleasant nor even very polite, just a cold, formal summons.

"Today at six o'clock. Can I count on you to come?"

Without hesitation Gondziłł replied that he certainly could.

He wasn't at all bothered by Hennert's tone. He considered it quite natural; that's how it was with businessmen. What did seem strange, though, were Nutka's efforts. He seemed to want to endow everything with the appearance of sociability.

Later that day, when Gondziłł arrived at Hennert's at the appointed hour, there was a new surprise.

In addition to the host, there was a third party in Hennert's dim, well-appointed, and rather oppressive office. On the table, covered with a diaphanous embroidered white tablecloth, Gondziłł saw a coffee service, two bottles, and even sweets of some kind—everything arrayed amidst the resplendence of uncommonly refined crystal and silver. So it was going to be a "little chat" after all…

Gondziłł uttered a few cordial words of greeting, just what was necessary, and settled comfortably into the seat that was shown to him. He accepted a cigar, lit it, and calmly waited for what they would tell him.

Right away, he felt exceedingly content in this atmosphere—sunk deep in his armchair, wreathed in plumes of aromatic smoke, joyfully disposed toward everything he saw. "Well, well, how about that Hennert," he thought to himself with sincere warmth and admiration.

The man himself was standing slightly off to the side, at the other end of the table, and was pouring coffee for Gondziłł (two cups, poured earlier, were standing on the table already). He was a short man, tidy and fresh, and, except for a barely discernible mustache that was already going gray, his face was smooth and bare. In any case, he was quite well-proportioned, slightly plump, pleasing to the eye. He shone with a special luster, one generated by good food, a comfortable bed, a first-rate tailor, a top-notch barber—it was as if his body were coated in a thin veneer of money.

In sharp contrast to Hennert, the unknown third party was rumpled, weather-beaten, deeply unimpressive. Although he was no older than fifty, his craggy face was furrowed with wrinkles and his shoulders were stooped, as though he were being crushed by the weight of his worries. His big hands, bony and red, rested on his lap, fingers firmly laced. The neck that emerged from his soft, colorful collar was long and sinewy. His accent was foreign, or maybe it was just that he was from the Borderlands. In any case, beyond the moment of greeting, he was as silent as Gondziłł—and likewise held a cigar between his black and incomplete teeth.

Only Hennert spoke. The smoothness and pleasant rotundity that made his appearance so charming also characterized his way of speaking. Gondziłł was listening carefully but understood very little. He blamed the absence of mental acuity on his unusually fine mood and this postprandial period in general. But, finally, an at least nominal understanding began to make some inroads into the delicious torpor of his thoughts: that despite the black coffee and the presence of a third party, this really was about business after all. Namely, some business about timber in the Borderlands or maybe Pomerania and—for some reason—his "close friend" Colonel Omski, or at any rate Major Bielski.

When Hennert's speech wound down and he arrived at the moment for taking questions, Gondziłł recognized that he was supposed to say something. Heedless of diminishing himself in the eyes of these gentlemen, he acknowledged good-naturedly: "I've never had a knack for business. I don't understand a thing about it—I'm more likely to make a mess of it than be of any help." This admission didn't seem to do much damage. Hennert didn't even smile. He continued along the same lines, only going into more detail this time and trying to explain it more clearly. In fact, the application had already been submitted to the proper place. Now it was only a matter of raising interest among suitable military circles. If Gondziłł would take the initiative, it would be enough to make the whole project come together...

At one point, Gondziłł heard the name Sasin.

He immediately raised his head, looking sideways at the silent man. He adjusted his position in his chair.

So this was Mr. Sasin! When they'd been introduced, Gondziłł—as usual—hadn't quite registered his name. What a singular stroke of luck! Could this be her father?

Now he heard plainly and clearly that Mr. Sasin had worked in forestry all his life, that he knew this particular area of economy and industry like few others. So he wanted to volunteer his experience and expertise—offer his services—for the good of the country. Especially since he'd lost his entire business, and together with his family—like so many of his fellow citizens—he'd ended up here, without connections, without means. He wanted badly to do something, but he was a complete unknown; he needed support and maybe even some encouragement...

Gondziłł was absolutely ready to provide him with both. He was passionately interested in this man's destiny. He was touched to the quick by the losses that Sasin and his family—his family!—had suffered on account of the war.

He worried only that he might not be able to be of much use. But neither Director Hennert nor Sasin shared his doubts. They both seemed to consider him perfectly capable, if only he were willing to try.

Together, Gondziłł and Sasin left the house; Hennert's role in the matter had obviously ended. Gondziłł blithely invited his new friend to Eden for a modest supper, maintaining that the best way to discuss business was over a glass or two.

6.

Professor Laterna walked out of the lecture hall and into the bright, beautiful world. Boisterous black crows flew through the blue sky and alighted on a low roof. Tree branches laden with big, sticky buds sparkled in the sunlight. It was spring, and it was wonderful.

The professor savored it all. He took off his hat and carried it in his hand so the warm wind could ruffle the downy gray fluff, so similar to chinchilla fur, which covered his head. He'd just finished a lecture and was still completely transported by the joy of teaching.

Beheld by the wide, eager eyes of his youthful students, he had spoken for an hour. He entrusted them with the most closely held secrets of his research, the most intimate details of his intellectual understanding of the world. He held nothing back. He sought only the words and expressions that best captured his meaning, the formula with which he could best seize and wholly encapsulate the shape of his thoughts. He acknowledged his bitter frustrations and resignations as well as his mind's most glorious achievements. He revealed the existence of these treasures unwaveringly—and thus rendered them accessible, self-evident, definite: they became fact.

He gave it away, this wealth of his. He gave it away with an open hand, pouring it all out to the very last drop—but in so doing, he by no means lost it.

He was struck once again by this strange phenomenon: there existed things of value that you could share as much as you pleased without diminishing their quantity or worth. Why, it was the same as that run-of-the-mill miracle that everyone knew, the miracle of the loaves and fishes feeding Christ's multitudes!

Never before had this thought occurred to him so forcefully. He felt that he'd truly made a discovery.

He had a reputation for loving young people, for having maintained his enthusiasm for learning, and for giving illuminating lectures. And this was exactly what it all came down to: he gave away what was most precious to him—and he continued to have it; he'd always have it—and he could keep giving it away.

This discovery—or merely his formulation of it—seemed to be of immeasurable significance to him. At such a moment, he thought, one should go running through the sunlit streets, leaping like a dancer, gray hair crowned with green laurels.

He longed to share this joy, to relay this wondrous news and explain it thoroughly to someone who would not only understand it, but would also grasp its emotional implications, so that they could be deeply moved together. But there were no familiar faces on the bustling street.

So he continued on his way, musing that this profound love of teaching must have a biological source: a surfeit of parental instinct, the primordial father's drive to pass down his vast store of valuable experience to the younger generation. He supposed that he would have felt the same delight lecturing, in ancient times, on how to make a bow and poison arrows.

The transference of these fatherly feelings to his pedagogy was facilitated by his circumstances. Fate had decreed that his own children would be raised far away from him, cared for only by their mother, who was a noble woman but too immature to be up to the task, to say nothing of her frailty and frequent illnesses. He hadn't known his youngest daughter at all; she died in exile shortly before the death of her mother. His older daughter, Zosia, and his son, Andrzej, had only recently arrived, and Laterna had seen them for the first time in almost eleven years. They were different than he'd expected, and he had not immediately managed to win their trust. The son, in thrall to new ideas from the East, did not seek his father's approval, and the daughter was sickly, timid, and seemed unable to shake off the depressive influence of the various atrocities that, before returning to her homeland, she had seen with her own eyes.

Laterna decided to take advantage of the couple of free hours he had and visit his daughter. He'd heard from Gondziłł that she was sick, and the news made him uneasy. Could it be that the illness of the mother was reoccurring in the child?

But Zosia's little room was empty. Andrzej wasn't home either.

So he headed to the nearby Gondziłł residence. He knew that Mrs. Gondziłł made daily visits to her sick niece. He wanted to thank her, find out more about the situation, and generally just see her. They had been friends for ages. Laterna might go a few months without visiting Binia Gondziłł, but when he finally did, it was as if they'd parted only yesterday.

He genuinely enjoyed her kind disposition and cheerful approach to life. More than once, her happiness surprised even him. He was also fond of Konrad, the older Gondziłł boy.

Since there was no other way to do it, he entered through the kitchen. As usual, linens were drying on the lines stretched crosswise from wall to wall. There were only large items today: sheets, duvet covers, tablecloths. Laterna made his way through, prudently ducking his head, but he couldn't avoid being damply stroked and caressed—only it didn't arouse the same ire it did in Gondziłł. Binia had once explained to him that since she did all of the laundry herself, she preferred to do it frequently, little by little, so that it wouldn't pile up. And she didn't hang linens in the attic for fear of thieves. This justification sufficed to satisfy Laterna's sense of logic, although for Gondziłł it remained, as ever, nothing but silly prattle.

Laterna found Binia at the stove, busily cooking for her husband and children. Watching her, he'd learned various little tricks and secrets about the matter of preparing meals, and, being the gourmand that he was, these details weren't wasted on him. He undid his coat and sat by the window, on a stool that was offered to him by a young soldier who had been peeling potatoes there. Hat in hand, he launched into a conversation with his sister-in-law, affably peering at her through the wet fringes of the nearest hanging sheet.

He learned that Zosia had recovered already and, as of two days ago, was back at the office. But it hadn't been good; Andrzej had called for the doctor several times.

Laterna was surprised that he hadn't been notified.

"Well, Julek promised that he would tell you. Anyway, everything passed quickly enough. There was some sort of complication with the kidneys, and there was fear that tuberculosis was a factor."

It struck an unpleasant chord. "But she's fully recovered?"

"Well, yes, she just has to stick to the proper diet." As she talked, Mrs. Gondziłł worked without pause. She told Laterna how happy she was since she had reconfigured the kitchen stove herself.

"It's very simple," she said when Laterna expressed his surprise. "Stanisław brought me some clay and a couple of new bricks. The grate was too low and needed to be raised—it was wasting so much coal, and you had to put the pots in so deep. But now you can set them right on top, and they almost never burn, and the entire dinner can be cooked with only a few pieces of coal."

How happy she was talking about it! Laterna, intrigued, lifted his great mass from the chair to get a closer look. Binia showed him the clean pots and pans and urged him to open the stove and peer into the billowing heat so he could see for himself how high the grate was.

"And the oven also bakes much better."

Laterna had a look at that, too. He did it without any sense of sacrifice. He didn't regard these little things as unimportant. Quite the contrary. It was a joyful occasion when something went well, when it was planned judiciously and carried out to the letter.

Binia shifted something, covered something else, lifted a lid (from which wafted the lovely aroma of roasting beef and stewed mushrooms and vegetables) and shook the pan, covered it again, and said,

"Now we can go to the other room. Stanisław will set the potatoes to boil and dinner will be ready. Professor, you're eating with us, right?"

Like her husband, she addressed her brother-in-law as "Professor" on account of the difference in their ages.

They entered the more modest of the two little rooms, and Laterna immediately thought, "Look how pretty and pleasant it is here. Look how hard this woman works, and how shrewdly, to achieve it. And she does it as naturally as a bird ruffles its feathers, hops, and chirps."

It was obvious that she was happy. She had her own quiet domestic pleasures that were unassailable, so to speak, that life's blows couldn't touch.

Her love of cleanliness had become her passion. It wasn't just that she couldn't bear dirt and disorder; tidiness instilled in her a state of unmitigated cheerfulness.

Only Gondziłł resisted Binia's influence in this regard. As for everything else that surrounded her—the kitchen and the apartment, the children's clothes, their faces and hands, even their servant's military jacket—it was all strikingly clean.

Little Konrad, at the sight of his enormous uncle, boldly approached to greet him and also to inform him that, during his walk with Binia that morning he had seen a camel. And a camel, even when it's angry, is gentle; it only spits.

This Konrad, with his clearly drawn personality and lighthearted disposition, was Laterna's favorite.

But the other boy—the pale, plump, timid Wituś—didn't want to move even a single step from the big rocking horse that Stanisław had assembled from two wooden planks and Binia had painted. The horse's one flaw was that you couldn't tell what it was from the front or the back, but from the side it looked real enough.

Quiet and serious, Stanisław generally played a big role in this house. From a simple plank he could make a table, a shelf, a chair, or even a small bed. Then Binia would coat everything with white paint and regret that she wasn't able to varnish it. But it would be too expensive.

"So what do you think of Andrzej?" Laterna asked Binia.

"Andrzej?" Binia thought for a moment. "He's a very good brother."

"Yes." Laterna nodded his head. "There's no doubt about that. He essentially raised Zosia, he hasn't left her side since their mother died. But apart from that, he himself—he doesn't seem strange to you?"

Binia thought some more.

"He loves her very, very much. So obviously he's a good person. But really, I've never seen such a…" Here she hesitated. "Such an unpleasant man."

"Truly?" confirmed Laterna, and he smiled.

"Because other people come back from over there, too," Binia continued, "but they don't look so…"

Laterna silently dandled little Konrad on his knee.

"Are you worried about him, Professor?"

"No, why? He fascinates me, that's all."

As they talked, she spread the tablecloth and set out plates. It went without saying that the professor would eat dinner with them. He didn't object. It was all the same to him, since he didn't eat dinner at any regular place or time.

"Ooh, Daddy's already angry," Konrad said suddenly, and he slipped off Laterna's knee.

Indeed, from the kitchen, a sort of uproar could be heard.

"It's Julek!" Binia was both happy and disconcerted.

Gondziłł came into the room, sputtering and irate. At the sight of Laterna, though, he immediately brightened.

"My dear Professor!" he roared, throwing his arms around his guest and brimming with joy. "What a wonderful coincidence! I saw Colonel Omski yesterday. We made plans for tomorrow, for the competition. Of course you'll come with us, Professor. Duty! It's our duty because of its purpose—and it's just generally our duty."

They were referring to the equestrian competition organized by officers to benefit the widows and orphans of soldiers killed in action. All their friends would be there, not to mention various personages... Laterna didn't take long to convince.

Gondziłł did not greet his wife in any way, nor did he acknowledge his sons, who were already seated on small benches across from one another at a small table, politely waiting for dinner in exactly the same pose—facing each other, each with a spoon in his hand, they looked like some sort of symmetrical children's toy.

Over dinner, Gondziłł divulged a new bit of gossip. Namely, that he'd managed to find out that Colonel Omski was engaged.

"He told you this himself?" Laterna asked.

"Not on your life!" Gondziłł was indignant at the suggestion, which would have greatly diminished his achievement. "I know from an entirely different source." He tittered bashfully. "A most reliable source."

So it turned out that Omski had been engaged for several years already and was most secretive about it. That's what gave him his mysterious charm and accounted for his resistance to temptation. The young woman was from an almost—*almost*—aristocratic sphere; she had been rich not so long ago, but nowadays she was a poor orphan and had to work. So if the love of a noble young man... Apparently she wasn't pretty or anything like that... At any rate, Gondziłł's source would point her out one of these days.

"But who told you this?" Laterna required more detail.

On that point, however, Gondziłł was uncompromising. He jokingly dodged the question, but lurking behind his embarrassment was no small amount of pride. For he'd come by this information via the charming Elżbieta Sasin.

Stanisław—full of care and concentration, following Mrs. Gondziłł's warnings and exhortations as if they were articles of faith—served the food. And Binia—beaming and attentive, pouring, distributing, offering more—was content that at least this time Julek hadn't been late and wasn't eating a dinner that had been left standing too long.

7.

It was Sunday, and everyone was headed off to the competition. The weather was perfect, warm and sunny.

Mr. Nutka was breakfasting at the Hennerts', from where they would all set off together. Diminutive, withered, gray, dressed in a gleaming shirt and impeccable suit, he cut a fine figure even against this sumptuous backdrop. Indeed, he was still going strong—majestic in his nobility, proud of his venerable age and his upright past. Furthermore, it had recently emerged that he had played a part—albeit a nonspecific and perhaps not completely active part—in an uprising. He'd also recalled that his apartment had once been searched, and Mr. Nutka had had such agility and presence of mind that he'd driven the interlopers into a corner. His family knew this tale well, and no one minded when, from time to time, some of the details underwent certain changes.

Open-handed and kindly toward their servants, gracious toward their guests, Mr. Nutka was completely at home in his daughter's house. He often had short, private conferences with his son-in-law and always left Hennert's office in a breezy, patronizing frame of mind. He seemed to feel that it fell upon him to play no small role in Hennert's projects, but—modest and unassuming as he was—he didn't see the need to confide it to anybody.

He had to have the first look at each new acquisition of art, furniture, or other luxury, which he then approved or sagely dismissed. In conversations with his son-in-law and daughter, he savored the sound of astronomical sums of money, which in these postwar times had become the standard units.[12] Currency devaluation gave him particular pleasure, just for the headiness of using such huge numbers. At "the young ones," he had a venue to experience the thrilling manifestations of his grand nobility. "You bought it for a song!" or "It was practically free!" he would tell his son-in-law as Hennert showed him a new appliance, item of silver, or piece of jewelry.

He was especially fond of his granddaughter, "little" Wanda, who, incidentally, was a head taller than her grandfather and already had her own extensive connections in the worlds of international relations and sport. She was attending the competition as "an enthusiast of horses and officers."

Partaking of breakfast was, besides family, one of "Wanda's foreigners." He was a very young-looking, thirty-something Englishman, mild, soft-spoken, and unfailingly serious. He had a mouth like a cherry, a full rosy face, and eyes of intense blue that looked around with an expression as innocent as a girl's.

Mr. Nutka, assuming—as he often did—a position of leadership, reminded them that time was ticking. His observation was duly registered, black coffee was finished in a hurry, and everyone was ready on time.

The small square in front of the gates was already jam-packed with fine carriages and automobiles, and still more were arriving. Indeed, the competition had drawn all of "high society." This did not necessarily mean aristocracy. These were new times, and the word "elite" meant something different.

Most striking were the dazzling uniforms of the dignitaries, both domestic and foreign, with their colorful military stripes, their emblems and gold braid shining splendidly in the full sunlight of midday. No less eye-catching, but in a different way, were the government ministers in their elegant black suits.

Everything was new, and everything was finally real. On a day like this, you could see that Poland really, truly existed. Amidst the hubbub of this overflowing crowd—long oppressed, cheated, and deceived, this distinct cluster of humanity—there was the hum of an instinct being joyfully fulfilled: the completely primal instinct of The State.

The stands were spilling over with a black flood of people—and there, one box decked out in flags and boughs of pine. It was still empty, but all hats were already turned in that direction, all eyes and binoculars fixed on it.

At last! It was *him*.[13] A quivering sensation rippled through the crowd, as visible as a wave upon the water. A strange emotion, both profound and bashful, swelled in their chests. Their hearts were gripped by an unfamiliar spasm: that sensual tingle—heretofore suppressed, envied of other European peoples—of monarchy.

Many had experienced it once or twice in regard to someone else, experienced it as a humiliation—in a foreign capital, at the seaside in Biarritz or Ostend, at the springs in Carlsbad or Wiesbaden. Some had seen, from close up, Emperor Wilhelm during his morning horse ride; others had passed the sleigh whisking Nicholas Romanov to Strelka. Some still recalled kind old Leopold of Belgium accompanied by the distinguished Mlle. de Merode, her hair always done up *en bandeaux*, or the unparalleled Prince of Wales, or, finally, one or another of the bourgeois French presidents.

But now there was no need for humiliation. That sweet spasm of sensation was no longer at odds with national affection, no longer violated patriotic principles. Now there was *Poland*—and everything happened here as it did everywhere else. Now there would be Poland's very own presidents and ministers, her very own senators and generals.

The diplomatic box was already filled to the brim. So many dignitaries! Now the society ladies no longer had to receive governor-generals from the East[14] in their drawing rooms. Their taste for international interlocution was satisfied by plenipotentiary ministers of allied states and heads of foreign missions.

Bows, smiles, noteworthy acquaintances, and actual friendships. But now everyone fell silent. Quiet in the stands. A crowd of pedestrians formed a dense circle around the low wooden fence. The show was starting.

Now, from under the low chestnut trees so recently emblazoned with yellow-green leaves, came the riders on their horses making their way through a narrow gap in the crowd. Single file, one after another. Each did exactly what his predecessor had just done: each crossed the sun-drenched square, rode up to the garlanded box, and stopped short for a brief moment of military salute. Then a few steps at a gallop, the first obstacle, turn, the second obstacle—a lap around the field, a larger obstacle—a ditch, an embankment, sets of rails. And then to the finish.

But each one was different. And each display brought a new sensation and new pleasure.

The first to run out, jumping eagerly, was a large, dark bay hunter—curious about what was coming next, paying no mind to the crowd or the emotional aspect of his task, having no desire for rivalry. He turned slightly for a moment, squatting on his wide hindquarters, and, bending his thick, bare neck—made larger by the crest of his short-cropped mane—lowered his good-natured head. He patted himself on the rump with his bobbed tail as if with a hand. This wasn't nervous energy, but rather a healthy appetite for sport. He knew his rider; he was sure that he understood him and that he wouldn't let his master down. He set off at a gallop, caring only that everything went well. With good faith and the best intentions, he took on the obstacles, one after another, all the way to the hardest jump. No one was anxious while watching him; everything went like clockwork. The applause surprised neither the rider nor the horse. They rode back toward the thicket of people, which parted for them again as they went through. The rider jumped off, patting the creature with a familiar, perfunctory gesture of praise and thanks.

And now a new rider came out. The dark bay horse underneath him was smaller, with an Arabian silhouette. Right away the bay noticed something unusual—he was unnerved by the crowd; he skittered sideways, trying to rear, champing at his bit. Sulking and glowering, he whipped his small head around on his long, curved neck. He was at his most beautiful in these silly caprices, in his anger and unease. He did not immediately take off in a gallop—rebellious and indignant, he balked. Finally he surrendered to the temptation of motion. Ah, how he flew, and with what perfect form—he seemed the embodiment of overcoming, of effortlessly conquering time and space! His hind legs, in constant motion, almost casually touched the flat earth and obediently extended backward. His forelegs were engaged in a delightful gesture of catching and scooping up the air underneath them. His small head, a little bauble, was thrown back,

snorting, ecstatic and enthralled in the throes of passionate movement. His mane fluttered in the breeze and his long tail, lifted high
above his rump, added to the impression of lightness, nimbleness,
panache. Hop!—the first obstacle. He clipped it with a hind hoof,
maybe even struck it. Vexed and restless, he stamped his feet for a
moment and again set off to take flight. He hesitated—he took on
the second obstacle none too willingly—but he was successful. And
then he ran as if he'd been given wings, nothing at all worrying him
now. Everything was going to be fine. Hop! Hop!—again and again.
To the right, to the left! Ah, how lovely he was, how smooth and
agile, swinging to and fro in an intoxicating gallop.

Now an English thoroughbred stepped out, a beautiful horse—
long, supple, and sleek. Underneath his skin the muscles rippled
as sinuously and distinctly as a foxhound's. His elastic body was so
self-contained and focused in its gestures, so efficient, economical,
and sure. His head was wise, and his beautiful, attentive eyes were
full of quiet composure. All his inner dignity, all the elegance of his
form—it belonged not to him, but to his breed. He himself didn't
strive to be anything special; he didn't aspire to fame or have ambitions of his own. He was a representative—and that was the only
motive for his cares and concerns, his claim to dignity; that was the
essence of his beauty and talent. Now he broke into a gallop. It was
hardly the windswept flight of an Arabian, conjuring up images of
the steppes of the Arabian Peninsula. This was a run perfectly calibrated to international turf standards. The horse was exemplary—
just enough jauntiness and excitement. He stretched out, lowering
himself a little closer to the ground. Here was a true *carrière*.[15] The
way he bent and straightened his legs was incomparable; he was all
breeding, entitlement, excellence. He moved steadily forward with
the infallible certainty of a machine. Although he ran calmly, his
speed was absolutely tremendous. A deeper squat before the obstacle; he flashed through the air—and again his body swayed to and
fro in the relaxed gait of his gallop. There was no trace of effort, everything seemed inevitable. He rhythmically turned here and there,
streaking through the air. Amidst the applause, a bow and an exit.

New horses came out. Again and again they did the same course,
but again and again each one was different. There were infinite

possibilities within the one pattern. In the movements and dynamics of an animal's body, the entirety of its nature—the whole of its identity and psychological being—was visible. Unlike humans, the important part wasn't the expression of the face, its glances and gestures. What was important was the tail, the legs, the windswept mane, the line of the back, the thump of the hoof. Clearly and surely, their dark, lustrous bodies sailed through the light, crystal-clear air. A horse's physiognomy is between the tip of its head and the end of its tail. Everything performs and affirms itself.

Here was one that was vain and proud, insecure, putting on airs. Such a surfeit of effort and teasing, half-understood coquetry. Right away he shrank from the obstacle as if, not wanting to do it in front of all these people, he had no intention of ever jumping. He was offended. He minced about, stamped his feet, went completely sideways and veered off the track. How much needlessly wasted energy! With considerable effort, he gracelessly—although he was very pretty—took the first obstacle. Right before the second, he suddenly got cold feet and turned, running off to the side. He was hit with a riding crop and, boiling with rage, quickly and angrily took on the obstacles one after another—panting, squatting, sulking, and straining.

Another objected to everything from the very beginning; he simply had a bad attitude. He didn't want to go into a gallop; he didn't obey the reins. Stubborn, gloomy, and spiteful, he did whatever he pleased. He reared and bucked, jumping left and right. The rider finally had to give up, so impossible was it to lead the horse to even the first obstacle. They retreated from the track to the crowd's amusement and maliciously hearty applause.

You could tell everything from the horses, but nothing from the riders. The Uhlans'[16] young faces, somber and focused, were all the same—their eyes tense and determined, their lips tightly sealed. Under their chins, the black straps of their shakos made them look even more boyish. In all of them, the hell of stage fright and prayers for the horse not to disappoint, not to fall, not to incur endless ridicule.

Right at the first obstacle, one horse toppled onto its back. The collective cry of dismay rising from the thicket of people was like a distant rumble of thunder. The rider immediately scrambled up from the ground and, hanging his head, lead the disgraced horse from the field—he, the unluckiest of men.

Again, a new horse was running—with every gesture, with every second of movement, he satisfied the laws of perfect beauty. He bent his neck, threw his legs forward, lifted his head, squatted, minced about, hopped. He had no idea that he was being observed, no notion of any of it; he was completely innocent—and, in his guilelessness, he was so beautiful. This was especially true at the moment when, galloping, he threw back his rear hooves and twisted his fetlocks so lightly, for a fraction of a second longer than was absolutely necessary—and then, in a flash, they once again transformed into steel. Running like so, moments of beauty were casually tossed from his body like jewels recklessly and extravagantly cast away. Anything he decided to undertake would be marvelous. Why, when his running slowed, did he champ at his bit and stretch his neck as though he wanted to break it? In this profound unawareness, in this senselessness of completely paradoxical gestures, there was an irresistible charm, an elusive but undeniable principle of beauty.

There were still other horses—brawny, nimble, well-performing, taking the obstacles successfully. But they were not beautiful. Their gaits and their movements did not inspire delight, their sulkiness was charmless, their trepidation and bravery did not win hearts. Yet they ran, jumped, and labored away, unaware that their existence was bereft of beauty.

The last horse returned to the soft, transparent shade of the low chestnut trees.

"Mama, Mama!" Wanda Hennert said quickly. "Did you notice the bay horse with the star on its forehead?"

Teresa smiled. "My dear, it seems to me that all horses are bays, and they all have stars on their foreheads."

"Oh, God," Wanda fretted. "Then we didn't spot Lieutenant Lin at all. They were all so much alike…and he told me what kind of horse he had—bay, with a star on its forehead…"

Awaiting the second part of the program, the black crowd was flowing from the stands and flooding the park's promenades.

8.

Gondziłł was so happy. He knew almost everybody here. He saluted and bowed left and right. He was able to tell Omski a little something about everyone.

Today Omski noticed a big improvement in Gondziłł's appearance. His uniform was new, his face was neatly shaved, and even his gloves were fresh and utterly white.

"Here's something you wouldn't expect." Gondziłł was offering energetic commentary on the recipients of his latest bow. "My nephew Andrzej Laterna, a recluse, a misanthrope, just generally a black character—and look here, see the company in which he finds himself. Colonel, see those two ladies? That's *the* Mrs. Hennert with her daughter. You wouldn't know it to look at them, right? They look like two girlfriends—only the little one is a head taller than her mother... I've known Mrs. Teresa since she was younger than her daughter is now."

He was clearly gratified by this acquaintance. He was proud of his nephew's lofty connections.

"The one mooning about after the young lady is Lieutenant Lin, although I don't think he has a chance with her. And that fellow with the pink face has all the trappings of an Englishman. He'll gladly recite Spenser on demand and play folk songs on the piano from different countries—Scottish, Irish, even German and Czech—that he arranges himself. He came here by a strange path: through America, India—and Russia. Finally, the fourth—why, the ladies are absolutely surrounded! Again, the fourth one is Teresa's admirer... He's only just appeared on the horizon, but—as certain indiscreet people say, and you really can't trust them anyway—they say he was a very distinguished young man back in the day. They were engaged once, after a fashion, and now they meet again after all these years—Oh, there's Mr. Nutka!"

Gondziłł was doing the honors as though he considered himself the host of the party. Since he took credit for Omski's presence at the competition, Gondziłł refused to leave his side.

"That lady, the one Teresa is greeting right now, that's General Chwościk's wife."

Indeed, this time General Chwościk had shown up with his wife. A fur coat was no longer necessary in this warm weather. The general's wife wore a greenish suit that was slightly wrinkled and a touch too short and tight; her little hat was embellished with black lace and a single white feather.

Mrs. Chwościk, along with another lady, the Countess Oskienna—whose attire was likewise shabby and outdated—stood in a splendid circle of foreign officers and conversed animatedly and simultaneously in the languages of three different allied nations. The general's wife's small face changed with lightning speed; she winced, laughed, and raged, illustrating every word with a different expression. The countess's face was pale and plump, full of sweetness and what seemed to be a constant plea for an understanding that nobody appeared to be denying her.

Moving on, they saw Hennert amidst a group of men who had the sturdy appearance of state officials. This time, Gondziłł's jubilant bow received a cursory reply; he obviously had infinitely more important business to attend to.

"That's how it is nowadays," Gondziłł explained to Omski with no loss of self-assurance. "He meets, after all these years, some dear Stach, some great Józef. They're all old friends, all fine fellows. 'Good Lord, there you are, a senator now!' 'Well, and old Edek's a general!' 'Gee, how long before that Felek becomes a minister?' 'Oh please, he'll land better than that…'"

Gondziłł—glad that at least other people were successful—wished them the very best and spoke without a trace of malice. And besides, he had his own innocent little victory: the people he'd mentioned had risen much higher not only than himself, but also higher than Colonel Omski. And that made the two of them closer…

They came to a stop at a little wooden bridge on the canal. The shallow, cloudy water was opalescent in the sunlight. Fresh leaves hung from the old willows' branches like unraveled golden netting.

They were about to turn back when Hennert appeared before them; he was completely alone now. This time, as if he'd been waiting for this very opportunity, he heartily greeted Gondziłł. It also happened that he badly wanted to meet this colonel for himself and introduce him to the ladies of his house.

However, the ladies were nowhere to be found at the moment. But they did meet General Chwościk, who was in the company of Professor Laterna and Mr. Nutka. This time, Andrzej Laterna found himself at his father's side.

Together, they all traipsed off in the direction of the stands. "Relations are improving, yes, relations are improving." General Chwościk spoke to the professor briskly and without pause. "Here, there, and everywhere. Europe, it's Europe. Style, culture, order. In short, aristocracy together. Democracy, too. And world superpowers. One horse needlessly fell down. But the officers, the officers. Indeed. I travel here, there, and everywhere. The People. And trains. In short, Europe. And so on and so forth. I'm proud. Poland is connected, bound, and united. Yes."

Unlike his wife, who had no difficulty speaking three languages, the general evidently had trouble speaking even one. He'd spent his entire life outside the borders of his own country. Nevertheless, his many years in the ranks of foreign armies gave him the experience and the professional expertise that was so valuable in his current position.

He had trouble, it's true, but it didn't discourage him in the least. On the contrary, it inclined him toward extraordinary concision and allowed him to encapsulate a multitude of thoughts in the space of a few minutes. As a result of this compacted speech, it was sometimes hard to grasp the ideas connecting respective sentences, to say nothing of making sense of any one of them. Professor Laterna gladly undertook the effort. He walked beside him, captivated, listening attentively to the words spilling out of the general. As usual, he carried his hat in his hand and let the sun warm the short, gray pelt on his large head.

The general's idea involved connecting officers, officially and socially, in such a way as to render obsolete the old differences engendered by their past affiliations with various armies and previous memberships in various political groups.

"Poland is united, and so on and so forth. In short, we are all united."

There was more: due to the various lands in which they had previously served, as well as the basic fact of wartime migration, a great number of military men had foreign wives.

"They went here, they went there, they went everywhere," is how the general articulated it. "And afterward, in short: Germans, Russians, Jews, Czechs, French, Italians. No harm in it. But these are wives, wives—our wives, our common officers' wives. And so on and so forth."

As he talked, he didn't once look at the professor; instead, his eyes roamed the area beyond him, intently searching for something. Finally he saw it—and suddenly, without finishing his sentence, barely muttering a perfunctory word of apology or even of farewell, he slipped away from the professor and, in two bounds, leapt toward some older gentleman who was walking alone. In the same tone and with the utmost urgency, he began to speak at once and was given an equally attentive ear.

"Prince Wiślicki." Gondziłł, who knew everyone, clarified what had just happened.

"Aristocracy together." Someone repeated the general's recent words.

Omski turned around: it was the heretofore silent young Laterna speaking for the first time. As their eyes met, Omski experienced a disagreeable sensation—namely, that the young man had been observing him for some time.

This young Laterna was a strange one. He was his father's antithesis. Equally tall, he was skinny and bony, his features—although seemingly regular—hard and unsympathetic. He was twenty-five, or perhaps a bit older, and on the whole, what with his big, dark, deep-set eyes, was rather handsome. His slightly protruding but hardly overdeveloped jaw and the bitterish shape of his mouth seemed to indicate strong will, to suggest stubbornness and energy. Meanwhile, the expression on his face was more neurasthenic than angry; it wasn't sullen so much as sour.

Jokingly called "my little boy" by his father, his criticism and acerbity stood in stark opposition to the elder's affirmation and cheer. His independent bearing, his perpetual tone of curt irony—it seemed an attempt to mask an internal agony of ambition, a self-dissatisfaction that was impossible to delude.

He'd been left to his own devices since childhood and owed everything to himself; he was hardworking, tenacious, and stubborn.

He'd finished school under grueling circumstances, completing his exams in some far-flung place. Oddly enough, he'd managed—despite his young age—to avoid any contact with matters of war, both while at home and in Russia. He'd never served in any army, never put on any uniform, and never killed anybody. He was in constant protest against the militarization of the world. But now, when peace had dawned, he felt no satisfaction.

Gondziłł thought to himself, "How did a fellow as nice as Laterna come to have such a horrible son?"

Because Colonel Omski was always gloomy, too—but you could feel a reserve of joy in him, you could feel his coiled impetus and strength. True, he rarely laughed—but the sound of his laugh was fresh as a mountain spring.

In any case, today the colonel wasn't laughing at all. The crowd of people, Gondziłł's nettlesome chatter—it was all just the belching of a stuffy city. Content, sated, lulled by peace, safe in the stale swamp of their lives, they all came here to gawk at the military displays, to feast their eyes on the picturesque scene of horses and uniforms, to amuse themselves with a harmless parade. This was what the army was reduced to nowadays!

He felt a sense of solidarity, of responsibility for the military's moral prestige. General Chwościk's latest role in this circle was equally distasteful to him. The grotesquerie of this figure pained Omski, a follower and champion of military authority. He by no means shared the concerns that the general had raised about divergent elements within the young army.

He himself—back at the beginning of the war, when he'd served as second lieutenant in the ranks of the foreign army—fought without hesitation or doubt, wanting only to be an exemplary officer. The geographical latitude of his placement simply meant that he found himself on this particular part of the front instead of somewhere else—and even then he didn't attach any particular meaning to it. He didn't now feel any hostility toward colleagues who'd been in different formations. He wasn't remotely involved in retrospective discussions and disputes over who'd been right politically or who was a better Pole. He thought that a good Pole was one who had fought well.

He just shrugged his shoulders at the animosity that erupted from time to time among officers over former "orientations" and old regional allegiances. He considered it stupid and beneath a soldier's dignity. The war had ended well; clearly everything was fine. He couldn't understand all these different schools that had risen from the rubble of old memberships and affiliations, all these pamphlets clashing up against and devouring one another.

These things served a purpose of some sort; they were undoubtedly necessary for something. You could obviously see it in Gondziłł, for example. The rank of lieutenant was a constant wound to his pride. But he never wasted an opportunity to mention how utterly indifferent he was to it. The reasons behind this unfortunate fate were indistinct and perhaps quite accidental. But Gondziłł, with certain intonations, facial expressions, and a knowing air, hinted at some higher and more mysterious meaning, with implications of far-reaching persecution and political martyrdom. He'd found some redress for his terminally injured self-esteem. After all, it was really by chance that he had found himself, as Omski had, on one part of the front and not the other. And he was certainly ready to serve the Polish cause in any way he possibly could.

The spring air, the scent of the still-damp earth and the young grass—today it galled Omski like poison. The sight of prancing horses, with their guileless, childlike souls, had reminded him of a sort of shared bygone province: war. War!

Once upon a time, he'd advanced amidst a flowing column of soldiers, woven into the march's current like a small thread in the shifting warp of fabric on a loom. Like everyone around him, he skirted the edge of his own death, steadying his exhausted but easily spooked horse with his knees. On the causeway that cut across the vast meadowlands, shells rained down on the mud and wet snow. There were endless horses, wagons, people. Sometimes one of the wounded would collapse—and the momentary hold-up would quickly be absorbed into the slow but ceaseless cadence of the march. Early spring clouds scudded low across the sky, dark against the patches of sunlight and the deep, glittering blue.

What exceptional power gushed from this brief recollection! The brutal strength of discipline, ambition, and will, of wrenching free from each defeat—of hope!

Again he felt an overwhelming disgust for life here and for the role he played in it. The city's bright, safe, tidy spring seemed to him as artificial as a theater set. What profound distaste he had for this world, for himself! He had fallen prey to some idiotic error. Living in a world of dry, almost platonic military calculations, predictions, and capabilities, shut away behind four walls, buried under maps and plans, he was suffocated by his excess of strength, this bound and useless strength.

The smell of last winter's fires still filled the young man's nostrils. At parties, concerts, and balls, in the fragrant darkness of theater boxes, in plush feminine sitting rooms—he wanted only to be tired. Just to be tired!

Trembling with impatience and rage, he made sweet, quiet conversation. He smiled and clouded over in turn, indifferent to temptation, burning with a different fire. He spoke caressingly to women he didn't love, masking his absent-mindedness, pretending to be happy.

Now he walked along with the others, listening to Mr. Hennert, his words smooth, silky, flattering, and almost slightly moist.

The director inquired about the location and condition of Omski's seat. He invited him to his own box for the second part of the program. Omski accepted, thanking him politely but unsmilingly. He was not remotely interested in knowing to what he owed the pleasure.

They broke off, because just then there was another flurry of bows. Miss Elżbieta Sasin was passing by. She walked jauntily down the avenue in the same ash-gray suit and little red hat. Accompanying her were her father and Mr. Niemeński, that young baron—a colleague from the office—who so frequently dictated translations of foreign telegrams to her.

She and the young man walked arm in arm, speaking intimately and laughing loudly. Unable to keep up, as it were, with the young ones, Mr. Sasin trailed slightly behind them, hunched as always, a chunk of cigar stuck in his wrinkled face.

Like the first time, before he knew who she was, a joyful and ad-miring Gondziłł did a double take at this lovely woman. It didn't even occur to him to envy the lucky man who was at her side. And, as before, Omski's gloomy face didn't brighten for even a second when he made his bow. Director Hennert's indifference seemed to equal his near-hostility upon encountering subordinates. Mr. Nutka, however, promptly left his companions and quickly caught up with the others. He managed to take Mr. Sasin by the arm and steer him off to the side for a longer monologue. And the young couple has-tened further down the promenade.

Finally they reached the stands and everyone dispersed, each heading to their respective seat.

With his usual sullen expression, Omski followed Hennert and allowed himself to be introduced to "his ladies," with whom, thanks to Gondziłł's report, he was already familiar. They both wore dark, almost black dress suits decorated with handmade appliqué—defying expectations, Omski knew quite a bit about women's clothing—and virtually identical little shiny black straw hats. It seemed to Om-ski that the daughter was already prettier than the mother. She was taller and statelier, and, although she'd inherited her father's too-small blue eyes, they were set off by a girlish oval face and a joyful expression of youth. She paid no attention at all to Omski, though. She offered her hand in a quick, casual gesture and immediately re-turned to her conversation with her foreigner. When Omski looked around, he saw that Hennert had already left the box. So he sat down in the empty chair behind the mother.

He effortlessly slipped into the role of polite party compan-ion and explained the different maneuvers in the show for Mrs. Hennert. From the little flashes he kept catching of her delicate profile, he noticed that she was still pretty. Which is to say: no longer young.

Omski felt better right away, as he usually did when in the com-pany of a pleasant and elegant woman. Mrs. Hennert clearly wanted to win him over with her kindness and charm. She thought it was a pity they hadn't met earlier. She mentioned the names of a few la-dies whom they both knew, mentioned a few houses in which they'd both been guests. How odd it was that they had never met until now. How unfortunate that it had turned out that way. Indeed. The colonel chatted easily and agreeably. Before long, he had promised to take part in a group excursion to the countryside (ah, if only the weather stays as fine as it is today!) and had unequivocally vowed to attend the banquet organized by General Chwościk's wife.

Meanwhile, young Laterna had somehow materialized in the box. He had something to say to Miss Hennert's Englishman, and something to tell her as well. It didn't take long, and after a moment Laterna stood in silence near the back of the box, arms folded across his chest, leaning against the wooden partition. Omski had the impression that Laterna—while supposedly following the various horses as they constantly went through their runs and jumps, which no one was really doing anymore except for maybe Wanda Hennert—was observing him in the same unpleasant manner as before.

"He's a very nice and capable man," Mrs. Hennert was saying about him.

Omski had a different view, but he didn't object. He'd already noticed that Mrs. Hennert had something good to say about everyone. This obliging attitude toward humanity appealed to Omski. There was a kind of honest feminine goodness in it.

New people were entering the box again, causing quite a stir. It was Mr. Sasin and his daughter. The blaze of her brilliant good looks instantly outshone the other two women in the box; they suddenly shrank, becoming colorless and irrelevant.

The colonel rose and offered his seat to Miss Elżbieta. Mrs. Hennert immediately turned to her with the same winning, enormously kind smile. Shortly thereafter, Miss Sasin had likewise promised to participate in the countryside excursion and attend the general's wife's party.

Suddenly Omski darkened. Pushing his way into the already full box with entitled ease was an older gentleman, one of those men whom Gondziłł had pointed out to him in the park. His name was Sednowski. Gondziłł had called him Teresa's admirer—but in a way that suggested something worse, even something completely vile. Only just now had it struck the colonel as offensive.

He approached the ladies and talked to them confidently, intimately, as if he were one of the family—again, of course, about the country outing and Chwóscik's wife's banquet. Omski felt a pang of hatred in his heart and, in that same moment, resolved to attend neither event.

He had to admit that Mr. Sednowski was very good-looking. Tall, a bit stout, with a symmetrical face and the slightly softened features of a voluptuary, he was full of palpable self-satisfaction. With a ringing voice and sweeping gestures, his speech and his gaze had a kind of indulgent, cheerful, patronizing superiority; like a lord, you might say. It was clear that this feeling of superiority required no justification; it was inborn, granted from on high—there was simply no doubt in his mind.

Without knowing why, Omski was angry. After all, it was no concern of his. But this Mrs. Hennert—so kind and delicate, so noble somehow—exactly, noble!—that she too could allow—and that tone alone! Let him talk to Sasin like that, but not to her! "Terenia"— that's what this "admirer" called her—"Terenia!"

The competition had just come to an end. Now the stands were full of movement. The clatter of hundreds of shoes resounded through the wooden platforms built over empty space.

Pushed aside by the surge inside the box—Mr. Hennert and Mr. Nutka had just squeezed in—the irritated colonel retreated toward the exit, where he found himself standing next to young Laterna.

There was no longer any doubt that he was looking right at Omski. Today was the first time in his life that Omski had seen Laterna; he had no idea what could be so interesting to the young man.

"Do you have something to tell me?" he asked at last, impatiently.

The man was quick to stand up.

"Yes." This answer was completely unexpected.

"Yes?" Omski struggled to remain indifferent. "And what might that be?"

"Your fiancée." Laterna began to speak with ungainly ironic elegance. "It is rather…"

Omski felt himself go unpleasantly red. He was extremely surprised.

"Whom do you mean?" he asked.

Mrs. Hennert had just risen from her seat and was looking at them curiously.

"Never mind. Actually, I have news for Miss Olinowska and only wished to take advantage of a good opportunity. Her aunt is back in town and doesn't know how to find her. In this day and age… And she's in the hospital."

"Basia's aunt?" Elżbieta asked gaily. "It must be Miss Lipska."

This completely innocent message generated an almost familial mood that the colonel didn't care for one bit.

He asked the young man for details and drily assured him that he would not fail to convey them to Miss Olinowska as soon as he could. All the while, he observed how, as Elżbieta made her way through the crowd at Hennert's side, her laughing face turned toward his again and again, animatedly explaining something.

9.

Early in the morning, having bathed with cold water, still shaking off the sleep that had been interrupted by her alarm clock, Basia Olinowska left her home and headed to the office. She could go by foot—there was enough time. The depths of the noiseless streets were milky with light spring fog. The sun was white, too, as it flooded the wooden cobblestone street and the stony sidewalks. A pleasant chill wafted from the shade of the chestnut trees, which were abloom with coral-colored flowers.

It was a great joy to be able to walk to work like this, completely alone amidst the flowering trees and the white sun. Alone with the spring and her breathtaking feelings.

The street was surrounded by gardens. Through fences' cast-iron bars she could see, above the vivid green lawns, lilacs blooming everywhere—everywhere! Among the dark leaves, there were white lilacs stuck stiffly to the ends of their rigid stems, and there were red lilacs that would be purple in less than a week, that were hard and just starting to open but would soon be velvety and bursting with fragrance. This was the most beautiful time of the year.

Now Basia knew that it was possible to pry fate's crushing weight off her chest, that it was possible to bounce back and go on living. The body tired of sorrow, and eyes eventually didn't want to—couldn't—cry anymore. After the death of her parents, after the loss of her home.

She'd become a different person. She felt the change within herself far more intensely than she felt her change of fortune.

At the time, that bygone world seemed to be the only possibility. It was the source of all judgments, the point of reference, the foundation for laws of living. Now that she had learned a new way of life, she saw clearly that this other one, lost to fate, was only a kind of expensive, pathetic oddity, something almost comically unreal.

Ah, what a home she had had—a home suffused with the warmest light of love. There they lived in a sort of cocoon of quiet happiness amidst the refined little comforts of the life they provided for each other, in the sweet concern and ceaseless care each gave the other two, in shy seclusion from the world's gaze.

There, the most important business of the morning was whether Papa was willing to drink the cream that had been set on his bedside table the previous evening. If he drank it, the day would be off to an auspicious start—the mood in the house would be completely different, the smiles and kisses different. Next, Basia would discreetly sniff the glass beside her mother's bed. If it didn't smell of ether, everyone was further pleased—she hadn't had heart palpitations and hadn't needed her drops. Before breakfast, which her mother took in bed, there was a new ritual, an entirely new lark: using a special machine, Papa himself squeezed the juice of several oranges into a glass, into which he had sneaked the daily lemon that had been prescribed to Mama. And Mama, moaning and shuddering, drank the nectar down, if only to spare the other two any distress.

Then came the hours of the day. Papa's every hunt, Basia's every horse ride—all were a source of mortal unease. Each return became a celebration. With relief and joy, they welcomed each other back as though after a long journey, hiding the alarm they'd felt, not wanting to burden their dearest ones and spoil their fun.

Each of their various little whims and weaknesses, each eccentricity and habit was, to the other two, the most sacred of laws, and they had perfectly assimilated this knowledge. Each had his or her own favorite cup at the table, a particular way for the coffee to be brewed and the lettuce to be seasoned. These little rituals were always remembered, always strictly observed, and were embraced and enjoyed by everyone.

Guests, tutors, and the household staff were all drawn into this system of consideration, comfort, and tender care. Everyone had to share in these anxieties, pleasures, and delights. The servants became much like the masters. Ah, that superlative little old lady, unforgettable Marianna, the cook, who treated her dishes like they were living creatures. She was always saying that every item "needs its own thing." Bigos "liked" a bit of Madeira wine, coffee "liked" to be served with fresh rolls, even an already-dead turkey "liked" things that would render him tastier to the masters.[17] Marianna remembered everyone's particular little fancies, delectations, and aversions. Her Madeira-liking bigos was rarely made, lest Mama be tempted and her arthritis provoked. Her unparalleled shortbread was baked three different ways to indulge everyone's individual preference. And her stuffing, "liked" by the chicken, was sheer poetry. After several dozen years of service, the old woman still trembled daily to satisfy her masters.

The circle of light cast by the fireplace in the dining room marked the horizons of the world. During autumn's long solitude, during all those winter nights, they were left solely to themselves to cultivate their peculiar, exaggerated affections. They devised little gifts and surprises for one another, innumerable little treats. Their intimate life seemed lit from within and swollen to excess. It bred an egoistic exclusivity, a subconscious disdain for the rest of the world. Neighbors, guests, and even extended family were all genially disregarded. Among these three most beloved to one other, no one formed factions or made comparisons. Each of them was the most important thing in the world to the remaining two.

Now Basia was a different person.

Now she could wake up in an empty room, set the tea to boil for no one but herself, and hurry to the office. Nobody put fluffy slippers beside her bed, nobody gave any thought to what she ate before she left. Her life—her entire soul—had been transformed to the very core. The few short years that had passed had wiped from the face of the earth all traces of this previous life. Not even a shred of its value was left in her heart. Only memory and incredulity remained.

And now Aunt Lipska had arrived and was in the hospital. Auntie Lipska—a stout, cheerful widow with a coarse face and wide shoulders, always slightly unkempt. What a joy it had been when she used to visit them! She had a broad sense of humor and liked to poke fun at the prevailing customs of her sister's home. "You all," she'd say. "Only looking after each other's stomachs. No one here can have a cold on their own—when one of you sneezes, somebody else wipes their nose; when somebody's belly aches, all three of you moan." She laughed at them. But when she arrived, of course, she had to have her salad specially prepared: no oil, only creamed egg yolks.

Yes, it was an impossible, artificial world, sealed in a sphere of glass, suspended over a complete void.

And now Basia was like the others: those mysterious working people previously unknown to her. In exchange for the work she did, work that benefited others, she was able to eat. She did something that was undoubtedly useful—she thought so, anyway. No one devoted themselves to her, and she was beholden to no one. This was independence. She considered it a source of moral strength; it allowed her to go on living and even to take some pleasure in it.

She often thought about that bygone time, about her former home. She considered it with aversion and distaste. Now she could bring herself to condemn it. So what if it was said, at the time, that they were the sweetest people on earth, that they were loved by their servants, that even the peasants... No, to live like that—it was a sin, a sin...

Only, she didn't know if her current self—this hardness, this particular emotional coldness—had already been poised and ready within her former self. Back then—indulged, spoiled, enfolded in the tenderest love, isolated and walled-off from the truth—had she been inside all along, this person she was today?

Certainly no one sensed it in her at the time; she hadn't felt it herself. But, after all, an entirely new approach to life couldn't emerge overnight without any groundwork being laid, just because of a simple change of fate. She'd already been different from those who were closest to her, and that was precisely why she was able to survive.

"Good morning, Basia!"

She stopped to allow Elżbieta Sasin to catch up with her. They were already in front of the office building. The broad Renaissance façade basked in the cheerful sunlight. On the lawn in front of the windows a gardener was watering the blooming irises with a hose.

"How is Mrs. Lipska doing? Were you at the hospital yesterday?"

They greeted one another like close friends, seeing as they'd known each other since childhood. Years before, Mr. Sasin had been the chief steward of Mr. Olinowski's forests.

Basia had been to the hospital, naturally, and replied that her aunt wasn't doing well at all. They needed to perform an operation, but for some reason they hadn't done it. Her aunt looked like an old, old woman.

"I saw your colonel again," Ela was saying. "You know, at the Hennerts'..."

Basia passed the wide-open doors of the typists' room. As always, it was pretty and bright, full of sunlight and flowers. The little tables were decked with bunches of narcissus, and there were sprigs of lilac stuck into water-filled bottles and drinking glasses.

The rooms and corridors were already bustling with clerks taking off their coats and greeting one another. The building was coming to life.

Basia—calm, serious, proper, a model employee—entered her office and got right to work. She took some files from a drawer and spread them out on a stain-spotted, cherry red desk cloth. Propping her elbows on the table and resting her head on both hands, she bent over the papers.

Coming and going through various doors were applicants, clerks, typists, and porters; they approached various desks, spoke quickly and urgently in hushed voices, submitted or collected papers, saw to their business, and left. The huge room was filled with hushed conversations, muffled disputes and attempts at persuasion, and the flow of constant movement. Basia had to plug her ears and furrow her brow in order to focus her thoughts. When she raised her eyes, irritable from the intensity of her concentration, she was met with a similar gaze from the clerk sitting opposite her at an adjoining desk.

It was completely different in here than in the typists' room. There was a certain hysteria in this kind of work; it was fast, frenzied, and exhausting. Everyone was on edge—leaping out of their skin, as it were—and their health and humor paid the consequences. The clerks smoked endless cigarettes, scattering ash on their threadbare clothing, undoing their fraying cuffs and rolling up their soiled shirtsleeves, always impatient, always in a rush. The women here were older and sterner, overloaded with responsibilities and concerns, earning more but dressing worse. Many had more education and better reputations than their male colleagues. Here was a place where problems were solved, where people needed to make decisions quickly and assume full responsibility.

At the desk to Basia's right sat a woman who was pale, sickly, and past thirty: Mrs. Bielska, who had a second job at a private office during the afternoon hours. She alone provided for three sons who were all in school. She worked with difficulty—she had migraines, vertigo, heart palpitations. She was constantly taking some kind of unpleasant-smelling pill, the odor of which hovered around her desk, creating its own atmosphere. She explained to Basia that the salary from her husband—a major—wasn't even enough to keep up appearances.

She worked diligently and earnestly, but with a strange passivity. It was always the same—she did everything within her duty, but beyond that she made not a single substantial move to resolve any matter. She had no sense of the connection between the work done at the office and real life. She lacked initiative and energy of any kind. Because of the way their work was divided, Basia was forced to make up for all these deficiencies and shortcomings.

Worse than the major's wife was Basia's closest assistant, Stefa. Likewise déclassée because of a twist of fate, she was spoiled, frolicsome, and clearly more cut out for the typists' room. She'd done everything she could to get her position, supplying diplomas and the best recommendations. She had support coming from every direction, and she'd assured everyone that she would manage. So finally she was hired—and immediately lost this indubitable self-confidence. She came to Basia with every little thing, supposedly for advice.

"Miss Olinowska, see what's happened here. It's too hard, I don't understand any of it. Somehow everything's gotten all mixed up here..." And she would dump the entire weight of her laziness on Basia.

At noon, tea was brought in.

Conversing with clients, they held their pens in their right hands and picked up paper-wrapped sandwiches with their left hands, munching and sipping without interrupting their work. At first it bothered Basia to eat amidst papers, dust, and general havoc. But now she ate like everyone else, with an excellent appetite.

In the succession of people coming and going, Basia noticed old Countess Oskienna slowly closing in on her.

Ruined by war, aristocracy from the Borderlands often wound up here. They arrived, disoriented and bewildered, to settle some pitiful bit of business, to seek support, to offer their services to the young democratic nation. Next to all the dirty collars and trampled-looking shoes, their exaggerated courtesy just seemed like importunate flattery.

Countess Oskienna arrived like the others. She had once been widely known and respected, incredibly rich, famous for keeping her profligate grandsons on a short leash, sparing with herself and her family but obliging with strangers. The servants worshiped her, and her relatives badmouthed her. Back then, she'd go out dressed in a thick leather caftan and men's shoes; she was scruffy, stubborn, and crotchety. In her old palace, among her venerable servants and her constantly favor-currying relations, this was just lordly eccentricity, to be treated with kind forbearance.

These days—utterly ruined, wearing furs despite the spring, muddy slippers despite the fine weather, and, with comical bravado, a felt hat—she kept coming in to beg some clerk to facilitate her equally ruined grandson's travel through the consulate or other diplomatic channels. Given the circumstances, it was impossible. The matter came down to a simple lack of money, to the price of the ticket; the request was shameless and, frankly, indecent. The impoverished lady didn't realize this—she, who had formerly done so much for others.

The clerk refused her. Not for the first time, he explained the situation patiently and politely enough. She doggedly insisted, her fat white face flushing with emotion. Finally, when she began addressing him as "my dear boy," he rose slightly to indicate that the conversation was over—he, who not long ago wouldn't have dared even to dream of sitting at her table.

Basia watched with harsh disapproval. This was fate's vengeance. This was proof of how terribly unreal that other life had been, that world like a glass bubble suspended over the void.

The countess, her smile completely new, uncertain, and conciliatory, came over to Basia to say hello.

"Sweet Basia, my dear," she began, exuding a stale air of musty clothing and elderly, carelessly bathed flesh, "I'm not disturbing you, I'm just..."

She knew she was doing exactly that, she knew how intrusive and unwanted she was—that's why she said it. Because she hadn't lost hope yet and was desperate for help, even if it came from this little Olinowska, who—well, who would have thought...

So no, she wasn't disturbing anyone. She only wanted to ask after the health of poor, dear Niusia Lipska, and she would run along in just a moment.

But she didn't run along. She even sat down—uninvited—just to give her tired old legs a rest. And as soon as she sat—without delay, she began to discuss her cause, the details of which Basia already knew all too well.

Basia looked at her watch and stood up. "Please excuse me, Countess, but I have to see the director right this minute. Yes, Director Hennert."

At the sound of this name the old woman's face lit up with a new flash of hope.

"Director Hennert, my God! My dear girl, couldn't you..."

But Basia had already slipped away. Indeed, she did have a one o'clock appointment with Hennert in his office to discuss the details and provisions of her new job.

In her work life there was a great change and a cause for joy and pride: this summons. A report from a meeting and several translations she'd done had turned the director's head her way. He appreciated good writing and was interested in giving her the position of private secretary.

In the corridor she mixed with the waiting crowd. She wasn't supposed to have to wait in line, so she sent a short note through the steward and waited calmly and self-assuredly. But, contrary to her expectations, the steward came back with the message that the boss would see her tomorrow at ten instead. During the brief moment when the door of Hennert's office was ajar she beheld, standing there in the middle of the room, Ela Sasin.

She returned to her office slowly, with a vague impression of failure. "She's so much prettier," she thought only now. The sight of Elżbieta's slender figure, the haughty profile and laughing mouth glimpsed for a second through the sliver of open door, lingered in her mind. The very same girl—dark, skinny, timid—who had been brought from the forester's lodge every Sunday so they could play together, the girl who was given Basia's crumpled old dolls and broken toys.

No wonder... "I saw your colonel again—you know, at the Hennerts." She'd already said as much.

Basia entered her office and saw with relief that Countess Oskienna had left.

"We've all changed somehow," she thought, sitting at her desk and cupping her bowed head in both hands.

10.

Breaking his dour resolution, Omski did take part in Teresa's excursion to the countryside, and he did buy a ticket to General Chwościk's wife's banquet.

He had somehow become a member of the Hennert ladies' retinue—together with Curll the Englishman, Lieutenant Lin, and Mr. Sednowski. Young Laterna had not reappeared in this company.

After paying a first visit, gloves in hand and stiff leather strap across his chest, the colonel immediately felt at home. He brought flowers for the drawing room, fed biscuits to Klinga the greyhound, and suggested ways to while away the remainders of evenings. He became a valued and trusted friend to the lady of the house and steered rather clear of the daughter. Several times a week he ate lunch or dinner with them—sometimes even among the close family circle.

He was not immediately at ease with the prevailing customs there, which were merry indeed.

After dinner, everyone settled into a small drawing room. Mr. Nutka, Mr. Sednowski, the colonel, Curll, and Elżbieta were always there, and often some young girlfriend of Wanda's, too. They listened to the Englishman's exotic tunes, which he happily played on demand, drank coffee with prewar liqueurs and brandies, and ate every type of sweet, even halvah and Turkish delight. In a corner of the room not covered by rugs, Wanda and Lin danced delightful tango figures, effortlessly tracing a square no larger than the surface of a table.

At Mr. Hennert's request, Elżbieta stood by the piano and, with Curll accompanying, sang arias from new operettas.

"What spirit, what spirit," Hennert said to Sednowski.

The beautiful girl's eyes were glowing, her shoulders and hips swaying in time to the music. Her ring-covered fingers showered the room with drops of light. Lascivious couplets floated melodiously from her lips. The music circulated like blood through her body, which was wholly taken with the rhythm's pulse.

"Encore, encore!" A beaming Mr. Nutka clapped his hands.

"And now you'll have more coffee," Teresa urged Elżbieta.

Omski sat there as if at a performance. Hennert had enthusiastically noted that Ela was really filling out—and, to illustrate this to everyone, he slid a sleeve of her amber-colored dress as high as it went.

Teresa watched attentively.

"Yes, yes, you're filling out. And it looks lovely on you," she said, with a winning smile.

Omski watched Teresa, searching her face for some sign. Could it be that nothing bothered her in any of this? She was so unlike her surroundings, so serene and noble. And she seemed to have no appreciation of just how different she was from the rest of them.

Again Hennert slid Elżbieta's sleeve up—this time to plant a kiss on her arm, high above the elbow.

Mr. Sednowski, lounging comfortably on her other side, was

less prone to romanticism, and only stroked the olive-skinned nape of her neck—a gesture of fatherly indulgence, or perhaps encouragement.

She half-heartedly tried to shake them off. Both her hands were busy peeling a tangerine over a plate that she held between her knees.

"Oh really, that's enough! I'll break this plate if you don't stop this instant."

But they somehow didn't stop. "Youth, youth!" Mr. Nutka said with relish.

The atmosphere was completely familial. Arms around each other's waists, Wanda and her girlfriend sat together in an armchair and looked on. Teresa, calm and cheerful, saw to it that everyone's cups were full of black coffee.

From time to time Curll stopped playing and amiably turned his eyes, blue and serious, to the amused assembly.

"Then again, maybe there's nothing wrong with it." Omski assured himself without conviction.

It was unclear why he was glad that Elżbieta appealed to Sednowski.

In any case, this kind of entertainment was reserved only for the closest circle. During their larger parties and high teas, Elżbieta modestly withdrew into the background. Even her beauty became more discreet.

Once a week, throngs of people crowded into both the small and large sitting rooms at the Hennerts'. The street in front of the gate was filled with honking automobiles, the pegs in the entrance hall were hung with hats and coats festooned with multicolored ribbons and threaded with copper and silver. Diplomats and foreign ministry officials, family names of the first order, and, especially, money—*money*. Omski knew their faces from the dozen or so other elegant homes in which he was received.

These occasions allowed him to admire Teresa's social and practical talent. How smoothly everything went, how happy and content everyone was! Guests stood, sat, milled around, chatted, came to a standstill, greeted one another, and said their goodbyes. Something was always going on, constantly and to an extreme degree. But after two or three hours everyone vanished, and it was as though no one had ever been there.

And once again, sitting down at the table, there was the small, most intimate circle, whose composition underwent only slight changes.

Young Laterna, to Omski's dismay, finally made another appearance. He'd just returned from some sort of travel around the country; this was his explanation for his long absence.

He arrived with Curll, rather formally, on the Hennerts' receiving day. Despite his ostensible lack of social graces, it turned out he had many acquaintances among the circles represented at the Hennerts'. Teresa gave him a warm welcome and later invited him to stay the evening. He eagerly accepted.

Today, this highest circle also included Mr. Niemeński, whom Hennert, his superior, had honored with an invitation.

After dinner, Curll had to play dance music only, since Elżbieta—never having had the opportunity to do so until now—wanted to dance with Mr. Niemeński. The languid and bored young man succumbed to the temptation, although the dancers kept bumping hips as they turned and spun on the too-small bit of floor they shared with Wanda and Lin.

"Well, if you really want to dance, I'll have the carpet taken up," Teresa fretted.

That was entirely unnecessary. This was fine. Perfect, actually.

Elżbieta was laughing and, head thrown back, looking deeply into the twinkling eyes of her dance partner. Her dancing revealed exactly what her singing did.

"Lively girl," Hennert told Sednowski under his breath. "But expensive as hell…"

Mrs. Hennert asked Laterna about his sister's health. Even though she didn't know her at all, she was sorry to hear that she had taken a turn for the worse.

"You're not enjoying yourself, Colonel." She turned suddenly toward Omski.

He smiled defenselessly in the beam of her crystalline gaze.

"I'm fine, really," he said.

When they stopped dancing, Laterna approached Lin and drew

him into a longer conversation. As the lieutenant wiped the sweat from his forehead, he listened with rapt attention to Laterna's impressions of his travels. The boy's lean young face took on an expression of seriousness and concern.

Laterna had returned from the Borderlands, where it just…there you could see just what we've come to, what we paid such a price for—the cost of torrents of blood.

The lieutenant had also thought about this. Belarusians, Ukrainians—after all, it was the same for them. Nowadays, "reasons of state" determined everything; nowadays, talk of the people's liberation had ceased.[18] And Poland, which for so many years had writhed in the shackles of her captivity (the lieutenant was a poet)—now Poland herself…so this is why we fought? So this, *this* was independence? Here people sit, locked in prison, simply for professing the highest, noblest ideas…and nobody protests, and everyone is silent!

Laterna, nodding curtly in agreement as though it gave him no joy to have found a fellow believer, encouraged the lieutenant to unburden himself. He made as if to soothe him, but, with his unpleasant irony and indulgent superiority, he fanned the flames of the lieutenant's youthful passion instead.

"That's right. Such is Poland. One shouldn't have expected anything different."

It wasn't the first time he'd noticed this young man—idealistic, truculent, disenchanted. Laterna knew that, despite his capering disposition, Lin regarded global matters with serious concern, that he had a "deeper" nature, that he was prone to illusions and disappointment. During the war, he'd written poems in which dying for the fatherland appeared to be the best way to go. And now he sometimes regretted that death had not come for him then—like it had for so many, many others.

Laterna was looking for such people. But he knew that this particular type was needed only at the first moments of an upheaval, that such people could come in handy during the initial, grandiose, declamatory convulsions of revolution, when slogans were needed to mesmerize and subjugate the masses. By the next day, such people would have doubts about whether it was advisable to use terrorist practices in the service of an idea, they'd be mortified by the military necessities of revolution, they'd revile the dishonor of compromising with the toppled order, they'd be outraged over "state considerations." Such people were good for making revolutions, but they must be devoured on the very day of victory, put in prison, condemned to quiet disappearance.

Laterna didn't like the ideological part, but for the time being he had to recognize its value. He sat off to the side with Lin and asked him whether he'd be willing to...whether he would able to... Considering the fact that in Poland ideas alone could land you in prison, the people suffered persecutions and torture, there were even plans hatched for—supposedly accidental—assassinations. The fact that in this reclaimed and independent fatherland the shameful czarist institutions had been preserved intact—the gendarmerie, the police, the spies...[19]

Curll approached them. He was looking empathetically at them both, sensing something with his delicate intuition. He didn't understand the words they were saying, but he could feel them seethe. And he was on their side.

"It doesn't mean anything as long as Asia is there," he said to Laterna. "The Soviet Union collapses without Asia. They shouldn't look to the West when they have the entire East before them... If communism isn't chipping away at the colonies, nothing is certain. India, India—there's the first task. A rich, marvelous country. And it's ready, offering itself up, craving liberation from the British yoke."

Laterna was familiar with this pipe dream. He made promises, he egged them on. It was all fine with him—both the ideological pathos of a naïve officer suffering from unrequited love for Poland, and the far off political plans of an Irish aristocrat and monarchist who, anonymously crossing the world, was chasing a vision of his own mighty, resurrected fatherland: the ill-fated, longed-for Kathleen.[20]

11.

Basia was surprised that the next day—and the days after that— the director still didn't have time to see her.

Mrs. Bielska, her exhausted face flushed from her efforts, was working more poorly than usual. After breakfast, she complained to Basia about the burdens of military life. An officer had to put in an appearance everywhere, had to maintain his contacts with people, had to participate in formal dinners, conventions, and commemorative celebrations, had to pay membership fees, endless membership fees, and had to be decently dressed, lest he diminish the army's prestige. But where did one find the money for all this? Where?

The couple recently had had to sell another mahogany dressing table, and Mrs. Bielska couldn't get over it. There had been so many compartments in each drawer, and now everything was constantly a mess; there was nowhere to put the little odds and ends. The surface and frame had been decorated with inlaid designs, and there had been an oblong mirror and thick, beautifully curved legs. For as long as she could remember, it had been the place where her mother brushed her hair. "These days, old pieces are all the rage, so of course people are eager to buy, and they pay quite a good price."

Mrs. Bielska swallowed a migraine pill with her tea. Her eyes were red, and her hands trembled as she helplessly rearranged the papers on her desk.

Shortly before Basia left for the day, Elżbieta stopped by to offer her some candy. That ridiculous Niemeński had brought a whole box to the office for her.

With a sneer, she told Basia that he'd proposed. "He as well!" As if she had enough time for this kind of silliness. She also mentioned that he was playing the stock market now and was making more than he earned at the office.

"Let's leave together, because I don't want him to walk me home again. Someone's waiting for me today—my new flame! You'll see."

Basia already knew him by sight—that ridiculous fat old Lieutenant Gondziłł. She didn't believe for a minute that he could honestly appeal to Ela. There were often random men standing on the street in front of the office and sometimes even on the stairs: the office girls' lovers or fiancés. These men were greeted cheerfully with an affable frankness born of feminine independence, of a life without family or obligations.

Omski had never come for Barbara. She considered it proof of his tact and respect.

Indeed, Gondziłł was waiting for Elżbieta again. At the sight of this Sancho Panza figure trying to woo her she exploded in irrepressible mirth.

She was not, however, entirely cruel.

"Papa complains about you," she said, opening a thick-handled little umbrella as the first drops of rain began to fall. "You're not being straight with them. Time is of the essence. Every day, we lose a few thousand... You're obviously a rich man if you can afford to waste that kind of money..."

She was marvelous—the harmony of her figure, her clothing, the way she moved. Her narrow pumps flashed against the pavement, which was rapidly darkening with rain.

"And you still haven't done anything about Bielski, have you?"

On the contrary, he had twice bought him dinner and had really softened up the ground.

"The ground?" Elżbieta laughed. "The ground is always soft. You have to act faster."

"And Omski—" Gondziłł began, but she broke in again.

"I know Omski myself. He's a fool..."

As they walked, she stopped in front of the shop windows, safe and dry under her umbrella while the rain poured down on Gondziłł's collar. She looked at the dresses on display, the blouses and skirts. She pursed her lips and, in the most refined tone possible, said, "Trash."

In front of the display window at the jeweler's, she said, "Ooh, this is the pin that I need. One lovely stone and nothing more. When you and Papa make good money, you both must buy it for me."

Meanwhile, Basia went to dinner—alone, as usual. Sitting at the restaurant were groups of people, or couples, or even solitary men, all drawn by the inexpensive meals served at that time of day. But it was only the unaccompanied women sitting there who were at a disadvantage; the staff ignored and disdained them.

At a restaurant, a man—even if he comes all by himself—always drinks vodka before his meal and always has an appetizer or two.

A working woman eats humbly, orders the cheapest item on the menu—only what's absolutely necessary—and chews and swallows without appetite.

The only luxury Basia sometimes allowed herself here was the pudding with cream. But old Marianna had made it so much better at home.

Basia never went anywhere with Omski. At the beginning, she was still in mourning, so theaters, concerts, and places with music were obviously out of the question. But it was the same even later. Her little room was the only place they saw each other.

Basia explained this state of affairs to herself as what was necessary for maintaining a good reputation. She also considered that it wasn't in Omski's nature to let love get mixed up with other matters in his life. Not wanting to cause him distress, Basia also kept it secret. Only Elżbieta knew, having once unexpectedly dropped in on Basia while Omski was there. But she probably took it none too seriously—she who had so many male acquaintances herself.

Critical thoughts, suspicious ideas—these did not easily penetrate Basia's consciousness. She still had great reserves of self-regard from her past. There was always an instinctive, subconscious sense that she was still the Miss Olinowska who might encounter unpleasantness, who might encounter unhappiness—but never humiliation.

Right after dinner , Basia went to the hospital where her aunt lay ill. Mrs. Lipska was staying in a room with three other patients. The principal and most important operation had not yet been performed; the only thing that allowed her to breathe was the tube they'd put in her afflicted throat, the opening of which was located in her neck, under her chin. The tube's nozzle was fitted with a metal ring—like the hole in a rubber doll that squeaks when you press it. At first she'd been so tormented by the dryness of her mouth and nose that it seemed like she wouldn't be able to bear it. But she eventually stopped complaining.

She endured unspeakable suffering. Her only treatment was the constant administration of new drugs.

The cancer had spread from her throat—through her neck—to her back, and there it caused the worst pain. A constantly festering ulcer throbbed under her distended, swollen armpit.

But worst of all were the attacks of dyspnea. Blood clots formed in her trachea, and they couldn't pass through the tube. Her coughing didn't sound like everyone else's; from the tube there came only a sharp whistle.

Basia was always informed of her aunt's condition by a nun in an enormous cornette and a coarse gray habit with an apron and rosary beads. Hidden deep within this severe form was a good, simple, young girl.

"Last night we thought she would suffocate," she said. "I didn't know what to do to, she was suffering so. I thought to myself, 'It makes no difference now, whatever happens is meant to be, I will try,' and I removed the tube. And luckily the clot popped out and flew all the way over here, to the middle of the room."

Aunt Lipska listened to the story and confirmed it with her eyes. That's how it happened, it was all true.

Despite her suffering, she never moaned. She couldn't moan; she couldn't make a sound. When she wanted to say something she blocked the opening of the tube with her finger. But even then she could barely whisper.

Basia listened with concentration. There were never complaints, just small, insignificant details about her illness. Her life consisted entirely of when she fell asleep, when she took her pill, and which doctor had come to see her.

Basia felt guilty when she wasn't able to catch something. Then the nun, who better understood the whispering, would repeat her aunt's words.

Afterward, though, Basia always tried to talk a while, to tell her aunt a little something. When Basia relayed something funny, her aunt smiled silently—with her mouth only, a slight movement of her lips.

And today Basia talked as usual. She never mentioned the past: her mother, her father, the house. She only talked about what was happening at the office, the work she was doing, things like that.

Mrs. Lipska signaled that she wanted to talk. She put her finger on the tube's opening. Basia leaned in to listen to the whispered words.

"If not for faith, it would not be possible. Do you understand, Basia? I wouldn't be able to bear it. If not for the faith that my suffering is needed by God."

Basia nodded her head to signal that she understood.

She kissed her aunt's hand and left.

Enclosed in the walls of this hospital room was everything that remained of her past.

She recalled that in the Krzywe parish, to which Chowańce belonged, the cemetery was atop a hill. Her aunt had a plot next to her husband, who had died a long time ago. You could see the river from there, down below, flowing between the trees, deep into the meadows, the gently undulating hillsides downy with grain. But she'd come all the way here—and here she would die.

It took quite a long time to walk home. She was tired. Her lips were tightly pursed, and the expression in her eyes was more harsh than sad.

She found Omski waiting in her room.

"I didn't forget that you would come today. But I couldn't get here any earlier."

Their greetings didn't require smiles.

"Were you visiting Mrs. Lipska?"

"Yes."

Omski didn't even ask about her aunt's condition—no doubt there was nothing to be done. It sufficed that he was glum about it.

"I was just going to have some tea," Basia said. "And there's something that you like. Here, have a seat."

There was a small gas stove attached to one of the walls in Basia's room, and she set the water to boil over its silent flame. Glasses and little plates of victuals had been tucked away on the lowest shelf of her bookcase. The something that Omski liked turned out to be smoked tongue.

Her little life was organized in a way that indicated a nervous orderliness and a full acceptance of reality.

Basia's round, ruddy face, with its low forehead and slightly bulging eyes, bore—despite its almost childish features—an imprint of seriousness and decisiveness, earned by a life of independence and relying only on one's self.

Feeling vaguely self-conscious, Omski watched her bustling around. Her movements were deft and energetic but not at all rushed; she was always completely calm. Both her hair and her shoes were neatly kept, and she wore an inexpensive, fashionable black dress—the type you could buy ready-made.

Her room's appearance was also striking in its lack of any tradition. Her furniture was minimal and new, purchased recently and all at once: what happened was that they'd sold a ring and had immediately bought the furniture. There was a small desk, a wardrobe, a little table, and a set of chairs, all of identical "mahogany-style" wood. There had been beds, but Basia sold one of them when her mother got sick and the other after she died. Omski himself had helped her with these transactions. Instead of a bed, there stood, diagonally to the wall, a small and deeply uncomfortable pink sofa. The window was covered with cheap but spotless lace curtains, the parting of which revealed a lilac blossom in a narrow glass vase.

Looking around the room, Omski remorsefully reflected that it had been a very long time since he'd sent Basia any flowers, and he resolved to make amends first thing tomorrow.

He felt some indefinable sense of guilt. He never felt good here, never experienced joy or even restfulness. He felt inhibited, dispirited, ashamed, although he had nothing specific in mind and was subject to no reproach. It was just him and this feeling that he was somehow to blame. The only one accusing him of anything was himself.

"In Chowańce—do you remember? The lilacs were blooming when we saw each other for the first time."

He spoke so softly, as if he were asking for approval. He wanted to offer her compensation for these thoughts that, though she didn't know about them, were so unfair to her. The thing he wanted to resuscitate didn't want to live anymore.

Basia rose to pour the tea. She didn't respond. They had met there, right there—at Aunt Lipska's... She didn't want to think about it. She didn't like memories.

And only through allusions to their past could Omski see the Basia he desired.

That slight girl with the ordinary, unremarkable face, so nonchalant and indifferent amidst the luxury of that noble old house, enhanced and elevated by her background—how attractive she was to him back then! Her wide nose hadn't bothered him at all. All the

Olinowskis had big noses. According to the prevailing worldview there, merit by no means warranted love or pride. Certain features sufficed. Clearly, just being an Olinowski already meant so much. As a child of common riffraff, Omski was sensitive to this sort of thing.

But that wasn't the most important part.

The spell that had so enchanted Omski back then was bound to the very thing that nowadays Basia regarded as a risible Olinowski eccentricity: the excessiveness of their familial feelings. Their mutual adoration, the meticulousness of their sensitivity, the refined art of their love—the atmosphere it created was, for Omski, the paradise he had dreamt about since he was a little boy.

Omski had just recently returned to his regiment after a leave he'd spent, on his mother's behalf, at his family home. He loved his mother deeply—and through the years, this profound childish emotion had filled him with bitter, hopeless pity. He couldn't do anything to help her. He was powerless in the face of her bleak life. He'd returned from the home that had poisoned his childhood, filled with fresh memories of all the torments he'd suffered there. And the place where he found himself quartered was Chowańce, located less than a mile from Czarna Wieś, the Olinowski estate.

"What can I do?" the elder Omski had said to his newly grown son. "Really, I have nothing against her—she's hardworking, honest, a good woman. But she's ruined my life with her hysteria."

To his son, he was the most loathsome man in the entire world. He physically couldn't stand the sight of him, couldn't look at him without visceral disgust.

Old Omski was abnormally short, with a big head, a face full of fat, drunken features, and grotesquely small arms and legs. As a boy, Omski trembled with hatred for his father. With clenched fists, he dreamed about revenge, about escaping with his mother and going somewhere far away, about his father's death. How fervently he longed for it!

His mother had some memories of better times from her past. It was precisely these memories his father derided during the frequent scenes he started when he'd been drinking. All through their married life, he took revenge on her for her superior birth and upbringing, even though she never talked or even thought about it. With a special cruelty, with a rare gift for cutting her to the quick, he reminded her that it was she who had fallen in love with him, not he who had fallen for her. It was a wonder what she'd seen in him—but that was her affair. He hadn't pursued her, he hadn't even dreamed about her. She was the one who'd wanted it. She alone had gotten herself into this—so really, she should just be griping at herself.

He said this in the presence of the children, in the presence of strangers, deliberately and with no embarrassment. Mother was afraid of violent scenes; she did everything to avoid them. She kept silent, busied herself with work of some kind, reined herself in, stifled her tears for as long as she could. She pretended she didn't hear, didn't understand. But Father was relentless. He wanted to humiliate her, to wound the self-respect that had not yet been blunted by years of misery; with a method he'd fully refined, he drove her to the breaking point, to noisy sobbing, to loud scenes. He knew that this was her weak spot. He knew that she suffered more when the children and neighbors could hear. He didn't let up until he saw her tears, her despair, her deepest abasement. For she still seemed unable to believe that such things had befallen her.

The strangest—or rather the worst—part was that she truly did love him. Whereas he—despite his awful appearance—purportedly appealed to women and had plenty of luck with them. Maybe it was just his vanity talking. But at any rate, he considered it an advantage over her.

Because Mother's second weak spot, one he exploited, was her jealousy. And so—as though inadvertently, without any intent, wearing an innocent and cheerful expression—he talked about his lovers in the filthiest, most debauched way possible, using swinish street terms. They were seamstresses, maids, prostitutes. He preferred them over some educated ladies he could mention—they had their merits, you only had to find them, and they really knew how to make love. He went into detail, described his escapades, his lovers' charms and techniques: "Really, what a minx. I'm telling you—I don't know how she does it!" Mother would suddenly go pale and run from the room, wracked with sobbing, tearing at her hair. That was exactly what he would be waiting for. He followed her, mocking her, bursting with laughter: "What does she expect? So old and still so jealous. I can't help it if I prefer younger women." And, laughing, he'd watch the woman go berserk: she would choke, hyperventilate, and pass out. Omski and his younger sister gave her drops, massaged her tensed arms and legs. And their father would take his coat and leave, saying that, really, living in such a house was hard to bear.

Among these childhood recollections, one of his father's sayings was burned into Omski's memory: "Just touching her is enough to make her have a baby." It was in this form that Omski came to know "the facts of life."

Indeed, worst of all was the thought that his mother loved this man—she, so good and gentle, so noble. He was secretly mortified by it, although he never let on, not even during his most heartfelt conversations with his mother. He never admitted the deep resentment he harbored toward her, the blood-red shame he felt for her—because even after such humiliations she still brought children into the world.

Despite these memories—or maybe because of them—there remained in Omski's heart an inviolate belief in family. He dreamed of a home where the children were happy and able to love their father, where the mother was cheerful and didn't cry. He knew it was possible; he saw it at other houses, and in his daydreams he imagined it spread before him.

What he found at the Olinowskis' satisfied his deepest longing, allowing him to fully experience the harmony and sweetness of familial happiness. And so Basia became a necessary condition for realizing his dream.

Now everything had changed. She'd been severed from her past, and not a trace was left in her heart. If only she'd feel like a victim of fate, at least for a moment!...

When he wasn't with her, he still thought of her as defenseless, incapable of doing harm, requiring protection and care. But she didn't need a thing.

He had done her wrong a number of times, but he still loved her.

She didn't recognize the only power she had over him; she rejected it as a weakness. She looked for strength elsewhere.

"You know, a very nice thing happened at the office," she said.

"Hennert wants to take me on as his secretary. I'd do considerably better than I do now."

He looked at her—and could no longer find anything to love in her.

"Ugh, that office again!..."

Omski struggled against the aversion that had engulfed him. He had to ask her about something that had been weighing on him for a long time.

"Listen, Basia, where did that Laterna character get the idea that we...we were engaged?"

"I don't know. I don't know him. And anyway, we aren't at all..."

"Yes, but someone must have spoken about it in those terms."

"I honestly don't know. There was that one time Ela Sasin saw you here and maybe she assumed something. She could have said something to that lieutenant, Gondziłł..."

"Yes, yes...Laterna is his nephew."

Watching him scowl, she said, "So at that point I should have asked her to be discreet? You don't really think that."

Omski was disconcerted. She said it so haughtily that, for a short moment, he fell under the same old spell. He found himself in that other world—the one in which being an Olinowska already meant so much.

"Dear Basia, if I put it that way, it's only because it's how you yourself wanted it."

It was how she herself had wanted it. This was true. It was at her request that they'd once cloaked their engagement in deepest secrecy. Her father had so many prejudices, and, after all, her mother had heart trouble.

He started to explain that he himself sincerely wished he could visit more often, that they spent too little time together.

She deftly reassured him.

"I know what an officer's life is like, dear. Mrs. Bielska almost never sees her own husband."

She understood the importance of his duties, the burden of the responsibilities and obligations he shouldered. Far be it from her to interfere with his work. She was not the kind of woman whose love would stand in the way of the consequential affairs of men.

This lack of suspicion was proof of her sureness of self—and of him. He could never detect in her even a shadow of jealousy. Her trust encumbered him more powerfully than the most despotic affection.

He suddenly saw it so clearly. The tenderest gratitude flooded his heart.

"I am yours, Basia, I am yours always," he said, kneeling in front of her and pressing his forehead to her knees.

And so he ardently assured her of that which she had not for a moment doubted.

12.

It was Saturday, and Stanisław, the Gondziłłs' orderly, was cleaning their small apartment. As usual, he was silent and serious, full of unswerving, almost childlike respect for the work he performed.

Binia was touched by the way he lay down the rugs he'd taken up, shifted the furniture, brushed the picture frames with a feather duster, wiped the very smallest items with a cloth before carefully putting them back in their proper places. He meticulously removed dust from each little nook, from behind each leg of furniture, dust as stubborn and ubiquitous as an earthly element. He oiled the door hinges so they wouldn't, as he put it, "squeal." But it was the hardwood floor that was the heart of the matter, Stanisław's greatest pride and joy. He devoted an abundance of effort and ingenuity to maintaining its color and shine. Here he scraped at some small spot with his large, black fingernail, there he rubbed it with wax, over here a cloth, over there a brush. He put his face to the surface, watched how the light struck it, ran his hands and feet over the smooth oaken slabs. And even then he was never fully satisfied with the results.

Binia, whose sensitivity to cleanliness was such that she needed it like she needed air for breathing, worked with him arm in arm. She cleared the dust from the little leaves of the spiderwort that hung from baskets of woven reed.

Stanisław spoke very little; he inhabited an inner life of his own. But from time to time he felt the need, characteristic of the human species, to share his thoughts with someone. He had great trust in Binia. She valued him, too, and they lived together in warm mutual understanding.

Kneeling on the floor, he broke off from his work for a moment and, not taking his hands from the brush, turned his gaze toward her.

"A cat is very hard to kill," he said.

"Is that so?" Binia asked.

"For example, if you take it by the tail and smash its head against the stones until it's covered in blood, it pretends to die. If you leave, it lies there for half an hour and then picks itself up and goes away. It's better to take it, step on its head, and give the tail a good yank from above. Then there'll be something like a moan inside it—and it won't get up anymore."

There was a knocking at the kitchen door, and Binia went to open it. She was very happy to see that it was Professor Laterna.

He was not at all put off by the cleaning in progress. He sat down in a corner chair and watched benevolently as they labored.

"One is constantly cleaning—and still, there's always all this dust. Where on earth does it come from?" Binia wondered at it.

Laterna was thoughtful. "A little from the carpet, a little from a dress, a bit of human skin and boot leather, small feathers from pillows, a little bit from the ceiling, paper from books and newspapers, various dried food... It all drifts down as dust—it no longer wants to exist separately. It's a tendency that accords with the nature of things. Only man likes to isolate everything."

Binia was keenly interested in this topic.

"I was just thinking that nature doesn't like order. Although some animals do lick and shake the dust off their fur. But what's the point of licking across the top of the fur like that? Just think of it: the fur of a live bear—a bear that's already quite old, for instance. What wouldn't you find in there, my Lord!..."

Laterna continued. "Washing, scrubbing, and dusting objects are means of individualizing them. In defiance of the natural order that blurs boundaries, man is constantly demarcating everything. Man's orderliness aspires to make the surface of an object the boundary of its essence. A clean human is entirely contained within his skin. And the fur of a live bear, which you would no doubt want to shake out, it's like a border zone between him and the forest. There's a bit of the animal's sweat and grease and a lot of mud, moss, pine needles, resin…"

"Man would like to be contained within his own skin," Binia broke in. "But he's not. And to me, for instance, the thought that I'm made up of the same things that I see all around me, the thought that I'm mixed in with all that, is very unpleasant. That the world and I are seeping into one another…"

"Yes," agreed Laterna. "It's troubling for our self-regard. The gospel of human supremacy craves some sort of chemical confirmation—but in vain."

When the cleaning was done, Stanisław went to pick up the boys, who'd been left at the park that morning with a reliable caregiver, and Binia headed to the kitchen to start dinner. The professor, as usual, accompanied her.

Finding conversational partners was the most agreeable concern in his life. He had a particular psychological knack for finding such partners amidst dense crowds, in completely unexpected circumstances, in any kind of situation. And he was never disappointed—it just wasn't possible.

By no means did the partner have to be an "interesting person" endowed with an extraordinary mind, character, or fortune. Laterna had no particular regard for remarkable people. A partner merely had to be someone whose presence was pleasing as he ruminated and sought to express his thinking, someone whose friendly curiosity and avid interest encouraged his contemplation, someone who provided—as a concert hall does for sound—good acoustics for the professor's words.

According to Laterna, Binia was one of these acoustic people—even though Gondziłł had, a number of times, shown the professor on his palm the narrowness of his wife's intellectual "horizons."

Because, for Gondziłł, the measure of a thought's value was its subject, but for Laterna any subject was a good one. He was fairly undiscriminating; he didn't accept that there was a hierarchy of topics.

Indeed, Binia thought about the commonest things, her home and her family. But, my God, wasn't the tiny world of hearth and home also, in a certain sense, a reference point for everything?

Binia's thoughts were far from lofty, chiefly concerned with the creation of some project, some finely detailed plan for a perfect system under which the mechanism of life would operate smoothly, and which produced the continual joy to which Binia was so receptive. In fact, these were entirely valuable attempts to uncover and explore the laws of economy on which, with cheerful and sustained effort, she could build her life and happiness.

Laterna often listened with surprise as she confided in him. And he fully approved of the means she devised to justify and excuse life's difficulties. It was all to establish and ascertain a basis for happiness.

Now she lit a fire in the oven she'd refashioned herself and set the cookware, shiny and clean as new toys, on the stove. She sprinkled flour on the white pastry board and made the dough that would later become noodles. The professor was interested in whether they would be firm enough and whether the strands would separate.

"Of course!" Binia said. "I don't add a single drop of water."

She suddenly looked worried.

"My God, I only hope that Julek won't be late…"

Knowing his brother-in-law as well as he did, it often occurred to Laterna that Binia must not be a very happy wife. But she never complained—it was out of the question.

At most, Julek was "nervous," overburdened with work, beset by problems. But he had the best heart and was always ready to share his last penny without asking anything for himself…

So Binia said. Underlying this paradoxical form of self-reassurance was the need for faith, the necessity of consenting to this life. Often, though—in the face of unmet household demands, of increasing deprivation and the new debts that were revealed again and again— she had moments of doubt. Then she would formulate a whole host of arguments against her uncertainty. She would tell herself that she wasn't right after all; she was exaggerating. Julek had said she was stingy—maybe she really was. Her father was stingy, although he was always sending her a little something—albeit secretly, so as to keep it from his son-in-law. After all, men had to have their vodka, their card games, their various entertainments. After all, he worked so hard and was entitled to recklessness from time to time…

But the facts, accumulating over months and years, constantly battered this system of faith.

However—even when she succumbed to weakness—Binia had, deep down inside her, a fortress impenetrable to doubt.

There was an unshakable certainty that Julek, though reckless, was honest to the core. A certainty that he was a decent man incapable of anything truly wicked.

The ironclad limits of Julek's recklessness and Julek's honor: this was the gospel of Binia.

"And things are going your way, Binia," Laterna said. "Lately, even Julek is beginning to be contained within his own skin. Shaved, dressed up, nice and clean—he's a pleasure to behold."

Binia was flushed and confused; it was unclear why.

"I'm really not sure I can take credit for that," she said with a smile.

Ah, so she already knows, Laterna thought with surprise. And he was a little confused himself as she looked at him now.

Binia was one of those women who, when young, are described as "lovely girls," and who quickly lose their looks as soon as they get married. Surrounded by children, housekeeping, and cooking, her pretty face had faded and was increasingly covered with fine, dry lines. Only her dark eyes and her smile had remained young. Her handmade clothing did her figure no favors, and her restless form, small and too thin, didn't turn any heads.

She sat down on a low stool, her elbows resting against her knees and her flour-covered hands crossed one over the other, far from her body.

"If someone's acting badly, it's better for him to stick with it... don't you think so, Professor?"

Laterna didn't understand.

"Well," she explained. "I, for example, personally prefer it if it's unintentional, if it's—unconscious... For me it's a great—comfort... And I think that's why, in the same situation, a clever man is always a little worse than one who simply doesn't know any better... It's not that he gives himself permission to be bad, he just doesn't understand that he's being bad, and he's not aware of his guilt at all..."

"And you prefer that, Binia?"

"Yes, that's what I prefer..."

After a moment, she added, "And it's very important that he's not told about it…that he doesn't find out somehow…"

Slowly it dawned on Laterna. He realized that Binia had to reach very deep within herself, very deep indeed, in order to find the basis for her happiness.

13.

"Society" was assembled once again at the spring rout held by General Chwościk's wife. There came again the people who'd come to the equestrian competition, who'd filled the Hennerts' salon, who saw each other seven times a week in ten different salons—those people without whom there could be no national, state, or municipal celebration. They were immediately recognizable by the honking of the cars outside the gate, the colorful hats with gold braid in the cloakroom, the gowns and jewels in the hall.

The day was drizzly and cool, perfect weather for the last party of the season.

That's what they called it: a rout. Indeed—a lady in a low-cut dress sang an old French song, a little-known musician—garnering no additional recognition—played a program of Chopin, and a completely unknown actor, to whom no one was listening, recited irreverent political rhymes. People strolled back and forth between several rooms, sat at little tables, chatted. It was so bright and warm. Through the windows, which here and there were slightly open and offered glimpses of ancient gardens languishing in the courtyards of old tenements and hotels, one could feel an invigorating chill and hear the rain beating against the leaves. The guests drank excellent black coffee, sweet wines, and liqueurs. They ate candies, pastries, and a walnut torte. They greeted one another with such animated joy, with eyebrows raised so high on their foreheads, as if it were something completely unexpected, something that wasn't the least bit foreseen.

Prominently positioned in the room, fussing solicitously over her guests and shining with joy, was General Chwościk's wife; all the gradations of social emotion, all the twitches and grimaces, flickered across her face with lightning speed. In one moment, she thrilled to the French dignitary to her right, who "had the goodness to...," when suddenly she knitted her brow with acute concern that the wife of the high-ranking Italian officer to her left didn't deign to, or would rather not... Simultaneously, with an expression of utmost dismay in her darting eyes, she called over her shoulder, "General, by no means will I let you go..."—he wanted to leave earlier than the others—and, already paying him no heed, she again spilled over with affectionate joy, clasping in both hands the hand of a familiar duchess who'd just arrived.

She was operating at peak capacity: decked out in a heavy, variegated silk dress of many years' standing, colorful jewels bought once upon a time in Tula and Saratov, and a black velvet choker around a neck that, long and yellow, resembled a plucked chicken's. She was a native Pole, but on the surface she was pure East, exotic in her bright attire, her anachronistic hairstyle and accessories, her excessively deep bows, her smiles and displays of distress, and the insouciance with which, on her yellow forehead, she painted black eyebrows high above the few hairs that constituted the natural line.

Sticking close to the general's wife was Countess Oskienna, dressed practically in rags but maintaining a sense of splendor with the two enormous diamonds that stood guard on each side of her full, white face, which wore a disarming smile. These days, she adorned herself with diamonds only on extraordinary occasions. She clasped the arm of the lovely Ela Sasin, leaning on her slightly. Grateful to the bottom of her heart for the few favors that she did for her at the office, the countess called her "my good girl."

The Hennert ladies arrived with their entire entourage, among whom even Director Hennert found himself this time. The general's wife simply didn't have words to express her joy. Warmly she took the hands of each of them in turn, excluding neither young Lin nor Laterna. Omski, Curll, Sednowski, Niemeński—no one was missing.

Elżbieta approached this group with her countess, who'd affectionately entreated Elżbieta to somehow bring her together with the heretofore unreachable Hennert. Her wish was granted. And Hennert, in this context, was so nice, so approachable and decent, that the countess had to stop herself from addressing him as "my good boy."

Though it seemed that everyone generally knew each other, there was still the need for new introductions. General Chwościk's wife spared no effort. She listed everyone's respective name in every language, their title, rank, and position—and everyone striking up acquaintances was happy, and everyone enjoyed their titles and positions anew.

General Chwościk vigorously worked his own agenda, too. Everywhere he found himself, he constantly spoke "a lot, any which way, and fast!"[21] He stopped for a moment with General Uniski's comely young widow and, not letting her get a single word in, he himself answered all the questions he'd asked. While speaking, though, his eyes searched beyond her head, scanning the vicinity for someone more important—and, barely finishing his sentence, he bounded toward the sumptuous, massively obese figure of Countess Opocka, which had slowly glided into his field of vision. Nearby, he effortlessly located Prince and Princess Wiślicki and, in an animated, chirping torrent, ultimately expressed his joy at the party's success and its achievement of a goal "so worthy of support, recognition, and acclaim."

All of it, though, was unimportant and took place merely as a matter of form, as if only on the surface and only for the time being.

It was in the farthest room that, discreetly and unofficially, the heart of the party beat. An accompanist sat at the piano and, with a violinist, played for the dancers. There, people were eagerly moving about with quiet, happy smiles, trembling with impatience, each already on their way to gathering someone in an embrace. My God, how drawn everyone was to this quiet, measured, swaying spell!

The music—the monotony of its interminable repetition like the weaving head of a charmed cobra—seemed to fill the air with a narcotic liquid. Bewitched by this rhythm, men and women stepped in unison, in solidarity, as one—as if already bound by death and life. Left to their fate, they joined the dance: dance of slight, guarded movements, devoid of whirling and ecstasy, filled with a sort of ceremonial dullness, the stiff sensuousness of ritual, a fervent, devoted daze.

Women danced like priestesses—with naked backs and shoulders, with flat chests and hips erased by the straight lines of their dresses. Their foreheads, with the hair smoothly combed back, had a look of austere, immaculate purity, especially in profile. From under eyebrows drawn on bare foreheads, their gazes were defenseless and open. The way they danced did not suggest impulsive passion or temptation, but rather sad and quiet consent to whatever comes. Professor Laterna, who always seemed to be everywhere, found himself in this room, too. He didn't dance himself. Instead, he leaned his great body against the wall and watched with genial approval. He watched how the children of the world fortified their innocent hearts, how they found safety on this little piece that they had cut away from the rest of the world—a place to quietly make merry, even though around them was sickness and tomorrow was death.

They made three steps to the right and, moving in unison, like ears of grain blown by the wind, bowed their heads and bodies deeply, and now they reversed and offered the world the same bow after the same number of steps to the left. They went this way and that—as though uncertain, swaying, tirelessly seeking some kind of place of their own, or maybe it was merely a strange, unnecessary path to nowhere…

"To dance," he thought. "Actually means 'to go nowhere.'"

Nearby, Niemeński and Wanda Hennert had come to a standstill.

"Only in Poland is the tango danced like this," Niemeński remarked with disgust. "You'd never see this, Professor, in Paris, or in Vienna, or even in Gdańsk…"

He went on about details so subtle that they were completely lost on the professor. But he took Niemeński's interpretation on faith, trusting the authority of this young habitué—especially since Wanda, whom he was leading away toward further gambols, wholeheartedly seconded him.

The sight of Gondziłł was causing a sensation among his friends. He was dancing carefully and intently, and in his arms was General Uniski's widow—that "poor woman" who "was left to raise two little children all on her own." She truly was a beautiful creature and had been accompanied to the party by some young lion who was waiting for his turn, not doubting that it would come, but pursuing her with his eyes while she danced. It was only recently that Gondziłł had acquired the art of dancing, and this was the first time he had dared to show it off in public. He looked quite elegant and even seemed to be a little slimmer.

Nearby, weaving their way through the dancers, were Curll and, in his arms, Mrs. Hennert. Her small and slender body, still youthful, was swathed in a lace gown. Her exposed shoulders and long, bare neck gave her lovely little head a sweet, haughty charm.

Wanda Hennert was the lucky one who got to dance with Niemeński. Travelling around the world on diplomatic missions, he'd become intimately acquainted with advanced dancing techniques of foreign capitals—to Wanda, he was the authority. With the utter impressionability of youth, she adopted his doctrine of how to dance according to the European style.

While dancing, however, she sometimes looked in Andrzej Laterna's direction and, from behind her partner's shoulder, smiled at him with the teasing smirk of a mischievous child.

14.

Arms crossed, Andrzej stood against the wall next to his father and watched the dancing couples.

He felt infinitely superior to this crowd—vacuous, shallow, complacent—engrossed in frivolous entertainment. His silent face wore a grimace of contemptuous irony. But his irony was less than honest, and his bitter smile of superiority concealed something very different.

Andrzej didn't dance for the simple reason that he didn't know how—and his mind was occupied with too many important matters to be bothered with learning. His life had not predisposed him to lightheartedness or cheer.

Besides, for whatever obscure reason, he was convinced that he would dance clumsily, certainly worse than anyone here. There was no small amount of self-loathing in his disdain for others.

Omski and Lin had paused near the Laternas. The lieutenant was wearing civilian clothes.

Paying no heed to the protests of his new friend, young Laterna, Lin had just left the army; he wanted to live according to his "inner truth," which didn't involve epaulettes, decorations, and militarism. "He's made a revolution of putting on a coat and tails," Andrzej Laterna thought ironically.

It's not at all what he had wanted. He'd had something else in mind, drawing Lin into his confidence, devoting hours to conversation with him, working to raise his political consciousness.

Andrzej Laterna didn't delude himself. He found nothing of use in the ideology of independence, which had fallen apart and been horribly crushed by postwar reality. It was a waste of time. But even there he tried to scavenge something, making connections everywhere, collecting information, studying, trying somehow to utilize their disappointment—the central motif of all their activity, distress, and impotence—like you'd find a use even for a dead carcass. It was all so flimsy, though, so pretentious and pathetic.

He saw them here, too, those people. They were like everyone else, only slightly worse-dressed, and even then it was often just an affectation, a fond tribute to their high-flown, *sans-culottes* youth.[22] They had come into prosperity, prominence, standing. They had their own homes—no more safe houses for them—and legally wedded wives; they had…possessions.

Sensing their own powerlessness, they'd pinned their hopes on one man.[23] They'd abdicated all responsibility. And now it was upon this man that they'd piled the burden of their disappointment and regret.

Once, in a moment of frankness, Lin had confessed to Andrzej, as though admitting a secret, something which no one doubted: "He seized the wheel of the hurtling cart of revolution—" (Lin was a poet.) "—and his duty was to ensure that revolution would not be necessary." (Lin was an idealist.)

At the time, when the people had wanted a revolution, he'd placated them. But he had not kept his promises.

So Lin had made a revolution of putting on a coat and tails.

"It's true." Andrzej smiled contemptuously. "It's not that the revolution has now become unnecessary, it's only become…impossible."

Because who were these people upon whom Lin, in his naïveté, had counted, the people who were to carry out this revolution?

These gentlemen who had come here today? Nowadays, they were the party leaders: emissaries, senators, and ministers, as well as the heads of offices, firms, companies, and banks.

Revolution is impossible when the revolutionaries are afraid of even moving.

Hence Andrzej's belief that revolution only came from outside. Andrzej had inherited his father's interest in people. After all, the domain in which he operated was first and foremost psychology. But, unlike his father, he was not impartial; his curiosity was neither disinterested, nor friendly. His father's friendliness toward humanity was just...indifference...

Besides, the elder Laterna applied a different standard to everyone; he saw each individual in his own light. Whereas the son had but one criterion. From his perspective, the world was clearly and transparently arranged. People, relationships, their business and affairs— these were all merely tools.

Lin came closer. His new coat and tails made him look slimmer and taller; he appeared older than he had in uniform. His young face had assumed a look of severity and seriousness. Amidst this frolicsome, glittering crowd he was truly and thoroughly fixated on the "action" he'd taken.

He leaned toward Laterna.

"I never realized that form was such an important thing," he said. "You have to totally sever yourself from the symbol, otherwise you'll never be free of the inner delusion."

"That was completely unnecessary," Andrzej broke in.

Lin thought that when Laterna had advised him against leaving the army, it was with his best interests in mind; he thought that he'd wanted to spare him.

He spoke with emotion, as if to an intimate friend:

"I thought that it would be harder than it was. Not because of any silly personal hopes—in any case, they were based on nothing—not even because of my mother... But for all those years I'd been so bound up in it, so stuck in the thick of it. And maybe that's why the first moments afterward felt so strange to me. But I don't regret anything. Freedom is a treasure. Now I don't have to lie anymore. I'm ready for anything. I'm truly—yours."

He lifted his eyes—dark, gentle, and slightly sad—to Laterna and added, "I am happy."

"No doubt," said Laterna, and he laughed. "Colonel, sir!" He turned loudly to Omski. "Didn't Lin look better in a uniform?" Omski darkened and didn't respond. He didn't like his tone. But Andrzej Laterna was not so easily discouraged.

This very Omski—a model officer, so alien and psychologically loathsome—had an irresistible allure for Andrzej; he fascinated and intrigued him. He was riveted by Omski's taut posture, his consummate military appearance, his self-control, his curt politeness, even his good looks. How intently he watched him; he saw the longing for battle and action, the bitter defiance held in check by discipline and subordination, the calm that came only by sacrificing his entire nature.

For this was precisely the kind of man he valued as a tool: men such as Omski were brave, they loved war, and they fought well irrespective of the cause and which banner they were under. The blaze of the battle, the lifeblood of an organization—these themselves were enough; they provided sufficient reason to fight. The commander's directive dispelled the deepest doubts, the words of an oath replaced conscience.

Whereas those who fought contrary to their nature, who were carried away by slogans alone—enthusiasts of theories, worshippers of principles—those were the ones he feared. Only in men of ideas did he—a man of ideas—see dangerous adversaries.

People like Lin, who, had he stayed in the army, could have accomplished so much, could have found out so much; Lin, who already seemed to have been under control…

Everyone else—mechanical experts, financial sages, men of ambition, the careerists and captains of industry gathered here—they were all precious raw material for the inevitable overthrow. One day they would all be harnessed to the chariot of revolution.

One might think: Omski, this precise cog in the military machine, how on earth could he be valuable to the revolution? He, for whom everything was fine, who matter-of-factly accepted it all. He, a stranger to any ideology, harboring no regional or party ambitions, ignorant of the profound implications of the army's seemingly trivial rift. He had no particular reverence for any of the generals who stood, like banners, on opposing sides. But the moment he found himself in his sphere of power he would serve and offer his life to any one of them, no matter the cause. To him, a commander's order was an absolute decree, a revelation of life and death, the paramount truth.

Here was precisely the man—a believer in the axiom of power—that the revolution needed, Andrzej thought.

Having no inkling of the hopes that young Andrzej invested in him, Colonel Omski talked unconcernedly with the father.

They exchanged observations about the dancers. The professor, who thirsted for knowledge of anything and everything, held the colonel's every word in high regard.

Now General Uniski's wife was passing them. They both pitied her: she was in the bearish arms of Gondziłł, who was executing his *pas* with a neophyte's zeal. She danced sedately, and certainly with greater gentility than that other one who, nestled in the embrace of a colorful Italian officer, was just passing now: Elżbieta Sasin. Mrs. Uniski's participation in the dance manifested itself entirely in her faithfulness to the rhythm. One of her bare arms, on which some black lace was slipping down, quivered with each measure. She was slim, aristocratic, almost bony—and this small shivering ripple under the white skin of her upper arm contained more sensual expression than Elżbieta's singing, swaying physical lushness.

At any rate, the colonel didn't like Elżbieta for all sorts of reasons, not least because she was the only person here who knew Basia.

He wasn't dancing yet, though he was powerfully drawn to the spectacle of the dancers. Each recurrence of the insistent refrain roused him, awoke the desire—quite familiar to him—for tiredness, to be tired at any cost... As he talked, he watched the women. He seemed to be readying himself for this feast of the senses, prolonging his anticipation with deliberation and refinement. He watched, appraised, selected. Several of the women were very pretty, and their beautiful gowns increased their allure.

Still, he waited. And at the same time he tried to overcome a certain unpleasantness that he didn't immediately understand. He gloomily wondered at the tangle of motives and desires within himself.

Because as he observed and evaluated the women, he stubbornly avoided the sight of Teresa, who was now dancing with Sednowski. He couldn't reconcile himself to this absurd unpleasantness, and he had no inclination to understand it. But he'd already felt it as soon as he'd met her, just a few minutes into their first conversation...

Their attention was momentarily captured by the young Princess Wiślicka. She had long, heavy-lidded eyes guarded by straight, black lashes and a truly bizarre smile—far too sweet, wallowing in its own sweetness. She danced gracelessly but also with a strange fervor, biting her oversweet lip and flaring her nostrils.

There came a short break. Everyone scattered to the walls, and the empty dance floor made the middle of the room look darker. The musicians were silent. Some of the crowd drifted through the open doorway to other rooms.

When the dancing started again, Omski headed toward Wanda Hennert, whom he hadn't considered earlier. By the time he'd reached her seat, she'd already been escorted away by Lin. So Omski asked her mother, who had just sat down.

At his bow, she rose immediately—obediently, passively, almost submissively.

He was suddenly ashamed by what he was feeling at this moment. He nearly recoiled when she stood up like that—ready, unhesitating, completely entrusting herself to his arms.

Until now, he'd always wanted her to be noble, to be better than her surroundings. Inside himself he'd been on guard, so to speak, in order that she not be sullied by any dishonorable thoughts. She was so good, everything was so nice when he was near her. But now he, he himself...

And at the same time, he was struck by a strangely ignominious thought. After all, Teresa was older than he was. And it wasn't proper.

This was the exact expression that came to mind as he gently embraced her, with a peculiar shyness and a quiet, apprehensive happiness. There was a moment when she even looked at him. When their eyes met.

Light, slender, supple, she danced evenly, without excitement, without passion. She didn't abandon herself to her submission. Rather, there was a certain hesitance and dreaminess in her placid movements, in the stillness of her head as it seemed to float high above her shoulders.

Beneath the silk and lace, Omski felt her shoulder blade shifting under her skin, felt the soft warmth of her body.

"You aren't tired?" he asked.

She replied that she wasn't. And, knowing nothing of what was going on inside him, she looked up sweetly and serenely.

Then, for the briefest of moments, he shut his eyes tightly in order to withstand, to somehow endure, this happiness—this happiness beyond his control. He even thought that this couldn't possibly be real.

The music abruptly ended and, surprised and motionless, he continued to hold her against his chest a moment longer.

After she sat down, he stepped away from her chair—there's no knowing why. He returned to his old place by the wall, and he slowly relived everything that had happened just a moment before. Yes. In his breath, in the beating of his heart, in his warm body—the ecstasy of her recent closeness filled every part of him.

He didn't approach her again—he only watched from a distance.

Now she was standing before a large, single-paneled window, slightly ajar, which looked out onto the darkness and through which a few shiny wet leaves poked in from the black night outside. She was talking to someone Omski didn't know, some lively, cheerful, gray-haired lady.

And she herself was, as always, calm. A damp evening breeze fanned her bare neck. Omski was concerned that perhaps it was too cool; he feared she might catch a cold.

She clearly didn't feel cold, though. A velvety sable dangled from the hand that hung at her side.

Next to Omski, Wanda (her daughter!) was breathlessly speaking to Lin:

"I know, I know what you're thinking. You're better off dancing. I know it all by heart already. But what am I supposed to do? I don't feel that way."

She fanned herself with a crumpled, soiled glove.

"I don't need anything, I don't desire anything—what kind of talk is that? Perhaps others have trouble admitting it, but I, for one, am satisfied with the world."

"You can tell at first sight." Professor Laterna laughed kindly.
"Good Lord! It goes without saying..."

"Isn't it true?" Wanda turned to him. "Why does everyone deny
that they're completely fine? And they keep denying it..."

"I don't," the professor replied. "Now that does need explaining."

"Oh? I'm very happy for you. Your son, on the other hand—oh
my! He's just like..."

"Like Lin?" Andrzej interrupted with clearly contemptuous irony.

"Yes, like Lin—Or maybe not... After all, Lin is a considerably
better person."

"Of course!"

And Andrzej thought: I am unpleasant, stiff, disagreeable. And
that was the thing that was hardest to reconcile. Because usually
it's against ourselves that others' likeability is measured and judged.

Teresa approached the group in order to collect her daughter and
say good-bye to the others. They were just about to leave.

Omski bid them farewell. In the brief, dry kiss he planted on Teresa's finger was the full intensity of his gratitude; yes, his entire
soul, dying of gratitude.

He later walked behind the others as they passed through the
emptying rooms.

Nearby, he could hear Gondziłł's coarse laughter.

"Look, Professor," he said to his brother-in-law, whom he'd taken
by the arm. "No one could tell that only ten years ago she sat behind
a counter and hawked her wares."

Indeed, Laterna was not familiar with the exact details.

"When I left, Teresa was a young girl."

"I remember her from those days, too. Why, she was my first
schoolboy's crush—and my first broken heart. Oh, Hennert and
Sednowski—what a pair! Now Sednowski does some mighty big
business through him. My God, who's capable of such lasting gratitude nowadays?"

"Why gratitude?"

"What do you mean, 'why'? After all, Hennert's entire fortune—it
all started with Teresa's dowry, with that silly few thousand as...
compensation..."

15.

Andrzej joined Laterna and Gondziłł willingly enough for supper at Eden. And on their way Gondziłł, with his characteristic enthusiasm, was able to persuade a "demoralized" Lin to take part in this worthy cause.

They found a free table in a small and completely empty room. Everything was coming together perfectly.

The professor poked fun at his "little son," joking that he ate everything like it was grass, never probing the sophistication of the dishes or the robustness of their flavors. For him, food was merely a way to satisfy hunger; he didn't yet know of food's perversity, of its hysteria.

"In my day, you read Huysmans' *À rebours*, and then you were a man. But now..."[24]

Andrzej was not easily cheered. That said, he was apparently trying to be pleasant. He treated his father with good-natured condescension—as though he were some tractable veteran of the revolution.

"It's obvious that my papa is 'an aficionado of humanity.' Just look at the way he reads the menu," he smirked.

He took the bill of fare from Gondziłł's hand and carefully perused it himself.

"All of this proves that we are a nation of patriots," he said. "This feeling of national distinctiveness: Polish-style beef medallions, Polish-style chicken, Polish-style crayfish."

"It's very typical—that is, this patriotic tone: the search for identity," Laterna mused loudly and eagerly.

"And understandable."

"Poland, situated in the very heart of Europe, this great crossroads of war and commerce, this vast swath of land with no natural borders, a place of marches, battles, and historical calamities, the intersection of all paths of European culture, the arena in which all influences clash head-on—pay attention, this is really very interesting... Her soul, open to every sway and pull, curious, receptive, elastic, rich; to the East, we represent refined culture, to the West, exotic barbarism—she combines, blends, and unites all possibilities and realities..."

"In short, as Słowacki said: 'The peacock of nations you have been...'"[25]

"Exactly!" Laterna was delighted. "Because this rare, marvelous quality, this boundless multiplicity, it's unsettling and incomprehensible to Poland herself. It exceeds her capacity, you could say... And this anxiety gives rise to the need for self-expression at any cost: my kingdom for a definition, for a formula, for—individuality! And look: in other places, the national characteristics of life, of art, of writing—they're just by-products of life and creation; they're defined later or observed from the outside. In other places, life and art transcend the local characteristics—for higher, more universal forms. And their methods of transcendence, the very ways and means—they're unintentionally national. Genuine exoticism must be unconscious."

The professor's way of gesticulating consisted of repeatedly poking the empty space in front of him, more or less at face level, with the rigid index finger of his right hand.

"But with us, that national identity is a way of life; in fine art and literature, it's not so much an effect as a prerequisite. Here, we impugn a book or painting by suggesting that it could have been made equally well by a foreigner. National characteristics are sought after for their own sake, imposed by theorists as the goal of creative endeavor, as a duty, as gospel. Not only this 'peacock and parrot,' but what Mochnacki demanded, that literature allow a nation to recognize something of its own being, and Norwid, consciously trying to invent a national style, designing a Polish architectural arch of two scythes with intersecting blades.[26]

"With regard to our own folk art—" Laterna was becoming indignant. "—we're like foreigners in some barbarian country. That which is unlike anything elsewhere, which is 'native' and primitive—we immediately snatch it up, we preserve and value it above all else. We toil and sweat to create what, in other places, comes into being naturally."

"You said that it's understandable." He turned toward his son. "Yes, of course. It's a matter of shaking off imposed influences, of straightening back up after the pressure of political subjugation. But this stubborn, relentless self-liberation is a vestige of our captivity. For God's sake, let us finally be truly free already... Poland lies in the center of Europe, she is its heart, she must absorb any number of its influences and pressures. Like no other country, she is able to escape nationalist exclusivity and narrow constraint."

"'Like no other country,'" Andrzej mocked mildly. "Such disarming modesty... Papa dear, it seems that here we already have a bit of that constraint..."

Gondziłł came to life.

"But aren't we free? Independence—it's here already, it is. There are borders. We have everything that others have, everything we were so jealous of everywhere else. There's domestic bribery, self-interest, favoritism, mob rule, great scandal, great fortunes, and business—above all, business. And there's contempt for the army already, too, a turning against military power. We have everything. This is how a democratic society rewards its soldiers for their sacrifices, for their victories. But they were singing a different tune when their skin crawled with fear..."

"Yes, yes, Papa," Andrzej unexpectedly seconded Gondziłł. "Frankly speaking, every one of you here is a failure, after all. Only Papa—thanks to his love of food and books—has somehow retained his astonishing cheerfulness. But really, having wasted his youth in the various prisons of European Russia and Siberia for his efforts to liberate the fatherland—for 'the workers,' and let's be honest, that was merely a façade— Papa has to be at least a little surprised by the product of his labors..."

Laterna was listening with heightened attention, though he continued to eat.

Excited, Andrzej continued:

"Resting on the faded laurels of fruitless revolution, Papa gives himself over to molding the young minds of liberated Poland, entertaining himself with harmless ideas; he's asocial, apolitical, and loyal to the core. This is the way Papa dodges responsibility for what happened, for what he himself had a hand in making. But it's not possible. Your efforts were in vain, Papa, because nothing's changed: prisons are overflowing, and the unemployed crowds in the street are dispersed with rifle butts. This is what your Poland looks like!"

"'Your Poland,'" Laterna repeated. And now he really was interested. Fork in motionless hand, he didn't take his eyes off his son. "Because for you, it was only about independence. Social revolution was just a cover for an ordinary national uprising. It was a lie—and this lie has backfired…

"Yes, yes, it was a lie," he said again, not allowing anyone to interrupt. "And that's why you're all failures, you who've lived to see this moment, this realization of your dream…"

"It's true," said Lin, who until then had only been listening.

Andrzej was silent, sneeringly awaiting his father's rejoinder. But Laterna didn't say anything.

Lin was also quiet for a moment, his gaze nervously shifting from Andrzej to the older Laterna. Suddenly, as if overcoming some internal barrier, he began to speak quickly, with unusual passion.

"It was a lie—but it shouldn't be you who says so."

"What do you mean it shouldn't be me? Why not?" Andrzej was amazed.

Lin looked him straight in the eye. "Any ideologically consistent position, any allegiance to an idea or a man—it's a way of not seeing the truth, of covering your eyes in dismay in the face of reality… Because in order to come into being, everything must renounce itself and enter the world only at the price of its debasement. As soon as anything comes to power, it needs to be combated—"

"Aha," Andrzej interrupted scornfully. "I guessed what kind of person you were right away, Mr. Ex-Lieutenant."

But Lin wasn't listening.

"After all, in politics the truth is a terrifying thing. To see the truth—it's to weather a blow; to contemplate the truth—it's to suffer! Only with your eyes closed can you stand by the idea as it's actually carried out. You can stand by the idea only with hands covered in mud, hands covered in blood…"

"Poetry! Poetry!" Andrzej laughed contemptuously.

"The truth is terrifying not only for the heart, which burns in anguish, but also for the will, which continues to yearn, which yearns for reality…"

He broke off—and, surprised, as if he'd made a sudden discovery, came to a close:

"Because the enemy of reality is truth—yes! Yes!"

He looked at Andrzej with fiery eyes and, pressing his hands to his trembling jaw, asked him, "Why didn't you want me to leave the army? Why? Why?"

"Calm down," Andrzej said in an ironic tone. "You're not going to frighten anyone here."

"Let's put it simply." Laterna spoke up. "An idea materialized is an idea falsified. I still don't see the drama here: the reality does not conform to the idea, does not do it justice. It cannot be completely encompassed within the mind's limited framework. Well, what of it? We live in an epoch of the collapse of every ideology, an epoch of the tremendous, absolutely marvelous proliferation of reality. Slogans haven't been taken seriously for a long time. The most sacred beliefs have been renounced on all sides. Political parties are still at each other's throats, but what once divided them no longer exists: now they're at each other's throats in order to gain power... Should we lament the wrongness of it, devise a course of rescue, call for help? No, no! The disaggregation of ideals only does life good. The words of manifestos have been blown apart, leaving a wonderful, new, unexpected, and still incomprehensible sense of meaning... The truth is, it's getting better every day. The manifestos have not come to life—but life has managed to look after itself. And it prevails..."

Andrzej Laterna laughed at the top of his voice.

"Ha ha! It's extraordinary!" he cried. "In Papa's eyes this is all— an idyll! For Papa, it's enough that 'life looks after itself'... This is something bigger than the standard resignation that goes along with gray hair, this is truly..."

He didn't finish. For Lin suddenly rose from his seat and, propping himself on his arms, bent his entire figure toward the professor as if he needed to communicate something important, something urgent that could not be delayed. But he'd barely opened his mouth when, with a sudden and equally violent motion, he fell back into his chair, clutching his head in his hands. Laying his head against the edge of the table, he convulsed with dry, hysterical sobs.

Gondziłł was filled with alarm and heartfelt concern:

"What's going on, sir?" He bent over him. "What is it?" He

turned to Laterna. "But he's hardly had anything to drink!"

The professor was pouring water into a glass, occupying himself fully with this activity.

Lin, red with shame, reached for the water. "Please excuse me, gentlemen, truly, I don't understand it myself... I am an idiot..."

"There's no reason to be upset." Gondziłł kindly comforted him. "Andrzej here is a black character, but he has a heart of gold. You can't judge him by what he blathers on about. The professor doesn't give a fig about his prattling..."

Lin drained his water, blowing air from his nose into the glass and dribbling onto his bulging shirtfront.

Andrzej smiled condescendingly at Gondziłł's praise.

"That's enough, Julek."

And while Laterna was busy with the bill, discussing something with the waiter, it was with this same derisive smile that Andrzej turned to Lin, who was already getting up.

"I don't understand why you're so nervous," he said in a low voice. "After all, the entire note is typewritten."

Lin recoiled as if stung. And when he looked at Andrzej there was hatred in his gentle eyes.

"I know the man," Gondziłł was still insisting. "He's a good fellow, a heart of gold, he just has a wicked character..."

16.

When he returned home from the rout, Omski was absolutely out of his mind. Everything he had heard pounded in his head like an infernal hammer. Arguing at length with himself, he swung from the fiercest hatred all the way to tenderness, to a mouthful of ashes, to fiery longing—it was an inexpressible torment that he had never known before now, that he never could have imagined possible.

Her, her!... Suddenly the abominable hatred, the torturous jealousy, the basest humiliation—it all came rushing back. He was filled with contempt and disgust; he burned with shame—for her or for himself...

Because what had brought all this on? Why had he experienced it as a terrifying surprise, this truth which he'd known since the beginning, about which there had never been any doubt, despite his attempts to drive away these humiliating, clearly improper thoughts? He had known from the beginning. But it was as if he had only recognized it the moment he heard Gondziłł's words.

And now it had become inevitable. This once distant and inconsequential matter now meant something completely different to him—abject unhappiness, the most profound, personal defeat...

He berated himself. "So how could this have happened, how could it have happened that I'm wallowing in this mud...? Who is she, this woman?" And he told himself exactly who she was...

And suddenly he pictured her perfectly, amidst everything, against the backdrop of the ballroom. He pictured her perfectly—and yet he couldn't truly behold her. And the full measure of his torment, his indignation, his contempt—it was suddenly transformed into a single, terrible yearning.

He was in no position to calm down; he couldn't just sit here on the edge of his bed, clenched hands folded in his lap, his head on the wooden banister. He sprang up, ran back and forth between the furniture in his cramped and gloomy room, pounded the walls.

The noise he was making restored his presence of mind.

He grabbed his coat and hat and slipped out of his room. In the dark of the stairwell he felt the touch of a cold, wet nose on his hand. It was Laterna's friendly little dog, whose daily strolls left unsightly smears all over the hallway and stairs. Passing the door of the professor's apartment, Omski overheard irate, unintelligible muttering. It was Laterna's longtime mistress, a simple French girl, who had been roused from her sleep by a doggy whim. She'd been plucked from the wide world and now lived here at the wise man's side, a stupid life devoid of friends and family, all her days spent cooped up with a dog in a small, dirty room filled with books.

The rain had stopped, but the wet streets and sidewalks shone dully in the light of the overcast spring dawn. An eastern wind shook cold drops from the trees that lined the street.

Omski despised himself for what he meant to do, but abandoning his plan was out of the question. He had to be there—on her street, near her house, under her window...

Not far from the gate, Omski ran into Professor Laterna, who was returning to his apartment, as well as Lin, who was evidently accompanying him home. He was shocked to see them, as if their presence here were something wholly inexplicable. Without waving or smiling, he offered them a mechanical bow as he passed.

He quickly headed off, looking only at his feet. But when he reached the street where the Hennerts lived he stopped and suddenly turned back. He was utterly exhausted.

Finding himself at home once again, he quickly undressed and fell into bed, feeling more depleted by this walk than by a long-distance march.

Despite the late hour, the professor's apartment was not quiet. It caught Omski's attention for a brief moment, since the professor was not in the habit of talking to his life partner. He assumed that Lin had gone upstairs with the professor.

Omski sank into a deep sleep, but it didn't last long. It was light when he awoke. He looked at his watch; he'd hardly slept an hour.

He closed his eyes—and surrendered himself to his suffering.

A hundred times he swore that he wouldn't see her anymore. He could easily obtain a transfer to somewhere in the Borderlands, and he would leave, he would leave. Half-dreaming, he endured months and years of separation, of fervent, futile longing, feeding off that one night of bliss—before he'd heard, before he'd heard...

"That silly few thousand as...compensation..."

That cloudy morning, fragrant with flowers and greenery, he didn't remember anything—he was sealed off in his office, immersed in work, focused and determined, kept in check by the tasks and business matters which buffeted him one after another. Each time the door opened, each time a new person appeared on the threshold, it was a new, difficult, harsh question that life was asking of him... Only inside his body did there remain, like a small splinter in his finger, a memory of his anguish. At the end of the day he was tired; in his muscles, from his head to his feet, he felt the pain of exhaustion.

But when the work day ended and those matters fell away from his consciousness, a heavy boulder of rage immediately rolled into the freed space in his brain; a flood of hatred roared in. Ah, if only he could somehow find someone to pay for this shame in his heart, this gross insult to his soul.

As the evening approached, his resolution to leave her abated. In its place, he was overwhelmed by an unquenchable desire for revenge. That evening, he freshened up and went—grim, yellow, torment-ed—to the Hennerts'. At the moment he crossed their doorstep, he reached a compro-mise, so to speak. That is, he hadn't come here to exact straightfor-ward revenge—in short, to kill—but rather to "clarify" things. On the one hand, it was a gateway toward departure and separation; on the other, it was a more refined form of revenge.

He entered, greeted everyone, and sat down. Sednowski wasn't there. Sednowski wasn't there! What a relief! And Omski suddenly felt much better. He was wistful, full of gratitude—all because of something that, after all, meant nothing.

It was just the immediate family, Mr. Nutka, and, again, Lin. Om-ski ate something at the table with the others. Sednowski wasn't there—but he could arrive at any minute. Ecstatic and tormented, Omski sat and watched. Lightning seemed to flash from his eyes, and his face was the wan yellow of a Christian martyr's.

And so the time came for departures. They all stood in the en-trance hall saying their goodbyes and continuing their conversa-tions. In a hushed tone, Omski drew Teresa aside, leading her to the recessed doorway that led to the living room, a place, however, where they were still visible to everyone. She looked up at him pleasantly, sweetly, a little questioningly, but still with trust in her eyes. And the cold cruelty of her ignorance suddenly roused in him the fullness of his hatred, his boiling, churning desire for mortal revenge. In the blink of an eye, his normal face—until now pale and sullen—was strangely transformed, as if into a wild animal's. His dilated pupils stood alone against the whites of his eyes, and his thin lips bared long, fierce teeth.

"You ought not receive your former lover here! How dare you receive your former lover here!"

As he spoke these words, he felt himself being carried away by passion and risk. Another moment, and he would seize her by the shoulders, shake her furiously, throw her to the floor. She leapt backward. Her look of indescribable shock, her terror, her com-pletely animal terror, in the face of danger—it filled his body with reckless joy. It gratified him to see, at last, this wild panic, this dark flush of agony that suffused her cheeks and brow, even these tears that were filling her eyes—she who had always been so composed, always emanating an air of safety.

Having achieved his aim, Omski became proper and ordinary once again. He stepped away and, as though nothing had happened, made his final bow of farewell.

He left with Nutka and Lin and parted with them as soon as he could. He headed home.

He was breathing heavily. He knew well what she must be feeling, he knew well how deeply he had insulted her—he, a relative stranger—and how completely defenseless she was before him...

He felt no remorse at all, no mercy. Ah, no! He laughed. He knew that there was no one she could tell. Would she say anything to Hennert, who—knowing everything...? Would he be outraged? Stand up for her, demand satisfaction?

Not only would she not tell him, but she wouldn't even dare not to receive Omski if he, for example, decided to pay her a visit; she wouldn't dare not return his bow in the street.

Ah, what contempt he had for her, precisely because of her fear, because of her meekness in the face of this blow. She wasn't at all indignant or angry, she didn't say a word; in all of her terror, she cared only that they weren't overheard, that no one noticed them.

And for his part, nothing mattered—let them hear everything. He would not be afraid of a scandal or a duel. He took vindictive delight in the advantage he had over those for whom things still mattered.

He had taken revenge! He had been able to cut someone to the quick and get the most powerful rush of joy in return. What on earth was this? Until now, he'd never experienced anything like it, but at the same time it wasn't entirely new to him... It had been waiting there inside him, ready, quite familiar, welling up from the depths of his childhood: the sudden calm, the joy at finally seeing defenseless terror, tears of helpless despair...

"Yes, yes," he thought. "Now I'm just like my father. I'm exactly like him. It doesn't matter."

The following day, and for a few days after that, Omski stood by his decision never again to cross the threshold of that house. He was fiercely determined, vindictive, deeply satisfied with the harsh medicine he had used to cure the disgraceful weakness of his heart. But on the fourth day—suddenly, easily, and without a moment of hesitation—he changed his mind.

He went and calmly crossed that threshold, certain of his impunity. He even thought, "And if she's told anyone, so much the better."

In the entrance hall, he was greeted by Hennert, pleasant and polished, suavely apologizing that just now he had to rush off… But "his ladies" would be more than happy…and "Oh, I apologize…" and "I am at your service…"

She hadn't told him.

Omski let himself into the large drawing room—passing Wanda, who stood arguing with Andrzej Laterna, he offered the kind of cursory greeting given by household members—and found Teresa sitting by herself in a small parlor. She was embroidering a handkerchief by the light of a small silk-covered lamp.

She rose immediately as he entered, standing pale and stiffly upright. She didn't say anything; she just watched with widening eyes as he came toward her. And in those eyes there wasn't even hatred.

It was rather Omski who had the cheerless face, the slightly offended expression that demanded consideration and particular sensitivity. He went to her and took her by the hand—she did not attempt to pull away—and kissed it briefly, in an ordinary way, while bowing. Then, not releasing her hand, he pulled Teresa toward the window, beyond where they might be seen from the open doorway.

She stared at him, waiting for words or action—and once again she was entirely at his mercy, defenseless and frozen with terror.

Without the least resistance, she allowed him to crush her against his chest and kiss her hair and temples.

He understood that she was falling into this as if into an abyss—from fear alone, without the slightest affection—and again he curled his lips in hatred, baring his long, white teeth.

"Why do you torment me so?" he asked her, instead of the other way around. "Tell me why!"

"Mother of God," Teresa whispered, wringing her hands and pressing them against her mouth, trying with all her might not to scream. Her eyes were wet with tears.

"What does it mean?" he thought. "This is unendurable. I could die from this suffering."

"Don't worry," he reassured her when she tried momentarily to break free. "If anyone enters, I'll kill you and then myself."

It was such torture! Nothing—not kissing her hands, her mouth, her bare neck—gave him happiness. "You don't understand what it is to love like this," he whispered hoarsely, sliding his arms down her body until he reached her feet.

He lay on the floor and kissed her small slippers. He couldn't tear his head away from them. Pinned by his embrace, she stood in place, motionless, her head tilted slightly toward the floor.

After a long moment, when he himself pulled away, she sat down helplessly and, overcome with horror, began to speak:

"My God, how could you, how could you?"

Shortly afterward, they went to the theater with Wanda, Andrzej, and Curll.

After the scene in the parlor, Omski had become calm and mild, burning—quietly—with agony. He was humble and did his suffering in silence.

Sednowski wasn't there—and that was enough. The terrible snake of jealousy had lain down to sleep.

Omski loved without return and without complaint.

17.

Binia sat by the window near the narrow box filled with blooming geraniums, the sunlight streaming in through the sheer cambric curtains. Piled beside her on the flowered cretonne sofa were freshly ironed linens awaiting mending. Binia had two hours of pleasant work ahead of her before it would be time to prepare cocoa for the boys.

She wiped away tears as she sewed. Ever since that letter... Because she'd had a moment of weakness, because she'd been so ignoble as to read what she'd found at the bottom of the wardrobe—a crumpled and dog-eared letter that had clearly already been carried in the pocket of some uniform for a long time. And since then she was ready to cry over anything...

Binia cried over the washtub, over her Spanish lace, while taking a stroll. But she could stop instantly when she decided to do so, when there was a need to do so. Because Julian must not guess that she knew; he must not suspect anything for even a moment.

What she'd told Laterna was true. It wasn't for her that Julek had become so elegant. Around the house, he wore the same strange outfit as before: collarless nightshirt, morning slippers, suspenders swinging behind him. Around the house, he was always tired and ill-disposed, his "head full of problems." And when he dressed himself in a clean uniform, put on a fresh collar and cuffs, pulled on soft, beautifully laundered white gloves—it was obvious what *that* meant.

Binia avoided the memories with which others might console themselves. But when she was sitting alone, any number of these thoughts—intrusive and unwelcome—ran through her head like an endless reel. And sometimes, despite herself, she was forced to think about the first time she saw him: in the hospital, a simple, ordinary soldier, a dying hero. He was expected to die, and he didn't die. They performed six operations where his leg was wounded at the hip, and she'd had to change the dressing dozens of times, during which he sweated profusely and lost consciousness from the pain. She was forced to think about his sad fortitude, the quiet, hoarse moans that he tried to conceal during the night. She had arrived solicitously at his bed, and he had gloomily averted his eyes, not saying anything, not wanting anything—he was beset by months of fever, sleeplessness, and suffering.

She was forced to think—she didn't want to—about his love, which flamed from the highest peaks of his soul. Back then, he'd experienced love with the same dogged pride, with the same visceral strength that he'd brought to his experience of pain. The surliness and silence were identical. But he would perform any prank or folly to make her smile; for every kiss, he was willing to pay with his life... Back then...

But no, no... Even when, in spite of herself, she found herself remembering, even then she knew for certain that nothing had changed. It was just that he didn't love her anymore—but deep inside, he was exactly the same as he had been back then, he was...

still himself. Through it all, she'd maintained her faith and pride in him. There remained an immutable sense of solidarity and an approval of his overall quality.

Binia wiped her eyes and thought that the past, even the happy past, was always worth less than the present.

Because, first of all, the past didn't exist anymore. She had discussed it once with Professor Laterna. And second, the fact was that bygone times, even happy ones, were all the more meager for not having gone through later experiences.

We're always simply seized with dread at the thought of how stupid we'd been just two or three years before. What kind of happiness can we possibly have in our youth, when we still don't have the slightest idea about anything?

And the present day, with all its trials and tribulations, how precious it is…

Gondziłł had not been home for lunch that day, and neither had he come home for dinner. As usual, Binia waited until the last minute, then she stopped waiting, and then she waited again.

The evening hours passed, and so did the hours of the night. Every rustle seemed to be a sign of the much-anticipated return.

For a long time, the night beyond the window was darker than the room inside, until slowly it was the room that became darker.

Binia closed her eyes and then opened them again. Those same thoughts were unspooling through her head like a long reel—ceaseless, unwelcome, trite… Until suddenly everything stopped, froze in its tracks—only her heart beat slowly: thump, thump…

It was Stanisław who leapt up from where he slept in the kitchen and opened the door, its chain rattling. Overcome by the importance of this task, full of unswerving respect, he eagerly rushed over to admit the lieutenant, who was returning home at dawn.

One door clicked, and then another. Binia lay with her eyes closed.

"Are you asleep?" Gondziłł asked, entering the bedroom.

She immediately understood the question, sensed its purpose. She knew that this softness in his voice could only mean one thing.

They had not made love for a long time—for a long time even before the discovery of the letter. They had established a firm mutual understanding that it was not possible to have more children, that life was hard enough with just two… She was silent for a moment, deliberating quickly.

"Are you asleep?" he asked again.

"No, I'm not…"

She didn't betray her panic. Her sad thoughts streamed through her head alone; they didn't concern her heart, which was quietly beating with profound tenderness and joy.

In the brief flare of the match, she saw his face, peeved as usual. Gondziłł was angry with himself for having "surrendered."

She understood that, too. But she had no idea what had caused this sudden change, this—return. What had happened to the other woman? Had it been something important, something meaningful? Or was it some fleeting moment?… Oh, it didn't matter… Now she only cared about not showing her surprise, about hiding her tears so he wouldn't guess that she—she knew…

She slid away from the edge of the bed like she used to do—as if nothing at all had changed—and made a place for him next to her, opening her arms in the gray darkness.

And now she had to expiate his guilt and even his pity, convince him that there had been no break in their happiness, hide from him the truth about himself.

So she gave herself up to new motherhood, to feeling no more anxiety or fear. She thought that if she bore him a daughter this time, he'd be happy, he'd be cheerful and good—and then everything would change.

She joyfully felt how the flame of her happiness and love swept him up in ecstasy. Silently, with a single kiss, she revealed to him what was inside her—and that it would never change.

Through what she felt, he became better, more beautiful, more precious than anything. So she had to feel this way.

Her entire body was suffused with the light of her soul.

This reconciliation was achieved in darkness and secrecy, with silent caresses—as if hidden from him to spare his humiliation. So that he would not know the sadness, the emptiness and devastation from which this night of momentous happiness had blossomed.

18.

"What did you do to my Lin?" Wanda scowled.

Andrzej shrugged his shoulders.

"I didn't do anything to him," he replied. "And anyway, what's he to you? When he was still in uniform and flaunting himself at competitions, that I could see... But now..."

"Oh, don't be so jealous. I know perfectly well what's happened to him. Ever since that evening, he's been disagreeable, he hasn't visited a single time... It happened after those secret dealings with you... I'll find out everything from Curll, just you wait!..."

Andrzej just smiled condescendingly.

He had come in hope of finding Omski. But Omski wasn't there. Teresa sat by herself in the other room, embroidering something.

Sednowski slipped out of Hennert's office. She was surprised and seemed almost frightened at the sight of him.

"I had no idea you were here," she said. "Is Józik not home?"

Sednowski kissed both her hands and took a seat on the same small couch, spreading himself out right next to her.

"Hennert's here," he said in a soothing tone. "But Sasin came flying in just now with a terribly frightened look on his face and some bit of news about Gondziłł. They're busy conferring about something, and I didn't want to be in the way."

"Perhaps it's about Ela's marriage?" Teresa asked.

"No, nothing like that. Ela's marriage is completely settled."

Teresa was doubtful.

"Is that true? Is it possible, do you think?"

"Is it possible? Oh please, why not? If only Hennert consents to losing a secretary."

He laughed loudly.

"There's no misalliance here: Elżbieta is an only child with quite a dowry."

He laughed, as did Teresa—but she immediately grew serious and looked around uneasily.

"You're not in the mood?" he asked, leaning closer to her. "Or aren't you feeling well?"

She was unsure. She spoke shyly, with difficulty:

"It's wrong of you to take this worry of mine so lightly. Because it's not trivial, it's not just my imagination. I would very much like it if you didn't come here—at least not for a while... After all, it's not long until we leave..."

Sednowski gave a full-throated laugh, the ringing laugh of a man full of self-confidence and self-satisfaction.

"You are without parallel," he smiled, holding her around her waist and toying with her hands. "You're always so rational, so reasonable—and now this childishness... Do you really believe that this young man is in love with you? He's a sly fox who knows how to make a career for himself. Quite simply, he needs Hennert for some reason, I'm sure of it. He wants to charm you, he wants to flatter you with his jealousy, nothing more."

Teresa relented. She gladly allowed herself to be steered away from troubling matters.

Now she sat, feeling safe and cheerful, and listened with pleasant absent-mindedness as Sednowski talked.

Their relationship was like the friendship of two close cousins or a peaceable old marriage.

Sednowski, always so sure of himself, unconstrained, dominating every scene—with her, when it was just the two of them, he was completely different. He allowed himself to be sincere, even to be weak. For him, it was a kind of psychological *dishabille*.

He groused about having already grown old, whereas she had remained so young. He had some arthritic complaints and a heart condition that had prompted him to stop smoking and drinking. He spoke of various concerns of his, assorted little problems. He was supposed to bring his wife in from the countryside, and he didn't want to. He didn't know whether he should buy an apartment here—he felt so fine and so free at the hotel. He grumbled about Hennert as well, how he had taken advantage of his trust and his naiveté, how he had unceremoniously robbed him of their joint profit.

"It's true that he issued me a concession—but the principal capital was almost all mine! And my name—after all, that means something, too... And today he tells me..."

Teresa listened with her hands folded in her lap, serene and slightly bored. Suddenly she broke in:

"But if he arrives, my dear, go right back in to Józik. Promise me—it really does make me nervous..."

Sednowski squeezed her again and, leaning toward her, kissed her neck and hair. "You're just delicious, Terenia, a frightened little doe, at your age... My word, I like it..."

He shifted away slightly, amused and aroused.

"My word, you're even prettier now than you used to be. You get prettier every day..."

He lowered his voice.

"How long has it been since you were at my place?... Think, you naughty girl..."

Her eyes grew round with horror. And Sednowski shook with laughter—once more he'd gained the advantage; he was filled with indulgent superiority, condescending and benign.

"Well, don't worry, don't worry... These are not the days of poison and stilettos..."

Laterna came in to say goodbye to Teresa. Neither he nor Wanda were surprised by the intimacy between her and Sednowski. He had privileges in this house.

Andrzej explained that he planned to leave again for quite some time, and Teresa wished him a quick and happy return.

After his departure, Wanda dressed quickly and left the house.

She didn't know where it was. She had never been there. But she remembered the address—and, without anyone's assistance, she found the street, the house, and the dirty door in the black wooden stairwell.

She rang the bell nervously, not sure that she would find him. Fortunately, she heard footsteps in the entryway. An old woman whom Wanda mistook for the maid—it was Lin's mother—opened the door.

With excessive eagerness and courtesy, but also with embarrassment, she led Wanda to the back of the apartment. They had to pass someone else's dining room, where a fat woman in a hairnet was reclining on a bed pushed against the wall, playing solitaire on the soiled quilt. Down the dark hall, they came to a little room alongside the kitchen. Lin was either sleeping or simply laying on a sofa. He leapt up at the sight of Wanda.

"And you came here all on your own." He spoke with almost no surprise, as if with compassion or pity.

His face had the look of someone who had not been sleeping. He was pale, and his eyes glistened.

"Of course I came," she replied.

Only now did she greet the old woman, who had remained in the room and was looking at her expectantly. Looking around, Wanda understood that they both lived in this tiny room—together.

She sat on the edge of something that might have been a bed, gazing at Lin with growing seriousness.

"What happened to you? What's eating at you?"

She was alarmed by his disheveled appearance. He had on an old military jacket, and his hair was uncombed.

He tried to smile.

"Nothing, I was getting down to work, to writing—here, you see..."

On a card table positioned next to the window she saw some strips of paper and an unstoppered bottle of ink.

"I was getting down to writing, but somehow it wasn't coming along..."

"And?"

Lin forced himself to smile again.

"I only wanted to organize it a little bit..."

They both fell silent and sat quietly for a moment. Wanda realized that Lin's mother was no longer in the room, although she hadn't noticed her leaving.

"I've become convinced that I have no will, that I am a man incapable of action," Lin finally admitted.

He rose while he talked and began, as if unconsciously, to turn over the papers on the little table.

"So what?" Wanda asked. "What sort of action?"

"Well, for example, I think that I ought to do a thing, and I make the most concerted effort to carry it out, and I achieve this superhuman victory over myself—and later it turns out that it was exactly—"

"What's the matter with you?" she interrupted him impatiently.

"No, because I'm talking about something else. This isn't about that... It's just that if I was able to bear the thought of it, I should

be able to bear the act. That's all. And I can't. Don't you see? I can't,
I can't bear it."

"What act?"

Lin didn't answer.

"But do you know what it is to be 'a man of strong will'—the kind
of will that Curll has, for example? A man with that kind of will
doesn't understand the need for doing anything he doesn't want
to do."

After a moment, she added instructively:

"It's precisely this 'man of will' who never overcomes himself."

Lin listened to her carefully, but he didn't understand. When she
was finished, he looked silently at the young face shadowed by her
hat, at her vivid, knowing eyes.

"Laterna has just been to see us," she broke the silence, slightly
discomfited.

Terrible pain distorted Lin's pale face.

"My God, what's going on with you?" she asked again nervously.

She stood and went to him. "You're not being honest. Why aren't
you telling me everything? Don't I have a right to ask?"

That's what she said: Don't I have a right to ask? And her young
eyes shone with pure emotion. And Lin thought despairingly that
only now, when it was already too late, that maybe now...

He shrank back as she approached, wobbled strangely, and fell
upon the sofa, where there lay a pillow already flattened where his
head had been, Wanda sat by his side and took his hand.

"It started a long time ago," he said, his head hanging low. "I didn't
want to turn away, I didn't want to cover my eyes. The dilemma is
everywhere around us, jutting out of life like a bothersome plank
from a fence. It's right before your eyes here, there—all the time.
I began to wonder if, when that crucial moment arrived, I would
be able to...if I would have the strength to renounce—the man...
Because the idea, separated from the man, can easily become a chi-
mera, a cheap dream for which you might, at the very worst, lose
your life."

He faltered.

"For which you don't need to lose your honor...

"They speak of 'strength of spirit'.... There's such sweetness and flimsiness in those words when you're standing on your own and giving nothing of yourself. But to take on the responsibility of others' blunders, others' guilt, just lining up for action, standing in solidarity no matter what—it's the only redeeming thing about…reality. Because it's easy to follow your own truth, which is pure and good, and which, out of all the others, you consider to be the one. It's easy to stay off to the side and just 'be in harmony with yourself'.…

"And yet the moment arrives when the idea demands to be realized, when you have to take the appropriate measures, when, in the name of the idea, you act—basely."

Wanda listened, her eyes alert and questioning. Lin suddenly laughed.

"This is how Laterna put it: The fatherland. Its moral significance goes completely unquestioned as dogma. They say: My language, my fields, the forests, this land in which the dust of my ancestors rests, in which I too will rest—it's not what it's about at all! The fatherland is 'the highest cause'—that's how he put it. There where reason and justice don't suffice, there where conscience doesn't suffice—that's precisely where we need the fatherland, don't we?"

He tried to laugh again, but he only grimaced.

"So there you are, that's the gist of it—for them, the highest cause is…revolution."

He slipped his hand out from under Wanda's, clasped his hands together and clenched them with all his strength.

"But I understood it just a week, maybe ten days—too late."

He took a deep breath.

"Yes. As long as I didn't truly understand, everything seemed to be in order. It was simply a continuation, the natural result of my certainty, one step further down this same path that led to the world of 'action.' Inside, I had no hesitation whatsoever, I had no doubts: it was too monumental for there not to be some kind of sacrifice… Yes. Sacrifice and—heroism…

"And afterward—" (Wanda didn't know what he meant) "—I spent nearly the entire night at his father's, at old Laterna's."

"And did you tell him?"

"Oh, I wasn't there to confide in him. I didn't tell him anything.

I listened. And now…maybe now I'd be able to think like he does, maybe I'd be able to—to accept it. Not only nature, which, with its suns and stars, with its blue heavens and green land, should be taken entirely as a gift, as a source of eternal, full-blown joy and complete fulfillment. Not only the animals within it—spirited beings, strange creatures, thinking themselves so necessary but living without the slightest care about what their existence amounts to. But to accept humanity…

"One can consider the miraculous role it plays—small and dark amidst the mysterious space of the world. One can consider it and burn with exhilaration, with amazement and delight, admire everything and sing its praises: the roaring chug of a train, the rectilinear conception—unprecedented, found nowhere in nature—of a city, the whirring vibration of the iron organisms in machine shops… and those animals harnessed to the mechanisms of human ambition, understanding nothing, yet trusting that this is the only way…

"Right now, both the known and the unknown live within and around people. And maybe now I could contemplate those who stoop low, watching, those who closely observe—who *know*. And here on Assyrian tablets, on papyrus, on parchment, on fibrous handmade paper—full of joy and suffering, delicate apprehension and intoxicating hope—they speak to each other. And it's with a strange, serene faith that they send their words out into the world—through the epochs and ages. They wait so long for an answer, but they're never impatient… It's enough for them, what they have been able to pick up, what they've heard from the past; it's enough for them to experience the exquisite sweetness of brotherhood with those long dead—through the darkness of years and the veils of foreignness, these identical sorrows and smiles, the eternal loneliness of people, the priceless, incomparable thrill of mutual understanding.

"Maybe I myself could live in this miraculous world, not in conflict with anything, in a world of internal harmony, praise, and joy…

"But it's too late. Just like your having come here.

"Because now I know that I could have not done it—but I did do it. And there was a moment when I hadn't done it yet—such a day once existed in the world!…"

Lin held his head in his hands and whipped it back and forth, delirious with suffering. Wanda leaned closer to him and, holding back tears, asked:

"My God, what did you do, my sweet boy, what did you do? Why do you torture yourself so?"

He kissed both her hands and moved them away from him. For a moment he looked her in the face.

"I will tell you and you alone."

But he remained silent.

"I will tell you: I wrote a note, a list, a complete list of the whole regiment—that's what. Almost entirely numbers. One note. And I don't even have anything to worry about—after all, he told me himself that the list was typed…"

Again she leaned over, enfolded his head in her arms, and hugged him tightly to her breast. Tears fell from her eyes as she spoke, as she attempted so childishly to "comfort" him…

She asked him to shake it off, to forget all about it, to stop thinking about just this one thing. If he truly was guilty, he had the rest of his life to make it right.

He refuted her stubbornly. "I know, I know it's possible to think like this, to think that good and evil are equally necessary, that crime is a necessary condition for penance and redemption. But even if I somehow clear myself, confess, atone, make amends, what is it to me? So what if I find some sort of forgiveness somewhere, if there's that falseness at the bottom of everything, the impossibility of truth. Of course—politics must have compromise. Not only politics: compromise is the very core of revolution. There's no escaping that."

She asked him to leave with her. To spend the evening with them, like he used to. But he refused.

She left alone. In the dark hallway, Lin's mother rose from the trunk on which she'd spent the duration of their conversation.

"What's the matter with him?" she asked in a frightened whisper. "Have you learned anything?"

"No," she replied, not knowing what else to say. Then she added pleadingly, "Please look after him. I'll be back tomorrow."

When the old woman returned to the room, her son neither

raised his eyes nor said a single word. She thought that he was angry with her. But it was something very different.

Again he tried to set about organizing his papers. Here were some older poems—naïve, patriotic, bellicose. And here were new ones—about cities, trams, cars, and buildings, about revolution... And he thought to himself that if only he had been able to publish them—with his little book ("my sole consolation...") he could have entered the ranks of those who have waited patiently for recognition through the ages, for the sweet reward of being understood...[27]

When his mother, having first made up his sofa for the night, finally fell asleep, Lin lay down on the bedding, still in his clothes, and tears streamed from his eyes to his temples.

He had to think about it again: the death of his young setter Ralf, which he was never able to remember without choking back a lump in his throat. Oh, he was the embodiment of goodness, friendliness, and delight. With his melancholic muzzle, his droopy jowls and floppy ears, he was always brimming with frenzied puppyish excitement. Who else but Ralf could rejoice so at the arrival of his master, offer his paw so gladly on demand, look into the depths of one's heart with eyes more golden?

He'd always wanted above all else to guess his master's wishes, to read his fate in his master's face. Whether or not he succeeded in this, it was always in the best faith, burning with eagerness, with joyful haste and enthusiasm. If he erred, it was only in his flightiness.

And then it came time for him to die, and there was no longer any hope for him. He didn't begrudge the fact that it was happening this way; he didn't utter a single moan. He let them pull his lips away from his muzzle to pour medicine down his throat, which made him vomit and didn't help at all. He let them apply a compress for his sick lungs, even though it made breathing even harder. Maybe he thought that that was the way it had to be.

He'd gotten up from his bed in order to make his way onto the sofa somehow, where—this time—nobody forbade him to lie, where nobody was angry with him... He climbed down again, slowly advanced a few steps, came closer on unsteady paws, and lowered himself hesitantly onto the bare floor. Was he thinking about where would be—best?...

Then Lin took the dog's head in both his hands, embracing his soft, velvety ears—as gently and delicately as he could, so not to disrupt the accord he'd reached with death—and whispered beseechingly, "But maybe you won't die, little Ralf."

And then he sat at a distance and watched Ralf for a long time as, again, he lay down on some spot on the floor, avoiding the patch of sun.

He didn't approach the dog, didn't say anything, and he didn't touch him so as not to disturb or exhaust him... He sat at a distance and watched as his golden eyes grew dim and dull, his breathing short and labored. But this was still not his final place...

Ralf rose, stood for a moment—and began to walk, unaccountably, toward a door. Did he want to go through it to the other room, where there were no people? Was he, doomed to this terrible fate, still counting on something? He reached the threshold, and there he stopped at the open door, where anyone could go through, where there was at least—refuge...

This was the final place. He stood for a moment—and his hind legs shook, so he slowly squatted. Then he lowered himself down to rest on his front legs. But he spread them strangely—wide apart, elbows on the outside. He flattened himself and clung to the floor. And now he rested his deathly tired head—his brown, velvety head, which had always been full of doggish frivolity and just one concern: understanding what was asked of him and fulfilling it at all costs... He laid his deeply beloved head sideways on his left elbow, like a scared and lonely child. It was obvious that this was the end. His eyes saw only what was very near; they weren't dim and dull, they were simply still. His muzzle's serrated brown lips parted slightly, and he bared his teeth.

That was the end. He bared his teeth—he who was so good, who only barked from overexcitement and was always ready for another pat on the head: he who was never angry, not even when pushed away or struck—his gaze always warm and expectant, always full of the tenderest forgiveness, always ready for unreserved amity and reconciliation.

He became just a dead dog, a "carcass," as the people who took him away wrote on the receipt.

And tonight, Lin was dedicating his last memory to him. Every spurned gesture of dog love, every harsh word—it still felt like a wound. "The soul exists," Lin thought. "The soul exists in humans and in animals. But the body *is* the soul…" And, eyes still wet with tears, he fell asleep. He had a dream. He was able to make out a very bright autumn night, filled with fog from the ground to the heavens, fog that obscured the moon but was imbued with its light.

On a low, dark, flat patch of land was a village huddled on the plain, tiny amidst the emptiness, doomed to extinction. But this was the way of it: the inhabitants wouldn't die out, nor would the buildings crumble. The village would simply stop being real.

Dying in this way, it sent—out through the white emptiness of the fog, over the flat, black plain—one musical tone. It sent it to another village, further away, a village that would remain. And the tone, landing there, was lower by a third.

There was a fatal smile in that tone, a fatal and unutterably sad greeting. A sacrifice beyond strength, signifying death.

19.

One morning Omski received an anonymous letter at his office. The unknown author informed him that Infantry Lieutenant Julian Gondziłł was worthy of slightly closer inspection. From Saturday afternoon to Monday morning, the office safe was always empty. Each Monday, before anyone else arrived, Gondziłł showed up at the office with a suitcase. Together with another officer, a clerk, and a few "civilians," he was making quite a tidy profit moving state money around, and furthermore, he was speculating on military supplies. Next, the letter addressed Gondziłł's "kept woman," Miss Sasin, and a brooch with a large diamond purchased by Gondziłł on a certain day and at a certain jeweler's. Among the names mentioned were Major Bielski, Sasin, and even—Mr. Nutka and…Sednowski. At this last one, Omski seethed. The letter's conclusion pointedly read: "This is what comes of Polish officers."

Omski—despite his expertise in the area of military law and honor—hesitated for some time over what to make of this document he'd received. The letter had been written by an unsophisticated man, most likely some lowly office functionary, perhaps someone resentful of Gondziłł's poor treatment of him. Its lack of a signature and its naïve style were grounds for simply throwing it out. But the facts, precisely and quite specifically enumerated, demanded consideration.

After another moment of hesitation, Omski forwarded the letter to Major Bielski's immediate superiors and put it out of his mind.

He was occupied with his own affairs. His relationship to Teresa filled his entire interior life. In his daily visits to the Hennerts, in her presence, he experienced a terrifying ecstasy that rendered the rest of the world a desolate wasteland.

In his obsession with her, there was no one physical detail or individual feature that captivated his senses, that became the object of his tormented lust and the inexhaustible quarry of his longing. Teresa had neither a special expression to her mouth when she smiled, nor was there any particular harmony between her tooth enamel and her gums, nor a singular pairing of her upper lip and the line of her nose—nothing that would madden the senses, nothing that couldn't be replaced by the stunning beauty of any other woman. Nor had she the kind of eyes one last glimpse of which was worth your life. Nor had she catches in her voice by which you could know your destiny, finally make it out among thousands of other paths, after years of searching...

It was impossible to overcome Teresa. You couldn't itemize her charms, reveal the secret of her magnetism—you just couldn't fight her.

Her allure was completely within her and around her, as though it were somehow in the air that surrounded her. Her pleasant eyes, none too large, so ordinary that it was hard to remember or reimagine them, the regular lines of her temperate smile, her nose graceful but without character, her oval face, her complexion—they constituted an entirety that did not lend itself to differentiation. Her body's shape with her clothes, her brow with the style of her hair, her form with its movements, her mouth with her words and voice—all were components of her appeal, which consisted of balance, accord, and the harmony of everything together. Nothing stood out, nothing drew attention from the whole; from everything together there radiated the gentle charm of safety, order, and calm.

He was helpless in his nights of longing and torment; he was hungry: he had no specific quarry on which to focus. He could not gorge and intoxicate himself—as other lovers did—on one particular word or gesture, on a particular detail of her body. He had nothing. He desperately needed to be close to her—in her sphere, breathing her air, there at the center of her harmonious relation to the world.

Even after seeing her, there was nothing he could take home with him. She was sparing and contained in her beauty, economical, centripetal.

Thoughts that might satiate him, that might ease his suffering, were powerless before her. Nothing—nothing! Total emptiness filled him the moment she was gone.

Once he thought, "It's strange, as though I love not her, but her presence."

It was an awful love, allowing him no memories, no extraordinary passion—so difficult, so unable to be deceived by anything.

And so he was forced to want for so much... Even if she fell in love with him, belonged to him... Even if—like other secret lovers—they were able to hide away together for a few days, arrange clandestine encounters of caresses and endearments, living on the memory of their last meeting while waiting for their next... No, no—none of this would do—only to be near her, constantly, day and night, breathing her air, feeding on her presence.

The fact that she did exist, somewhere, was by no means a consolation.

Tormented, humiliated, furious, bereft of pride—again and again he would go there as a friend of the family: always recognized, having certain rights, embarrassing no one.

After some initial scenes of reproach and confession, Omski gave the appearance of calming down. He was dogged in his sadness, having renounced hope and revenge. And Teresa, accustomed now to the daily presence of her quiet admirer, somehow forgave him his unthinkable impudence and seemed to forget the insult she'd endured. She was once again as calm, trusting, and sweet as she'd been at the beginning.

But he had not forgotten a thing.

Sednowski's disappearance did not reassure him in the least. The very fact of it gave him vast grounds for suspicion and speculation. But he was so afraid of the truth he found neither the courage nor the strength to ask her. Consumed by unrelenting jealousy, mad with suspicion, he often secretly followed Teresa so he might learn something, so he might finally achieve some certainty.

Knowing she wasn't at home, he waited for a long time in the street. When, at a distance, he finally saw her, she was returning alone. She was returning alone! Such relief, such immeasurable happiness, such wonderful safety and calm—if only for a day, if only for an hour...

As usual, he found himself walking her way. The whole of her figure against the dusk, her movement as she walked, the color of the air that surrounded her, her smile, the nod of her head, the way she offered him her hand—it filled him with delight. He took the key from her purse. They entered the elevator together. Then, bending over her and lifting her chin with one hand, not even embracing her, he kissed her on the mouth.

"You mustn't do that," she said to him gravely as they stepped out onto the stairwell.

He turned away without saying goodbye, without bowing. Swept on waves of grim fury, hatred surging from the very depths of his body, he quickly left.

He couldn't understand, he was entirely unwilling to accept that if she were to love no one, she would have to not love him as well. He knew that Hennert had lovers, that he—indifferent, obliging, complacent—meant nothing to his wife. He refused to acknowledge the obstacles she had casually given: the difference in their ages, her responsibilities to her daughter. He scrutinized the people who surrounded her, subjecting each male acquaintance to analysis and, after undergoing an agony of unwarranted jealousy, dismissing him as implausible. And his thoughts always returned to the one about whom he was certain: Sednowski.

But after an hour of pacing various streets he returned, taking the elevator up and standing at that very same door. He entered—sullen, determined in his misery, demanding consideration, kindness, and delicacy, but then docile, rendered powerlessness by anguish and fatigue.

There were times, however, when he didn't return.

He was deeply unhappy. He dreamed about shaking loose, about liberation, about escape. He thought about how it used to be, when Basia's love seemed to mean happiness. When, away from the dirt and toil of the front, the haze of smoke and vodka of the officers' parties, the stupid jokes and vulgar dalliances at the officers' mess—he found an escape in her girlish caresses, her gentle words, the soft warmth of her love.

He took the familiar route, climbed the shabby stairs. She opened the door—and choked on her gasp and turned pale.

He kissed her hand. He didn't have a plan. He didn't even know whether he'd come to her as a lover or as something else.

"Please, have a seat," she said in a low voice.

It seemed to him that there was some sort of expectation in her tone. But he recognized his mistake. Basia knew that his visit didn't mean anything.

He sat. He asked after Aunt Lipska's health.

"She's been buried two weeks already," she answered sadly.

He was quite surprised not to have known, though there was really nothing surprising about it. He told her how sorry he was, how grieved he was... She listened with downcast eyes.

He wanted to lower his head and nestle it against her chest. It was all the same to him what she thought of it. He was so accustomed to her persistent, irrational trust.

She was talking about the office again. Now that Elżbieta Sasin was betrothed and leaving her job, she would finally receive the long-promised promotion to Mr. Hennert's secretary.

She spoke in a gentle voice. But when he wanted to sit closer to her, when he permitted himself remorse, tenderness, irresponsible softness of heart, she quickly moved away.

She did it without fear or alarm. But he saw it in how her lips were set—their hardness.

He sat next to her and drank another cup of tea. Then he stood to say goodbye.

"I am sorry that I came," he said.

"Yes, it's not good that you came," she answered, not raising her eyes.

However, after a few days had passed, he came again.

Seriously and sadly, he told her that he was very busy, that he had many concerns. Basia didn't ask what kind.

He had thought about how weak he'd been before her, how worthy of contempt. He could not defend himself, there was nothing with which to justify himself.

Yet he wanted to shift the burden of the decision, the entire weight of breaking it off, onto her. He himself didn't have the strength to fix the moment and bear its responsibility.

He knew that, thanks to him, she would discover a new reality of life: she might meet not only disaster, but also humiliation.

She asked him, "Why do you trouble yourself so? After all, I already understand."

Even just hearing it, he felt better; after the torments and storms of that other love, it was a relief.

"I understand," she said. "Obviously it can't be any other way. So why torture yourself?"

Still, he had one final illusion: if she did reproach him, if, in a voice powerful with love, she demanded that he stay—then he might yet be saved.

But he did not ask her for salvation. He wanted nothing to do with deciding his own fate.

"I thought about it for a very long time," she told him calmly. "Obviously it can't be any other way, so let it be this way. Actually, it's all I've been thinking about…"

He listened in silence and found absolution in the calmness of her words. Yes—he didn't feel guilty. He compared her dispassionate resignation to the madness and torment of his love. What did she know of suffering? Did she even know how to love?

"I've been thinking," she went on, "that probably the worst thing about it is that it's impossible for me to see it in any way that could allow…"

She fumbled for words, but he was listening intently. And at last he heard:

"That would allow me to—still respect you."

He eagerly accepted the insult. Yes, yes. She was right, and so everything was as it should be. He was guilty, and he had been punished. Now he could leave.

20.

Professor Laterna, having read in the newspaper about the search and arrest of Lieutenant Gondziłł, went to see Binia that very same day.

He was certain it had been a misunderstanding, the result of the young army's overzealousness in carrying out reforms, and it would undoubtedly be cleared up in a couple of days or even hours.

Like everyone, he was intractable in his belief that nothing truly bad could happen to anyone close to him. For there are things one reads about in telegrams, in court reports, in police chronicles, which one learns about through the crude gossip of common folk in tenement courtyards or back rooms, but they never happen to, for example, one's brother-in-law, to cheerful, good-natured Julek, to kind Binia.

And even on this occasion the professor mused about how wide the range of perception of reality was when one faced the facts, how many degrees there were, and how each was equally, objectively real.

"Well, fine—they did a search," the professor conceded in his head. "But, of course, they didn't find anything. For God's sake, what on earth could they find at old Julek's?"

He found Binia doing better than he'd expected. She was utterly calm.

She confirmed exactly what he already knew from the papers. She agreed that she just needed to wait until the misunderstanding was cleared up. She really was calm, if not even a little indifferent or numb. And it was from this strange calm that Laterna caught wind of—reality. Here, in this apartment, it became evident what had happened.

Binia told the professor of her concern that Wituś was sick. This drizzly weather was surely bad for him; he'd caught a cough and come down with a fever, so she'd had to put him to bed. There wasn't any lunch. Binia offered the professor some of the watery, fine-milled porridge that she'd made for the children. Then she sat for a while beside Wituś's bed.

"Andrzej was here earlier," Binia said hesitantly. "He came this morning as soon as he found out… It never even occurred to me that he would care…that he would be so upset by Julian's case."

As she spoke, Binia didn't meet Laterna's eyes.

"He told me that he would probably be going away, and that he didn't know what was going to happen to Zosia, and that he was sorry to have to leave her behind."

Laterna shook his head. His daughter, whom he didn't know well and who was not especially dear to him, was ill again. The several times he'd visited her, Binia was often there already. Zosia was looking worse and worse. There were black circles around her eyes, and her cheeks had the vivid flush of constant fever.

She spoke rapturously about Russia, there where children didn't know what hunger meant, where workers' children got as many cookies as they wanted. She told him that no one was oppressed there, no one was disregarded, and that everyone had to sweep his own steps, peasant and aristocrat alike.

Seeing how crucial these details were to her feverish faith, Laterna decided not to voice his skepticism.

Shyly and tactfully, Binia asked Laterna whether he might perhaps pay her a visit today.

"She would be so happy…"

"Of course I will!" the professor assured her, rising at once to say goodbye.

Binia rose as well and, holding Laterna's great hand a little longer, said emphatically, "And please let Andrzej know that it would be better if he didn't come here to make inquiries…"

"What?" He was surprised. "Binia, why?"

Wrinkling her brow, Binia attempted to explain. "I can't see him anymore, do you understand, Professor? I'm just not able to see him, I can't, I can't…"

And seeing the professor's undispelled surprise, she added, with effort, in a quiet, tired voice, "I don't trust him…"

Having said goodbye to Binia, Laterna made his way to his children's apartment. This time Andrzej was there. At the sight of his father, his face lit up with an ironic smile.

"Ah! Honorable professor, respected father! Welcome, welcome… A rare guest…"

He led him into his room.

"Zosia was in tremendous pain all night," he said in a completely different tone. "She was given opium, and she's sleeping now. So we won't wake her…"

"How is she?" Laterna asked, settling heavily into a small chair.

Andrzej shrugged his shoulders.

"She's taken a turn for the worse these last two days." He said it as though it were his father's fault. "Yesterday's test came back very bad… And there's been a complication. There are some matters that are forcing me to go away. Abroad, abroad," he added quickly and—noting his father's questioning look—reassuringly. "I'll be leaving in a few days, maybe even tomorrow. But you have to appreciate the fact that this shifts certain responsibilities, certain burdens, onto you…"

At this, Laterna felt bad.

"Of course I appreciate that fact," he broke in. "The one thing I can't do is bring Zosia to my place. And that's on account of Marcela, who would never agree to it…"

"Exactly right!" Andrzej was almost pleased. "Because it's out of the question to move Zosia, not in the state she's in. The thing is, she can't be left alone for even an hour, even half an hour. Do you understand, Papa? Someone has to stay here, someone has to be here day and night…"

"So we get a nurse…" Laterna ventured uncertainly.

"Do you think so? Indeed. But we need to find someone, hire her, and try her out. I can take care of it before I leave, if you see fit…"

Papa did see fit, of course. "I've just been to Binia's," he said after a moment of silence from Andrzej. "Do you know something more about this business with Julian? What is he actually accused of?"

Andrzej made a gesture of supreme distaste.

"It's a tremendously ordinary affair, far too ordinary," he said. He made symmetrical gestures with both hands, as if to drive away a surfeit of unhealthy curiosity. "It's simple. He took money from the safe and spread it around, he stole, he stole... What can I say? It paints a pretty picture of the prevailing conditions in our young country..."

Only now did Laterna actually understand the terrible thing that had happened. "This can't be, Andrzej. It must be just a misunderstanding..."

"Unfortunately, Papa, it's not... And I never imagined that Gondziłł would be so appallingly tangled up in it... I myself thought of him as someone who inspired confidence... And yet..."

"Are you sure of this? How do you know?"

"I'm sure of it. Papa, you once said that it's not so bad, that 'life looks after itself.' Well, here it is, life looking after itself." Andrzej laughed.

Laterna, surprised, didn't respond. He was thinking about Julek, who had suddenly become alien and incomprehensible, about what would happen to Binia and the boys. He was feeling humiliated, a low, common shame that it was someone in his family, someone close, and that everyone would know about it.

"In times of peace, there are remnants of war," Andrzej said. "And they linger for a long time. You know, Papa, this Colonel Omski of yours was right: war is necessary to uphold the army's moral strength. Because without war—what happens?... War demoralizes—that's how it might seem. But when we pull these dark demons from men's souls and bring them into the light, we give them beautiful names—names particular to wartime. When peace comes, the glory of these names dies away, but the demons don't. They merely shrink, hiding away in the little nooks and crannies of the soul—and there they quietly live, just waiting. Opportunities often arise... It's no longer heroism, blind courage, 'joyfully bathing in the blood of the enemy'—oh yes, instead we have petty criminal assaults, quiet crimes in dark corners, secret feuds...Well, and cases such as Gondziłł's..."

Laterna remained silent. He was experiencing an odd sensation. Here, in front of him, was his own son, whom he remembered as a small boy, toward whom he felt he had certain moral or emotional obligations. At the same time, this heightened consciousness of their blood relation seemed to him something unbelievable, even monstrous. He was more distant from Andrzej than any person—any stranger—he passed in the street.

"What's universally perceived as the evil of war," Andrzej said, "is people dying from bullets, gas, and disease. But that's by no means the most important thing. I'll give you, my good Papa, just one little anecdote, one of thousands. Driving through the war zone, I chanced upon a little village amidst willow trees and twig fences lining a sandy road. The village was empty, the peasants had all run away—only some black silhouettes of people in the distance, on the banks high above a little pond, in the shade of these willows and wild gooseberry bushes. So we went to take a closer look at this strange spectacle.

"Along the bank of the pond, each a few paces from the other, sat some Hebraic citizens, each with his head chopped off. It looked like they were fishing. Each one had a hand resting on a pole stuck in the ground, leaning toward the water like a fishing rod. Their poses—a bit artificial, a bit tired, a bit, let's say, sleepy—they all looked like people just sitting beside the water. You could have laughed. I counted them: there were seventeen. Each had his head resting at his feet."

"Where was this?" Laterna asked, wrinkling his forehead.

"Oh, here it is already: 'Where was this?' Where it was is totally insignificant, it's absolutely unimportant. The point is these things are necessary for something—besides being innocent, wholesome fun, they're also needed for something. That is to say, enemy nations hurl these events at one another like they were bullets. And this is the only reason why we need to know where it happened… They try to outdo one another in recriminations of savagery and barbarity. Things that happen everywhere, that discredit all people, get slung at one side of the front to discredit a particular nation. These events are needed as kindling. They're fertile; they're constantly breeding hatred and an undying desire for retaliation."

Laterna was listening with utmost attention. But he didn't say anything.

The issue was too enormous. Any judgment he pronounced would be a distortion of reality. Andrzej spoke like someone who had always stood off to the side, hardly touched, scarcely brushed by the great roaring chariot of war. He'd been splashed by mud and blood—he hadn't seen the laurels on its head.

And today—looking at the war through the lens of its peaceful conclusion—young Laterna saw before him a naked skeleton stripped of its crimson, pennants stripped of their gold; he saw victims and cripples, husks of human beings rotting in hospitals...and so he had for himself this ready judgment, this easy judgment: it's all lunacy and crime.

And yet—to think this, one must dredge up from the bottom of one's heart some incontrovertible value, feelings of reverence and deep tenderness, emotions that coincide precisely with those of this lunacy and crime, that run closely parallel to this lunacy, to this crime.

"In order to live," Andrzej said, "we must decide on certain truths, certain moral postulates. We can't do without them, even though in real life they're either absent or they mean something entirely different. But that's exactly why we need them. The principles of justice, of guilt and punishment, of redemption. They're constructed outside of life in order to impose them on life, in order to make life—possible. The principle of the fatherland serves the same purpose.

"The fatherland," he continued. "Here's a way of giving these same things a different name, of assigning different qualities to the same values. We judge nations by their patriotism and military virtues, but it's not until we apply the criterion of the fatherland that we have a positive or negative sense of them. What we deplore in ourselves, we love in our enemies. The German: a coward, a lay about, submissive—to a Frenchman, this is a good German. The Russian: a drunk and a slave—this is a good Russian to a Pole. Oh, but how we hate to see in the enemy anything that's desirable, any feature that's hard for us to come by! The world found such tremendous comfort, such moral relief, in hating Germany during the first years of the war. They unleashed the fight, and they fought superbly—if it had happened on this side of the front instead of the other, what could be more commendable from the standpoint of the fatherland?

They've become infinitely less hated since they lost. Their downfall and demoralization have aroused empathy and compassion in their former enemies.

"The fatherland always serves as a criterion for injustice. It is a postulate of a hatred of the highest order. So in the phrase 'God and Fatherland,' there is paradox and blasphemy. 'God' is what reconciles and unites people in their loftiest yearnings; 'fatherland' is what, under the influence of lofty slogans, divides them. The fatherland reinstates polytheism: each army prays to its own god for a victory. It would be better to remain silent before commencing to rip God to shreds, singing war hymns all the while—God, the father of men, who bestowed exactly one name upon us all: 'brothers'..."

"So you—you found God?" Laterna interrupted, suddenly raising his head.

Andrzej fell silent, looked at his father, and smiled faintly.

"We're not going to talk about that."

Laterna stood and looked around for his coat so he could go.

"When do you leave?" he asked.

"Wait, Papa, your salutary-sounding expression is that life looks after itself. You always did put too much faith in it—and I'm afraid... Because I'm leaving Zosia solely in your care, do you understand? Solely."

"It's not necessary to remind me," Laterna said with impatience and distaste.

Andrzej's face changed. He paled with sudden fury.

"I will remind you, and I'll remind you again after that... Listen, I was sixteen years old when my mother was dying there of tuberculosis... She died from hunger and deprivation—when the water froze right there in the room, when there was nobody anywhere close to us, when the dream of returning had long since disappeared, the return that you had promised, you'd promised... How she suffered, how she longed for you and waited for you!... How she loved you until the very end and never complained... She believed she had been trampled by the march of a hero... And yet how could she not know that you had...a lover there!..."

When his father had gone, Andrzej quietly slipped into Zosia's room. She was still sleeping, sleeping so deeply and peacefully.

He clasped his hands and, standing there motionless, watched her for a long time.

He gazed once again at her sharp, thin nose, her eyes like two black smudges, her small, bony face—it was so changed, so changed. If she were already dead, she wouldn't look any different.

He knew that she would last perhaps another week more, maybe ten days—and then this defenseless, exhausted child would die. The only person on this earth whom he loved with all the strength of his heart…

After a short life filled with sadness and suffering, she was going to die. There was nothing he could give her, nothing he could do to change her fate.

He approached the bed without a sound, knelt down, and rested his forehead on the edge of her blanket. He cursed his own fate, cursed that he couldn't stay with her until the end came, hold her thin hands in his own, remain in her sight.

The thought occurred to him that there might come a moment when Zosia would be afraid…understanding the inevitability, she might be terrified.

Hearing someone coming in, he jumped to his feet.

Laterna, who had just remembered Binia's request, came through the unlocked door.

He, too, watched Zosia sleep for a moment. Then he turned his eyes to his son.

"I wanted to ask you, Andrzej," he began in a low voice.

"What about?"

Laterna hesitated.

"Binia would prefer that you not visit her anymore…"

"Ah. Yes." Andrzej nodded his head to show that he understood.

They stood opposite one another, as if still hesitating.

"This must be very hard for you, Andrzej," Laterna said finally, and he opened his great arms to his son.

"It is hard," Andrzej replied.

21.

Omski arrived at the Hennerts'. Wanda was not there, and Teresa's face was sad.

"Oh, Colonel," she sighed when she saw him.

"What happened?" he asked.

"Lin shot himself late last night. The bullet went through his left lung and he's hemorrhaging. He's in the hospital..."

Omski made an angry face.

"I hadn't heard anything about it," he muttered churlishly.

For him, the most salient point was that she had known something before he had, and it made her a stranger. There was still this whole other world from which he wasn't able to isolate her.

Teresa was speaking softly.

"Wanda's there with him, I didn't have the heart to forbid it. The news has had a terrible effect on her..."

She invited him to sit, and she herself took a seat on the small sofa.

"Just yesterday we were at the theater. Wanda let him know we'd be there, but he didn't come..."

"You were at the theater?" Suddenly, he was outraged.

Yes, she'd been to the theater to see the new play by one of these very young playwrights, a play that inspired by turns scandal, enthusiasm, and sensation. Teresa was never particularly swept away by anything; rather, she displayed a pleasant curiosity and openness toward everything.

"I have the impression that it does seem strange and awful, but only for the time being. Professor Laterna was there. He knows Lin, and he said..."

Omski seethed and churned. He was of the opinion that these young people should be locked up and given a taste of the lash. It was ridiculous what they did.

He hated them, these blackguards who made a mockery of the army, of authority, of love for the fatherland. Lin was very much one of them—and you see where *that* landed him....

So he said, but inside he was thinking that she would always be able to go anywhere she wanted, that there was an entire world that separated her from him. She had been there—and he had known nothing about it. Laterna had been there, and each person in the audience, as well—only not him, not him...

His face clouded with anger, and he said goodbye. But by the time he was in the street he was already admiring her goodness, her allure, as irresistible as destiny. He saw that it was by the grace of heaven that—out of seemingly nowhere—she had thus entered his life. His soul was completely spellbound by this one beloved being, and he was filled with the tenderest gratitude for the simple fact of her existence.

He knew that he would go back tomorrow, he knew what he would say, how he would seize the wings of this miracle and hold it fast. He would bind it to his life, make it irreversibly real.

And immediately there loomed the problem of reality, the total impossibility of making what he desired come true.

And again he went back. She received him—not like other women, wearing such and such a dress, setting off this or that facet of their beauty. She wore some dress that was barely discernible but also couldn't have been any different. Teresa didn't have particularities, she didn't have any especially felicitous moments. Her beauty was general; her charm was spread evenly through her face and figure.

She had hardly even smiled, hardly even looked at him with her calm, sweet eyes. Before she'd managed to do or say anything, he was already feeling the entrenched anger, the longing to avenge his stupid dreams, the desire to humiliate the both of them. The tenderest trembling of his heart, his timid happiness, the bliss of his humility—suddenly these were transformed into this senseless anger, this anger of honor seemingly violated.

All at once, it became undeniably clear to him that she was a shallow, ordinary woman, an unremarkable sitting-room doll, just like all the rest.

With a gloomy face, he learned that Lin was still alive but that his condition was deteriorating. Teresa didn't talk about the reason behind his suicide attempt; perhaps she assumed that it involved Wanda, with whom Lin was infatuated.

Now she was waiting for Wanda's return. Later that evening, she was going out to some dinner with her husband.

She talked for a while and then fell silent. It was quiet and calm all around them.

"And again I'll leave," he said. "And again I'll be alone, and again I'll go mad."

"Oh Colonel, you're starting again." She interrupted him with a gentle rebuke, without a trace of fear. Her tone was almost maternal. She was well aware that she was loved. She took his impertinence and spite as the inverse of a formal declaration. She laughed indulgently when he accused her of vanity and coquetry, and frowned with mild distaste when his attacks became coarse and brutal.

"And now, again, she will go off somewhere," he thought. She always slipped away from him. She was beyond his knowledge and his power.

"I can't stand it any longer, I can't stand it…"

He started toward her in a frenzy of anger. As he neared, she got to her feet and raised her arms slightly. Could it be that she thought to defend herself? Taking her in his arms, he felt almost no resistance.

"I love you, I love you," he repeated through clenched teeth.

Now he kissed her lips. Everything was swallowed up in the terrible pounding of his heart. Like the first time, he didn't feel any joy, only a passion that left him both breathless and senseless.

He repeated the only thing he knew: "I love you."

He didn't feel any resistance; he had no idea what she felt. Her calm was so insubstantial compared to the unbridled strength of his emotions. Maybe once she softly moaned. He could feel her little teeth behind her lips and forced them open with a kiss.

What was this? But he wasn't mistaken. Something had changed in her—as if something had consented. There was a softness is her arms now, her whole body yielded—as if she were a possibility, as if she could truly be—attained.

What bliss! Could she really be returning his kiss? He still couldn't believe what he was feeling. Warm tremors of happiness flooded his entire body. He knelt, his head on her knees.

When he stood, for a long moment she didn't move from the spot. She didn't straighten her hair or her clothes. Her forehead and cheeks were slightly flushed.

He remembered that as he knelt, she'd gently stroked his hair and face.

He looked at her with gratitude, full of happiness, weak with joy. He sat at some distance from her.

"Why are you quiet? Why don't you say anything? I love you…"
No, it didn't surprise her. She had known, she had waited for it… She was lost in thought and slightly sad, although she sort of smiled.

"It's too bad," she said hesitantly.

Again he was before her, he had her in his arms, all of her, real, his.

"For such fatal love…"

22.

When the Hennerts went to the countryside, inviting all their closest friends to their villa on the lake, Omski was determined not to take advantage of the invitation and politely excused himself.

"Here's the perfect separation," he thought, "arranged by fate itself."

He would overcome his longing, he'd forget, he'd be free, free…

Ah, what did it matter that she was his lover now, that now she—passive, a little sad, a little embarrassed—consented to everything?

Her beautiful eyes filled with surprise and apprehension at his madness, his incoherent and impossible love. In his hands, she was like a soulless object, allowing herself to be steered but taking part in nothing. She was outside her own pleasure, never fully abandoning herself to it, never his, never unquestionably his…

She made him suffer; it was the suffering that a lover experiences when he loves a passive and affectless woman. She was so detached "during" that he suspected her of thinking of someone else, of having a lover other than him.

But when she went away! Then, with admiration and awe, he believed to the bottom of his heart that she was more soulful, subtle, and desirable than anyone, with a love as reckless, wild, and earthbound as his, could possibly live up to.

Then he'd remember moments of incomprehensible rapture, when no caress could possibly satisfy his longing for her, when he gazed at her face resting on his arm, at the eyelashes on her closed eyelids, at the sad, delicate half-smile on her lips.

How long could he continue to dwell on her downcast soul, never willing to give itself to him, never willing to lower itself to suffusing her body with the burning sweetness of passion?

Before spring was over, he went to her.

It was true that he was acting badly, that in some inexplicable way he'd become indifferent to his work, to his chief responsibilities. As any feather-brained officer who wanted a vacation would, he applied for a leave. He was completely entitled to one, but a leave would undoubtedly delay urgent business matters and it would reflect poorly on him—ah, but none of that mattered! And again there was something vindictive in his nonchalance. That was just it: he would never have left the front for the sake of a lover, he would never have gotten bogged down in love's stupid insanity—if there were a war, if the fever of his youth had had different temptations and his valor had been tested in other jousts. Alas, it was precisely this suffocating emptiness in his life that the curse of "fatal love" now preyed upon. He hadn't wanted it; he was not the guilty party...

The shuddering automobile deposited him onto the marshy gravel of the driveway. He looked around for a moment, dazed and uncertain, still deafened by the din of the drive.

He deliberately hadn't sent a telegram—or maybe... It was strange: he hungered after what he would find horrifying, after something he wouldn't be able to bear...

Before he climbed the stairs and rang the bell, he stood there for another moment. Had no one heard him? Was no one here?...

It was a gray stone cottage with a high red double roof. Balconies, terraces, rounded corners, windows and glass rendering it almost transparent, geraniums hanging from each window and honeysuckles climbing toward the roof making everything seem green and alive.

The front garden, which descended to the lake, seemed to him an amusing little ornament—full of wickets and croquet balls, with pyramids, hedges, and even whole walls carved from the bright verdure of the bushes. Little white lacquered benches stood here and there, and the smooth, even lawn was bordered exclusively by blue hydrangeas in bloom. And, calmly glittering beyond the gravel pathways and the green tunnels and colonnades of this playful trifle of a garden, was the vast, shining water of the lake.

Surprised at the silence, Omski rang. A servant with an unfamiliar face opened the door right away. "Neither the Master nor the young lady are at home—only Mrs. Hennert."

"Alone?"

"Alone…"

She was alone, and she appeared before him: paler, smaller, younger. He looked at her face searchingly, sharply—was she happy or was she merely terrified?

"But I'm happy, of course," she said, and her smile was cheerful, trusting, sincere. "I am happy, my dear. I'm all alone, see?" And she looked around to assure him or, rather, to assure herself.

He brightened and was immediately consumed by a mad, youthful joy. "Can I stay until tomorrow?" he asked. "You must stay—as long as you can… Hennert is always coming and going, we constantly have some guest or another… The Chwościks left just yesterday—." She provided names right away so that he would be pacified. "They stopped here on their way to the seaside… Curll, as well… And did you hear that Lin will survive, that he's improving?… Wanda will come tomorrow, and he'll probably come here, too, a little later…"

A room had already been set aside for Omski. He freshened up for dinner. He was so happy, he was really almost happy…

From the outside, the villa gave the impression of being a little house, but on the inside there were twenty-some rooms and an abundance of space. Hennert had bought it, already completely furnished, from some German who was fleeing the area. The room in which Omski found himself had walls half-covered with white lacquered paneling, and it was crammed with furnishings so similar in appearance to the wall that, for a moment, Omski didn't know where the wall ended and the bed began. Wardrobes, shelves, little benches, semicircular end tables—it all seemed half-melded into the wall. Over the paneling, the wall was covered with sapphire- and gold-checked upholstery identical to that of the white chairs and the sofas that stood on the sapphire carpet.

It delighted him.

In the dining room, where he soon descended for dinner, the wood was a different color, light yellow, but the effect was similar.

Identical china cabinets stood symmetrically on both sides of the room, an identical little triangular sofa stood in each corner, and there were large, identical "still lifes" framed in light yellow wood, hanging in a row and looking as though they were recessed in the wall.

At dinner they were not, strictly speaking, alone. There was a Miss Maria and a Mrs. Skąpska; the former kept the house, and the latter was Wanda's tutor, anticipating her return. Nonetheless, they felt like newlyweds—together for the first time, free and on their own.

Together, the two of them went to the drawing room to read the newspapers Omski had brought. And in here it was simply ridiculous. Colorful, splendidly embroidered linen tablecloths covered the wicker tables, and the wicker sofas and armchairs were buried under masses of similarly embroidered cushions. Finally, the wicker shelves were adorned with elegant Meissen china figurines, as well as little cows, calves, puppies, maids, and old ladies made from Copenhagen porcelain. And there were flowers absolutely everywhere—sticking out of everything, hanging, flowing down the walls.

"That cow is the work of Knud Kyhn," Teresa said, as if this were important.[28] And Omski laid his forehead against her hand and was happy.

That afternoon they went out on the lake.

The vast, calm water flowed beyond the shallow shore. It sparkled under the sun and danced with countless fiery sequins, but on the far side it lay flat—distant, glassy, milky blue. A long line of tall lakeside trees and dense clusters of bushes, highlighted by reeds that shone gold in the sun, cut into the frame of the water; right behind it stretched the lake, spreading out into a vast space where water was joined to sky. This liquid distance was like a gate leading into a separate, mysterious world.

Omski sat at the oars. The mechanics of rowing filled him with ecstasy. This fragile bauble of a boat, its long sides thin and aristocratic-looking, glided through the glassy water with extraordinary speed and silence.

The oars' blades pushed through the stubborn depths, surfaced and skimmed, and returned, again and again, to slice new triangles of water. Omski became one with this movement, as though each oar was just another segment of his own arm.

For the first time, he felt utterly fine in Teresa's presence. It didn't matter that Mr. Nutka had arrived, that Wanda had arrived, that Curll—who was making his farewells before his final departure from the country—had spent two days, that, along with her taciturn but determinedly confident admirer, Mrs. Uniska had arrived. Her children, with whom she'd been left all alone after her husband died, were somehow never really mentioned these days. It didn't matter that Hennert—smooth and suave, enjoying everything, content with everyone—constantly came and went.

There was such freedom! While others played tennis, took a walk somewhere, or even simply slept, Omski and Teresa went out on a simple fishing boat and caught crayfish and pike with a five-pronged spear. A young boy, indigenous to the area, bound to the water since early childhood, an inveterate killer, rowed with just one oar while closely observing the bottom of the lake. The boat moved with a gentle whisper through lakeside reeds bathed in sunlight. From between the stalks, the lake bottom glowed—bright pebbles and the shafts of last year's reeds, bearded and wispy with golden seaweed.

There were fish among the fragile, rippling, golden shade of the reeds, and crayfish lay on the bottom with the pebbles. They both watched as the fisherman, with a quiet, unhurried thrust, plunged the spear to the bottom—and immediately brought it up again with a fish on its end. Pierced by iron teeth, it struggled, silver and bloody, against the sun and blue sky. It traced a slight, quivering arc in the air and then fell, tossed to the bottom of the boat, onto the bloody, wriggling heap that rustled and scraped in agony as the fish dried. Among the silver masses, bleeding black crayfish with punctured shells helplessly waved their pincers.

The sun glowed as it rose to its midday height, the water was quiet, the sides of the boat brushed against the green, softly humming reeds. Somewhere off in the distance, a heron flew toward the shore and disappeared. Closer, gulls chased one another, their bent wings flashing like little white streaks of lightning.

Omski looked into Teresa's eyes—not so much with entreaty as with the deepest belief that she was as he desired her to be: pure, noble, true, already completely redeemed by his great love. She seemed to understand his wish and looked into his eyes for a long,

long time. Until both their eyes narrowed, pricked by tears of profound emotion, of heart-rending tenderness.

"How I love her!" Omski thought, terrified. "How I love her..."
But he was unable to say it.

Another fish was shaken off the spear and fell to the bottom of
the boat beside Teresa. It was a small pike, still young, with a long,
gray jaw and a wide, calm, indifferent eye. The harpoon's teeth had
speared him in such a strange way—he had one bloody wound just
below this indifferent eye, a second right under his gills, and, on
his side, a third and a fourth and even a fifth. It was as if he'd been
stitched by a torture-needle—and he was still alive, he was still very
much alive. He tossed about so much that he slid from the top of the
fish pile to the very bottom, down to the boards. And here, twitch-
ing and trembling, he beat against the wood with his tail fin, pouring streams of blood. And his silver body, accustomed to the water's
wet chill, dried and dulled in the sun.

23.

After Andrzej left, the elder Laterna simply moved into the younger's
room so that he could be near his daughter at all times. Because
Andrzej had disappeared so quickly that he hadn't managed to find,
try out, and hire a nurse.

Against all odds, Zosia's health had improved. It was warm; sunlight flooded the room all day. Zosia, fully dressed, lay on the chaise
lounge and basked in the sun.

Laterna's little dog, a fox terrier and bulldog mix, had moved in
with his master and now made his messes here. A moment after arriving, ignoring the reprimands flung at him, he jumped on Zosia's
bed with an innocent look and set about, amusingly and endear-
ingly, to win her affections.

Binia also visited, but these days she didn't stay as long as she used
to. She was sickly and wasn't able to help much. She had lost weight,
had become drawn and gaunt, but she didn't complain about it
at all; she somehow carried on, bravely awaiting the outcome of
Gondziłł's trial.

In her eyes, Julek was merely the victim of some intrigue, some strange tangle of circumstance. Someone was angry with him and had stupidly and despicably taken revenge. For what, she didn't understand. "He kept out of it," she said. "He didn't meddle around, he just did his work. What did he do to fall into such disfavor, to be persecuted like this? He was completely nonpartisan, even..."

At this, Laterna suddenly came to life.

"Nonpartisan, did you say?"

"He didn't belong to anything, I'm sure of it."

"He didn't? Well, it doesn't matter. But Binia, you shouldn't succumb to the common delusion that supposed nonpartisanship is an expression of some kind of moral superiority, something meritorious, a guarantee of impartiality..."

Binia looked at the professor with dull eyes.

"Because, you see, everyone who believes in something or who thinks about the world in any particular way—they express, involuntarily, some religious or philosophical idea, even if they deny any kind of affiliation. Anyone who has any particular wish for the good of the country or the good of humanity is, at that moment, a political partisan. You can deny your convictions, you can change them, but in the end, you cannot *not* have them.

"You see, Binia—" Laterna was getting excited. "Taking the side of some political party is a very positive, natural phenomenon. It's a moral articulation of oneself, it's self-recognition, but in the end, it's also always a certain sacrifice of one's egoism. After all, one can't actually define oneself completely and wholly without reservation. And not just because this occurs in the field of politics, under the rubric of state and social concepts. For one may hazard a claim that in each cross section, we can see all of a soul's qualities revealed because of the way they extend into any given field: from each individual feature of the soul you can draw a continuous line to each level of the cross section—yes, so that they intersect there, which means you can see them from another angle.

"So no, that's not the reason. The reason is that some of these extensions of the soul intersect levels of the cross section with their negative poles.

"I don't know if you're understanding me, Binia." Noting the dull gaze she fixed on him, he was suddenly concerned. "I mean to say that, for example, a conservative might feel that his party affiliation is a certain sacrifice of his individuality, if he's subjectively a religious skeptic; a national democrat—if, for example, he has an innate distaste for crowds, if he's disgusted by the common rabble; a socialist—if he's aware of how flawed human nature is, if he knows that all authority is actually bad and that the invocation of any ideal system is simply demagoguery. But they don't emphasize their reservations. They resign themselves to some extent; they renounce parts of their worldview for the good of the whole. That's why party affiliation is also a generalization of oneself.

"So who on earth is this—as you said—nonpartisan man, this nondogmatist, objective and impartial, ungoverned by any passion? He's a man who is unable to define himself, a man who has no individual conception of the state or of human relations in general. A person who neither acknowledges that the status quo is satisfactory, since that would define him as a conservative, nor who desires to change it, since he would then be defined by his choice of the something or other he aspires to reform. Because every critique of one party makes us supporters of the opposition. Any opinion about anything classifies us, in a certain respect, as partisans. Any position on modern goings-on can find its expression in some existing party platform or is ripe for use as a divisive catchphrase for some party faction. And taking any position is, morally speaking, already 'belonging' to a party... If someone says, 'I am beyond partisanship; the only thing that matters to me is the good of the country'—well, the way he understands what 'good' means makes him a partisan. And there's nothing particularly exceptional or tragic in the idea that our fatherland is 'torn apart by feuding parties.' All political battles are fights for the country's good—just different conceptions of 'good.' It's also said, correctly, that parties fight only for power, that they favor only 'their own people.' What of it? Winning power is the only way to carry out their platform, and 'their own people' is the only guarantee that it will be carried out according to the dictates of 'the only way that makes sense'..."

Laterna talked, but Binia was no longer the good, reliable, acoustic listener she used to be. Her thin face wore an expression of weary obligation. "Well, fine," she said when he finished. "But you see, Professor, Julek really was completely nonpartisan. He didn't care about anything—he just did his job. That's why I can't understand who could be so angry at him. He's completely innocent."

Laterna was surprised. Binia—so keen and insightful when it came to her own happiness, always so rational when confronted by her destiny—turned naïve and uncritical when it came to that faith which she couldn't live without.

And at this point he noticed that his own thoughts about Gondziłł had undergone a transformation. His case had ceased to be what it was at first—a blow, a surprise, a disaster—but had disintegrated into different little topics for discernment, revelation, and discussion. In this way, a tragedy is absorbed into life, dissolving into it without diminishing its value.

Binia wasn't staying for long these days, but Zosia's friend from the office, Basia Olinowska, was. Serious, severe even, she was able to clean and organize, make the bed, prepare food, and give meticulous orders and instructions to the Laternas' servants. But she did it without joy and appeared to take no pleasure in it. Despite their high opinion of her work, no one actually came to like her.

But Wanda Hennert, whom the professor had simply met in the street and brought up to his daughter, won Zosia over completely. She was so cheerful and full of life!

"You know, Professor, Lin has recovered. He's a new person, he's entirely back to life. We got engaged, and there was a big hullabaloo—it was 'against my parents' will,' but we love each other in spite of it all."

This fiancé of hers accompanied her once.

"Neither of us was supposed to live," Zosia said to Lin. They knew each other from when he used to visit Andrzej there. "We were not supposed to live...and yet..."

"And yet," Lin repeated with an embarrassed smile.

"That's just it!" stormed Wanda. "You act like it's an unpleasant surprise. Professor, he really is my fiancé, he just doesn't want to admit it… He resents me because I don't believe that someday, in some undetermined future, things will be 'better.' What on earth does that mean? One day he's a socialist, the next day he's a patriot— he doesn't know for himself. And still something eats at him. Hell, Poland already *is*, the one thing that's certain is that she *is*. She's not exactly what you wanted? All right, she is what she is. That's the only thing that matters, the only thing that's real—marvelous, even! After just these few years, she's already something she would never be in captivity, she's like any other country: ruined and thriving, brave and greedy, full of heroes and profiteers. We have somewhere to live, somewhere to act. We're citizens at last, like everyone else in the world—we're responsible, ready to fight, completely to blame. We're no longer just victims—we're the culprits. We no longer have any excuses, no more justifications. No more 'Christ of nations,' no more 'shackles of Siberia' or 'myrmidons of the czar.'[29] We're done with that! We are what we are—just like any other herd…"

Zofia, listening, smiled tolerantly, secure in her own, superior knowledge. And, despite Wanda's efforts to seize him and carry him off, Lin was far from sharing this *joie de vivre*.

He was still facing his court martial, where he himself would testify to his treason. He endured convoluted pangs of ambition and doubt—regarding both the court's competency in this matter as well as its qualifications in general. The sentence he'd already pronounced on himself seemed the only possible justice. However— since fate had decreed differently and, contrary to his best judgment and against his will, returned his life to him—he was unable to muster anything other than resignation and the desire to put the entire matter in someone else's hands.

Only Professor Laterna readily agreed with Wanda, and only he seemed satisfied. It was good, he thought, that people were so diverse, that our fatherland was "torn apart" by parties' "feuds." The representation of a nation seethes on the surface of a roiling sea of peoples like whitecaps on waves. It's a summing up, a digest of the vast reality of coexistence. Parties fight fiercely, they devour each other in their scrambling for greater power—only to come face to face with the swelling life of the state, to be forced to keep pace with the frantic, marvelous life of the nation.

"In these partisan battles," he thought, "life looks after itself, guarding itself against ossification, against—perfection..."

24.

One sweltering afternoon, Omski, dressed entirely in mufti, sought relief from the heat behind the lowered blinds of his white and sapphire room. Hands behind his head, he lay stiffly on the hard, benchlike sofa that seemed to melt into the wall.

It was hot, much too hot, oppressive, and everything felt strange somehow.

"There will probably be a storm," he thought.

He wasn't really thinking of anything—he was, rather, dreaming— when, amidst the suffocating silence, he suddenly heard the panting whirr of Hennert's "machine." He leapt up and ran to the window, though the arrival of the man of the house was of little concern to him. Peering through a gap in the blinds, he saw nothing apart from the automobile already driving away from the front of the veranda.

He lay back down and listened intently. But it was quiet downstairs.

Listening, he drifted off again. And he had a very unpleasant dream. He was confronted with a superhuman task: during the night, he had to go down a narrow street lined with wooden shacks and fences, down to the high-walled banks of a lake or sea, where, mired in the water, there were the giant black hulls of cargo ships, freighters, and barges. And from this embankment he had to jump down into the water, move past the standing ships, and swim, swim away as far as he could.

Now he was already down there! He could feel the dark, viscous water and the splash and slap of the waves amidst mysterious shadows, deepened by the night's blackness. He swam with effort and revulsion, squeezing past the bottoms of the ships, brushing against the black, perpetually slimy planks of the hulls as he made his way through the narrow, horrifying passage; high above his head, the ships' starboards were nearly touching. He swam past them in the darkness, and with fathomless sadness he glided further and further away—toward some dreadful, unknown aim, to the very middle, straight into the hopeless vastness of water under sky, where there would be no chance of rescue…

He awoke in mortal terror, sweating profusely. His cheerful room was filled with sunlight and a penetrating silence surrounded him. Omski struggled to recount the details of his nightmare. He understood now that it was a recollection of a particular night on the Black Sea. He had sailed past those massive, monstrous hulls as he left the harbor. But it hadn't been horrifying then; compared to his nightmare, it was an innocent lark—the thought had barely occurred to him that the safety of a ship's gangway was, so to speak, suspended over a mystery. Because everything underneath them was unknown and dreadful—it was permanent, it was forever—and not just when a boat sank to the bottom of the sea.

He fell back to sleep—and again he had a vision of night, but this time the sky was clear, the moon was full, and everything was bright. But there were strangers in the house, the house in Chowańce— they were the same bandits who'd sought shelter there that evening, but now there were too many of them, and no one could do anything about it. Gripped by a terror worse than the most blistering pain, Omski fled to the forest—he fled from Basia, who remained in danger—a forest flooded with light. He crawled over pine needles and leaves, searching for cover, trying to squeeze himself into some low-lying thicket, but there was nowhere to hide; the light of the moon still pursued him, the light was everywhere. And then—how bizarre—from behind a great, light-drenched old larch, the one that stood in front of the house, there emerged a terrible apparition, a living figure of supernatural enormity, its midsection rising above the tree branches, smiling with its great mouth, perfectly visible in the moonlight. The artificial smile that was supposed to be cheerful, the nod, the welcoming motion of its hand—it was Basia… She nodded, nodded, her mouth opened, her eyes searched for him— formally, somehow, politely—in the distance. Trying to conceal her fear, she called out for rescue—not knowing how close he was, just a few steps away, hidden by a little shrub made silver by the moonlight. He didn't hear anything, but he could see that the huge mouth was still calling for him, asking for him, smiling in an ostensibly casual way, inviting him to stay.

He hid without moving, without breathing. Oh God, so she'd come here, her spirit had arrived by night—to this old place, to this forgotten garden—and here she appeared, monstrously large and excruciatingly sad, smiling futilely at the emptiness of the trees, waiting in vain for his help…

He heard his own scream as he woke up. Oh, it was a terrible dream. His heart was pounding, and he was bathed head to toe in cold sweat.

"There's something wrong with me," he thought.

He put his head under the tap, dousing himself with water.

"You could lose your mind from this heat," he muttered, reassuring himself. He got dressed and went downstairs.

Sitting in the hall were Hennert, some unfamiliar guest, and—Sednowski. Teresa wasn't with them.

Omski stopped in the doorway for a short moment and then, scarcely looking their way, greeted them with his usual gloomy politeness. He understood that this was the day it would all be settled. After brief consideration, he joined them, seating himself in an armchair to wait for the imminent transition to the dining room. He confessed to Hennert that he'd wanted to leave that afternoon, but he immediately yielded to Hennert's hospitable persuasion and put off his departure until the next day.

The blood in his veins was like liquid fire. His suffering had become unbearable; death seemed like a paradise. He thought—should I flee? What, and leave them together? Never! Never!

This Sednowski seemed less sure of himself, less expansive than he'd been before. But his voice—good-natured, indulgent, patronizing—still rang out over the others. Omski couldn't look at him.

He heard only that they were discussing the Gondziłł affair. So it wasn't just misappropriation of funds—the investigation had apparently turned up evidence…

And then Teresa came in. Omski didn't take his eyes off her. She was smiling, but she seemed slightly pale and shy. She didn't greet anyone; evidently they'd already seen each other earlier. He also noted that they didn't say anything to each other—Sednowski and Teresa—and didn't even look at each other. She sat down for a moment, but almost immediately they all rose and went to the dining room.

"So this Gondziłł affair," continued Sednowski in that indulgent way of his. "Something completely different has come out, something apart from what he was originally accused of. It's much, much more serious... They've started talking about that favorite of yours: Andrzej Laterna..."

"What?" Teresa was surprised.

Yes, now he and she were talking to one another.

"Oh yes, my dear lady," Sednowski took a tone of paternal moralizing. "It's a very ugly story. And Lin, he was involved, too..."

Yes, Lin's involvement had already been established. But he had been rehabilitated—he indicted himself before the prosecutor, and in light of his remorse and his suicide attempt his prospects were good... But Laterna?

"Meanwhile, Laterna has disappeared. He's left the country altogether—he left with Curll—East or West, nobody knows..."

Omski remembered the names that had been mentioned in the anonymous letter he'd received about the Gondziłł case. He remembered and remained silent. What could he say, sitting here, at this very table... He thought only of the quote from that same letter: "This is what comes of Polish officers."

It turned out that the unfamiliar third man was someone from the ministry of justice. His position was that the earlier accusation against Gondziłł was simply baseless, that the case was really about a completely obvious political crime...

"Everything else is completely in order," he assured them. "Completely in order." And for the gentlemen assembled, only the "everything else" mattered.

So the conversation turned to Elżbieta's marriage to Niemeński. The ceremony had already been held, and "the closest" had barely received notice. Despite that, they were sincerely delighted. Even Teresa brightened, and she seemed to calm down.

Later, finally, they were alone together.

"Perhaps there'll be a thunderstorm tonight," Teresa sighed as they strolled through some green corridor of trimmed hedges.

"And you dare to talk!" Omski was outraged.

Her eyes filled with tears. "Oh God, so what do you want from me? What can I do? Tell me, please, what can I do? Do you think I wanted him to come?..."

She wrung her hands. Her lips quivered miserably.

"I already told you. If it's true, if you're not lying, then get your hat and your coat right now. Leave with me right now..."

"And go where?"

"Come with me—leave this place forever."

She looked at him in dismay, with the dawning horror that everything was crumbling around her, that there was nothing of this life—this nice, pleasant, pretty little life—that she would be able to save.

"Wait, just think," she begged him. "Is it really so bad, do you really not believe me?..."

His hand made a motion toward her face—and on her nose, between her eyes, she felt the touch of a gun barrel. She moved the hand with the revolver from her face and slowly backed away, staring at him with round eyes. He had no idea what was going on in her soul—maybe it was even contempt—but her eyes were pleading.

"Bear it in mind," he said. He looked at the small revolver and put it in his pocket. He didn't feel any shame, just helpless despair.

Whatever happened—whether she went with him or whether she stayed—it didn't matter. The mystery of her soul and her heart was an awful thing.

He smiled and kissed her in the very same place, right between her eyes. "Do you love me?" he asked.

"I love you," she answered, and sighed.

She allowed herself to be led down a familiar path into a dusky blue patch of closely cropped brush. "Here?" she asked gently, as he spread his coat on the ground. "My darling," he whispered.

It was already night by the time he came back to his room. But he immediately left again and went to the garden. He circled the house, stopping underneath Teresa's window. The white curtains were drawn; he didn't even see a shadow—just the light still burning, the golden light from the little lamp by her bed.

Sednowski probably had one of the guest rooms upstairs. Hennert slept in his office, one door down from her bedroom. But there was no light anywhere else.

Its gray fur nearly invisible in the darkness, Teresa's dog, Klinga, quietly approached Omski. He hadn't noticed it leaving. So it'd been in the garden—had it gone alone? Klinga nudged Omski's hand with its nose, and he stroked the dog mechanically. "Where's your mistress? Go find your mistress," he told it softly, while it didn't understand. From the shadows, its narrow gray snout moved toward him.

Omski wandered the garden in a futile, senseless search. He turned to the lifeless, illuminated spot beneath her window. "Teresa!" he called in a low voice. There was no answer from inside the house. Everything was quiet.

No. No, it wasn't quiet. Surely he heard something now. He circled the house again. Was there a voice coming from an open window upstairs, or was he imagining it?

After their recent intimacy his muscles were still full of pleasure, and his soul was full of torment. He was ready. He was completely mad.

"Teresa!" he called again.

Now he distinctly heard a rustling from inside the house, the patter of running feet—maybe coming down the stairs, maybe just on the floor... But the lamp in her room was still burning as she descended the steps of the veranda—and then was before him.

"Where were you just now?" he wanted to ask, but instead said only, "Come on..."

She went with him again—as usual—by the hand, through the same path, between the smooth walls of the hedges. In the darkness, they made their way down to the shore and then further out, to the place where the boats were moored. Without releasing her hand, Omski gropingly untied the boat from the post—it was that simple fishing boat.

"Come on," he said again.

She hesitated, he felt her slight resistance. "No, I don't want to," she blurted.

"Come on." He pulled her more forcefully, and now he understood—hatred flooded him—that she was afraid.

Without letting go, he transferred her hand to his other hand, took out his revolver, and shot her, point blank, right between her eyes. "Clap, clap!" A wet echo sounded across the lake, and she was already lying in the sand, right next to the water, like a little pile of something white.

Omski leaned down and, with some effort, carefully dragged her into the boat. He was calmer now that her body was lying on the bottom—in the same spot where, caught by the spear, the dead, bleeding fish had been. He sat across from her, on his usual little bench, and quickly, forcefully paddled away. Because, he thought, it would have to be the furthest spot from shore, out in the middle of the lake, out in the depths.

NOTES

1. *filet* (Fr.): An old style of embroidery in which a pattern is worked by hand into fine netting.

2. *new settlements for soldiers:* In December 1920, the Polish Sejm approved two acts that would allow demobilized soldiers of the Polish Army to apply for plots of land in the *Kresy* (Borderlands), which had been ceded to the new Republic at the end of the Polish-Soviet War. A major aim of the program was to polonize the area, including western portions of modern-day Ukraine and Belarus. Poorly managed and underfunded from the beginning, the program was suspended in 1923.

3. *She's from the Borderlands.:* The Polish *Kresy,* or Borderlands, encompass those territories east of present-day Poland that belonged to the Polish-Lithuanian Commonwealth before it was partitioned by its neighbors in the late eighteenth century, and that includes large portions of Lithuania, western Belarus, and western Ukraine. Although the negotiations that established an independent Poland in 1918 did not include these territories within the new state's eastern border, they were ceded to Poland following its 1921 victory in the Polish-Soviet War.

4. *aged Marcelain:* A brand of cognac prized in the late nineteenth and early twentieth centuries.

5. *two bottles of Chambertin:* A fine French red wine from around the village of Gevrey-Chambertin, in Burgundy.

6. *most recent enemy attack on the northern Borderlands:* Poland annexed the Lithuanian capital of Vilnius and its surrounding area between 1920 and 1922 through means both military and political. Consequently, diplomatic relations between the two states were not normalized until 1938.

7. *Each case in its own right would be sufficient as* casus belli.: From 1919 to 1922, several regional and international incidents reflected ongoing tensions

between the new Polish state and its neighbors and ethnic minorities, who disputed its borders.

8. *Shortly thereafter he was imprisoned for illegal educational activities and then sent into exile.*: Poland under partition (1795–1918) saw sharp restrictions on cultural and educational activities regarded by the partitioning powers as fostering Poland's ambitions toward self-determination. This was especially the case in the Prussian and Russian partitions. Those who ran afoul of the Russian authorities, particularly in cultural centers like Warsaw, could be arrested and sent into Siberian exile. Laterna's "illegal educational activities" may have included offering instruction in Polish, which was legal in the Russian partition only after 1905.

9. *she fell victim to the first wartime epidemic:* The 1918–1920 influenza pandemic, commonly known as the "Spanish flu," killed an estimated 20 to 50 million people, more than World War I itself.

10. *a certain old palace:* Ewa Wiegandt points out in her annotations to the Biblioteka Narodowa edition of *Romans Teresy Hennert* that Nałkowska's model for the "certain old palace" was the Namiestnikowski Palace—today, the Presidential Palace—in central Warsaw, where Nałkowska worked in the Office of Foreign Propaganda. Zofia Nałkowska, *Romans Teresy Hennert,* ed. Ewa Wiegandt (Wrocław: Ossolineum, 2001), 34.

11. *Biedermeier chairs:* "Biedermeier" refers to a range of functional, neoclassical furniture designs developed in Germany during the first half of the nineteenth century. Here, it demonstrates the taste and elegance of the office's décor.

12. *astronomical sums of money:* The Polish economy experienced extremely high inflation after independence in 1918, with hyperinflation taking hold throughout the early 1920s.

13. *It was him.*: The mythic figure here is Józef Piłsudski (1867–1935), who led the successful military campaigns for Polish independence during World War I and subsequently against the Bolsheviks in the Polish-Soviet War, even as he was serving officially as head of state. Nałkowska's novel is set during the period when Poland's right-wing opposition was maneuvering for Piłsudski to withdraw from national politics, which he ultimately did in 1923, only to reassume the reigns of state in a military coup in 1926.

14. *the society ladies no longer had to receive governor-generals from the East:* From 1874 until 1917, the portion of Poland occupied by the Russian Empire was administered by a Russian governor-general, who naturally enjoyed access to the most exclusive Warsaw society.

15. *carrière* (Fr.): A course or run.

16. *Uhlans:* Polish light cavalry notable for their traditional long sabers.

17. *bigos* (Pol.): A traditional Polish "hunter's" stew made with slow-cooked cabbage and chopped meat.

18. *Belarusians, Ukrainians—after all, it was the same for them. Nowadays, "reasons of state" determined everything; nowadays, talk of the people's liberation*

had ceased.: Poland's annexation of the eastern Borderlands thwarted the national ambitions of local ethnic groups and subordinated their interests to those of the Polish state. Many Poles who had harbored high ideals for an independent state before 1918 were disillusioned by Poland's new role suppressing similar ideals in others.

19. *the gendarmerie, the police, the spies…*: As elsewhere in the Russian Empire, the czarist regime maintained political control in its Polish territory through an intricate network of bureaucrats, police, and informants. Many aspects of this institutional structure were preserved in the newly independent state, where searches and arrests of individuals regarded as subversive, especially communists, remained commonplace through much of the interwar period.

20. *the ill-fated, longed-for Kathleen:* "Kathleen Mavourneen" is a ballad composed in 1837 and popular in the United States and Ireland. Its titular figure came to personify Ireland, whose independence movement offers many parallels to that of Poland. The Irish Free State was declared in 1922.

21. *"a lot, any which way, and fast!"*: This line appears in Tadeusz Boy-Żeleński's poem "In Praise of Adulthood" (1913), in which the poet lambasts the youthful attitude that seeks only to live "a lot, any which way, and fast!"

22. *sans-culotte* (Fr.): Literally, "without *culottes* (knee-length pants)." Because the young radicals of the French Revolution were drawn largely from the urban working class and wore full-length pants instead of shorter, more traditional *culottes,* the appellation *sans-culottes* came to apply to left-wing revolutionaries more generally.

23. *they'd pinned their hopes on one man:* Many Poles came to regard Piłsudski as the sole guarantor of Polish independence in an uncertain geopolitical environment.

24. *Huysmans'* À rebours: Translated into English as *Against the Grain,* *À rebours* (1884) is a mildly scandalous novel by Joris-Karl Huysmans (1848–1907). It is a major representative of literary Decadence in fin-de-siècle Europe.

25. *Słowacki said: 'The peacock of nations you have been…':* In his poem "Agamemnon's Grave" (1839), Juliusz Słowacki (1809–1849), one of Poland's three national "bards," calls upon Poland to cast off its "slavery" through spiritual renewal. Nałkowska's contemporaries would likely have heard the end of Słowacki's line, cleverly omitted in the story: "The peacock of nations you have been, and their parrot."

26. *Not only this 'peacock and parrot,' but what Mochnacki demanded, that literature allow a nation to recognize something of its own being, and Norwid, consciously trying to invent a national style, designing a Polish architectural arch of two scythes with intersecting blades.:* See Note 23, above. Maurycy Mochnacki (1803–1834), Słowacki's contemporary, was a major theorist of Romanticism in Poland, as well as an influential critic. Cyprian Norwid (1821–1883), who belongs to the second generation of Polish Romantics, was its most gifted poet. All three writers died in exile in Paris. Nałkowska is referring to a stanza from Norwid's philosophical tract-in-verse *Promethidion,* published in Paris in 1851,

in which the poet laments that no "Mazovian canvas" has "become a standard to art, that the ashtar / On Krakowskie Przedmieście has forgotten conversation, / That all peasant huts are crooked, that churches / Do not feature a Polish ogive…" This "Polish ogive," a fancy of the sculptor Henryk Dmochowski (1810–1863), is the arch formed by two intersecting scythes.

27. *"my sole consolation"*: In this opening line of an untitled poem by Stanisław Wyspiański (1869–1907), Poland's most important Neo-Romantic playwright and artist—"Pociecho moja ty, książeczko" (1905)—"my sole consolation" is a "little book."

28. *Knud Kyhn* (1880–1969): A Danish sculptor known for his stoneware figurines.

29. *No more 'Christ of nations,' no more 'shackles of Siberia' or 'myrmidons of the czar':* All three quoted phrases were popular slogans of Polish Romantic nationalist sentiment in the nineteenth century.